LAS VEGAS
Lucky in Love
CHERYL DRAGON

ELLORA'S CAVE
ROMANTICA PUBLISHING

What the critics are saying...

ONE HOT EXPERIMENT

4 Lips "*One Hot Experiment* by Cheryl Dragon was an immensely enjoyable erotic tale with a touch of danger and suspense. […] Readers who enjoy a good reunion story will love this. […] A delicious read from start to finish." ~ *Two Lips Reviews*

4.5 Blue Ribbons "Cheryl Dragon's ONE HOT EXPERIMENT is filled with non-stop action from the beginning until the surprise ending. […] The story is interesting, well written and will keep you sitting on the edge of your seat until the very end. […] It's a very good read. Enjoy!" ~ *Romance Junkies Reviews*

VEGAS STYLE

5 Angels "I appreciated the entertaining state of affairs Vivian had to deal with. […] Every novel I have read of Cheryl Dragon's has been wonderful. *Vegas Style* is no exception, so pick yourself up a copy today." ~ *Fallen Angels Reviews*

5 Rating "Scrumptious sex happens whenever they are together which spices up this totally outrageous storyline. Every naughty escapade feels deliciously right heightening the reader's senses and making the fast-moving plot more enjoyable. […] Ms. Dragon has successfully dealt with the lasting effects that leave their marks on impressionable minds in this world where relationships go bad by a dozen. *Vegas Style* is dazzling enough to pull its readers away from their hectic lives and get engrossed in a tale of two people who get hitched in a style most suited to the city-that-never-sleeps!"

~ *Just Erotic Romance Reviews*

An Ellora's Cave Romantica Publication

www.ellorascave.com

Las Vegas Lucky in Love

ISBN 9781419958403
ALL RIGHTS RESERVED.
One Hot Experiment Copyright © 2007 Cheryl Dragon.
Vegas Style Copyright © 2008 Cheryl Dragon.
Edited by Shannon Combs.
Cover art by Syneca.

This book printed in the U.S.A. by Jasmine-Jade Enterprises, LLC.

Trade paperback Publication December 2008

With the exception of quotes used in reviews, this book may not be reproduced or used in whole or in part by any means existing without written permission from the publisher, Ellora's Cave Publishing, Inc.® 1056 Home Avenue, Akron OH 44310-3502.

Warning: The unauthorized reproduction or distribution of this copyrighted work is illegal. Criminal copyright infringement, including infringement without monetary gain, is investigated by the FBI and is punishable by up to 5 years in federal prison and a fine of $250,000.
(http://www.fbi.gov/ipr/)

This book is a work of fiction and any resemblance to persons, living or dead, or places, events or locales is purely coincidental. The characters are productions of the author's imagination and used fictitiously.

LAS VEGAS LUCKY IN LOVE
ଚ

ONE HOT EXPERIMENT
~11~

VEGAS STYLE
~97~

ONE HOT EXPERIMENT

☙

Acknowledgement

๛

Special thanks to Joanna, Barb, Ang and Shawnna!

Trademarks Acknowledgement

๛

The author acknowledges the trademarked status and trademark owners of the following wordmarks mentioned in this work of fiction:

Diet Coke: Coca-Cola Company

Frankenstein: E.L.V.H. Inc. Corp.

Harvard: President and Fellows of Harvard College

OnStar: General Motors Corporation

Oxford: Chancellor Masters and Scholars of the University of Oxford, UK

Princeton: Trustees of Princeton University

The X-Files: Twentieth Century Fox Film Company

Chapter One

✺

"What is he doing here?" Maddie Simons glanced past her assistant Ginny's desk to the man walking with her boss.

"Looks a little dangerous, but cute. Who is he?" Ginny leaned over to look.

"Just someone I used to know." Despite the bad history, Maddie felt her pulse pick up. All the girls at college had whispered about Tim. He'd always been just a little too in control. Too walled off and moody to pursue. The bad boy they wanted but who was a bit too much to have.

"Tim Foxmor." Generally Maddie enjoyed Ginny's frankness—however cute didn't begin to describe him. He looked just the same as he had in college. Tall, dark brown eyes and brown hair with a hint of a challenge always in his expression. He was dressed in black pants and a gray polo shirt with a logo for Foxmor Security on his left chest. "He screwed up my life."

"Your life is fine." Ginny looked confused but put on a smile as Tim approached with the boss.

"Dr. Simons, I'd like you to meet Tim Foxmor." Dr. Bellows was a rich and eccentric inventor who looked like Santa Claus in a lab coat. Everything in his world was a production of his own making. He had recruited Maddie for his think tank right out of graduate school so she knew how to handle him. Tim was the man throwing her.

"Hello," Maddie said coolly. *When all else fails, be professional.*

Tim reached for her hand. "Dr. Simons."

The spark put her off balance. Maddie shook his hand with every intention of being only as polite as necessary when he mentioned their college association. But he didn't. Tim held her hand longer than expected—no doubt to show that he was in charge. He oozed silent power.

The longer he had her hand, the more uneasy she felt. There was too much heat in his touch and she pulled her hand away. It appeared as though Tim didn't think anything of what had happened in college. He'd probably forgotten all about it. There was no evidence that he even remembered her. Though she could feel his eyes analyzing her down to her toes.

"What brings you to our little think tank, Mr. Foxmor?" she asked.

"I hired him for the security project. Best in Nevada. We need to stop these break-ins." Bellows slapped Tim on the back as if he were his best friend. "Show him around, will you, Maddie? Billy and I are working on a little project." Bellows' son Billy had a summer job at the tank that encompassed whatever the college kid felt like doing. Not much, in Maddie's estimation. As long as she didn't have to baby-sit him it was fine with her.

She had bigger problems at the moment. Her blood began to boil and she couldn't immediately respond. Tour guide to Tim!

She was relieved when Ginny jumped in, "We'll have to rearrange a few things. No problem. I just need a moment with Dr. Simons in her office, then she's all yours."

"Take your time." Tim said and turned away.

Ginny urged Maddie into her office, closing the door behind them. "What's wrong with you? A good-looking man wants a tour, you give it to him. It's not going to kill you."

Maddie paced around her office trying to determine where to begin. "He ruined my life in college. He was behind my getting dumped by my boyfriend and all my friends. He messed up everything."

"You look like you've seen a ghost." Ginny frowned in concern.

"I have." Maddie leaned on her desk, doing her best to fight the queasy feeling as she relived the humiliation. It had been the icing on the cake of life—being a genius yet always feeling like a social loser. As hard as she'd worked to make her life a success since then, all the negativity had came crashing back on her the moment she saw Tim.

"He seems polite, if a bit quiet. What did he do?"

"He destroyed my one chance to be a normal person." Maddie sank into her chair and took deep slow breaths. If anyone had asked her yesterday how she'd react to seeing him again, she wouldn't have said with a panic attack. It made no sense that she was still this upset by him.

"Slow down and tell me what happened." Ginny sat primly in a guest chair with her legs crossed.

A motherly figure, Ginny was able to sooth Maddie's senses by merely her presence. "I never fit in." The admission was hard for Maddie. She took another deep breath.

"Most kids feel like they don't. It's normal."

"No, I mean I was never with my own peer group. Both my parents were teachers and I was an only child. So I was being educated all of my life. I was put in kindergarten for socialization. Then went straight to second grade. Then I went to fourth. Then sixth."

"I get the picture," Ginny cut in.

"I was ten when I entered high school. I never went to a school dance or a prom or anything. No dates, no boyfriends. It went beyond being a nerd—I was a freak. I didn't know what kids my age were really doing because they didn't want to play with me. I was in college at thirteen and the sideshow attraction there too. When I turned eighteen, I decided to try something else."

"That super brain of yours came up with something?" Ginny's face was covered with concern.

"I had undergrad degrees from Harvard. Since I grew up in Boston, my parents were right there the whole time. Not that year. At eighteen, I transferred to Princeton to take graduate-level classes. Because I was under twenty-one, they housed me in an undergrad dorm. No one knew I was a freak there. They just thought I was one of them." Maddie looked at Ginny for a reaction.

"You pretended to be an undergrad." Ginny adjusted her many rings. "How did that feel?"

"Amazing. I was just one of the crowd. Even in my graduate classes, I never mentioned my age so it didn't matter because I looked old enough. I made friends my own age, went to parties and had a few dates. I wasn't beating boys off with a stick but I had a boyfriend." It was a very brief time she relived often. Maddie loved the think tank even though it wasn't an average workplace.

"Tim was the boyfriend?" Ginny concluded.

"No! Tim was always quiet, brooding and antisocial. He never even looked at me. Tim was my boyfriend's roommate and he ruined everything." Maddie bit her lip. This was the part she hated reliving.

"Go on. We can't keep him waiting out there all day for this tour." Ginny glanced at the clock on the wall.

"Tim found out that I was actually doing graduate work. I don't know exactly how he found out but he told my boyfriend, Mark. So my boyfriend dumped me when he realized I was so much younger than he had thought. None of my friends would even speak to me because they felt I had been so dishonest. The kids in my graduate classes treated me like I had the plague. I had to get out of there."

"You lied to them." Ginny didn't seem surprised or upset.

"By omission," Maddie admitted. "I knew I'd never get that chance again. It didn't matter if I was eighteen or twenty-three. The age gap suddenly felt like nothing. I thought I was liked for myself so why give them a reason to hate me? It's not like I was pretending to be someone else."

Ginny looked at the wall showing diplomas from Harvard and Oxford. "I don't see Princeton."

"I didn't graduate. I had a Rhodes Scholarship my parents had pressured me to apply for. I got it and left Princeton. If Tim hadn't happened I probably would've turned it down and kept on being normal for a change. Instead I dropped out of Princeton to go home in order to prepare for Oxford." Part of her still wondered how her life might've turned out if she hadn't left.

"Did you ever confront Tim?" she asked.

"No. I left pretty fast. He barely spoke to me back then anyway. All the girls talked about his body. Tim really kept to himself. We couldn't figure out if he was a bad boy or just smug. I've never been good at confrontation outside of an academic sense. I did demand my ex-boyfriend tell me who told him."

"That explains your reaction in the hall. But it's history, dear. You need to let go and be a professional."

Ginny had this annoying habit of being right. Maddie knew that's how she should act. In every other way, she'd matured beyond college. Surely she'd grown past this. Now that the initial shock was over, she could put it behind her. "It's just a tour. He doesn't even remember me." She took another deep breath. Her body didn't seem sure yet.

"Exactly. It's all in the past. What's a week or possibly two of having him around? It's nothing. Your life is fine. You turned out great. It's not as though you have to work with him at every turn. Give him the tour, get the plan for security underway and then let him do his job. You have your own work to do." Ginny made it sound simple.

Maddie wasn't convinced. In the past, she'd worked with colleagues she didn't like, but this was different. Tim was at the core of the worst days of her life—a culmination of a lifetime of being someone who was excluded. On top of that, he had the nerve to forget her. Two could play. She'd mature and forget him…she hoped. "I'll try."

"Good. Now go before he thinks you've tunneled a way out." Ginny winked.

* * * * *

Tim wasn't at all surprised to see Maddie at the Bellows Think Tank. He checked out all of his potential clients thoroughly. Her name had sealed the deal. It was a unique business that shouldn't be too time consuming. In truth, he couldn't resist seeing her again. This was a job he'd handle personally.

College was behind them but he could never get her out of his head. Which wasn't like him. Tim had always had his life under tight control. She was his one weakness.

There had been no chance for them in college. She'd been packed and gone so fast that he never had a chance to talk to her.

To tell her the truth.

Rumor had it she went to Oxford. Hell, he'd barely had the money to cover the room and board his scholarship didn't. Cash for a long-distance phone call to try to talk to her — not a chance. That was fate. His life had been a test of endurance from his parents on.

Yet here she was. He wasn't a sullen kid scraping by with two jobs and a full class load anymore. He owned his own company. Not that money had been their problem in college. It was weirder than that. The twisted irony of being obsessed with your college roommate's girlfriend made him not say a word to her. Now it was all different.

Tim wasn't a romantic — far from it. Life had dealt him too rough a hand for that. However, he wasn't one to throw away an opportunity when he saw it. They were rare enough in his life. He was analyzing the hallway layout when the office door opened.

"Sorry to keep you waiting. Should we get started with the tour?" Maddie's smile looked strained.

"After you." He didn't want to be caught staring but couldn't take his eyes off her.

Maddie led the way down the hall. "What brought you to Vegas?"

"I grew up here. Came back after college. You?" He kept his distance as they walked so he wouldn't be tempted to push things. She was just as beautiful as she had been in college. Tall with long limbs, reddish-brown hair that brushed past her shoulders and green eyes that missed nothing. Her curves were downplayed but not hidden by the fitted skirt suit. She'd haunted his dreams.

"The think tank. I was recruited out of Oxford. I liked the flexibility of being privately funded and there aren't too many of them around. It means I get to select some of my own studies." Maddie seemed perfectly professional until Tim noticed the pulse on her neck picking up tempo.

Tim couldn't help but wonder what the private chat with her assistant had been about. Scheduling, probably—however his instincts said otherwise. His instincts were usually right.

The look on Maddie's face when she first saw him had been as controlled as her expression now. She'd always been that way. Even in college she was hard to rattle. Not that he hadn't seen her having fun and a few drinks at some of the parties. She never lost control though. He respected that. Understood it. She was the only woman who'd ever rattled him.

His outside persona had been crafted to keep people away. Off balance. As a kid it was self-preservation. By Princeton, it was habit. He'd never dropped the habit. Everyone thought he was the dangerous type and he certainly grew up on the wrong side of the tracks. All he really wanted was to invent and fix things. Until Maddie. "What type of studies do you do?"

"This and that. Some are commissioned. Some studies are our own ideas. Anything really. The group is very diverse. It's been a great place to work until these break-ins started. We're all on edge." She rubbed her neck as they passed by more typical offices.

The fact that she didn't have a clue what was on his mind only made him want her more. Unfortunately, with their odd history, he had no solid plan to pursue her. Tim wasn't going to push the subject when they should be focused on the job. The time would come.

He could smell her perfume, which was only making things worse. Maddie hadn't aged a day, or at least it seemed that way. Still gorgeous. He was a grown man. He could control himself. Not that it was easy. "That's understandable. The break-ins started about two weeks ago?" He had to keep his mind on the job for now. Discipline was something Tim had.

"Yes. At first we thought it was just carelessness. Nothing was really missing, just moved around. We've used the same cleaning service for years. They know better. Then things turned up broken or missing and we knew it wasn't one of the cleaning staff or us. A one-time mistake we could understand. Someone could've left a door unlocked or a window, but it's happening every few days now."

"Must be the same person. Thinks he'll find something worth pawning. Your typical Vegas burglars. With so many people losing their money, the crime rates are always high."

"We're not exactly on the strip, Mr. Foxmor." Maddie turned to him.

"Tim," he corrected. Clearly she was holding him at a distance. He couldn't blame her. He would try to change it.

Maddie's cheeks had a tinge of red. "Fine, Tim. We're in the desert. The exterior of the building isn't exactly flashing cash."

"You're right. It's probably locals who know you're here, looking to find a vulnerable source."

"Vulnerable is right. I've been trying to get Bellows to upgrade security since I started. It never took priority with him because no one ever bothered us. We all trust each other enough not to touch the experiments. It's just so strange." Maddie chewed her lower lip in anxiety.

The innocent act had Tim counting to ten. She was just chewing her lip. He had no idea what had gotten him so stuck on her but it wasn't gone. Something about her intense focus drew him to her. He loved a challenge. "Don't worry. I'll start with the exterior. That'll make sure we know if anyone is illegally gaining entry. First I'll have to do a detailed evaluation though. I'm guessing your internal security needs to be improved as well. Smoke and heat sensors, CO_2 detectors and everything. Code just isn't enough for what I imagine goes on in here."

"Probably not." She smiled. "Better do it now. Bellows doesn't like change so just get it over with. He'll learn the new security procedures all at once. It'll be less stressful for all of us."

"He's the boss?" Tim knew Bellows was in charge. Beyond that it seemed like the place revolved around him. He respected that—it was how he ran his own business.

"The boss and financial source. We have to be privately funded by someone." She opened the next door. "This is the pit."

"The pit? Bellows keeps problem employees in there?" Tim glanced into a dark room.

Maddie laughed. "No. It's used for testing anything flammable, explosive or hazardous. Soundproof and fireproof but it probably needs upgrading too."

"The job's bigger than I expected." More time with Maddie was all he could think. No problem at all. Tim ignored the arousal she triggered. His control would be tested.

"I'm sure Bellows can find someone else if we don't fit into your schedule. Maybe you could recommend someone." Maddie looked indifferent to that alternative.

Tim knew he couldn't walk away. Even if there were more lucrative projects for him just then. His other teams could handle it. He didn't do much hands-on anymore. For Maddie he'd be very hands-on. "No, it might take longer than I planned, but it'll be better than Fort Knox when I'm done. It might help to go over my notes later. Make sure my plan is on target for your needs."

"I'm afraid I have meetings all afternoon. Bellows didn't give me any warning about today. I gave you the quick tour. If you want to poke around on your own, you'll find most people willing to talk. A lot of science geeks, so don't be offended if they're a bit skittish at first. Just tell them who you are. It'll be okay."

"Perhaps over dinner if you're free—you could fill in any holes in my research." Tim kept his cool, not wanting to appear too eager. She might accept it for the job but otherwise he knew it was a gamble. No way. No way would she be interested in him after she barely knew he existed in college.

"Dinner's good. Leave the time and restaurant where you want to meet with my assistant," she said casually.

"No, that won't work. You should come to my place. I have my computer, blueprints and prototypes there. It's more practical." He wanted her alone on his territory.

Maddie chewed her lip again.

How was he supposed to think when she did that? Was she trying to kill him? Was she going to say no? He'd offer an out to ease the pressure. "Unless that's a problem?"

"No." Her reply came quickly this time. "No problem. I'd like to see the prototypes."

"Seven o'clock. I'll leave my address with your assistant." Tim gave her no chance to change her mind this time.

"Fine." She glanced down at her watch. "I have to go prep for a meeting. Are you okay on your own?"

"Always." Tim had always been alone and was getting tired of it.

* * * * *

Maddie paced her office with frustration and arousal. He was still the sexiest guy she'd ever met. She'd just spent more time alone with him than in all of college. Yet he hadn't mentioned college at all. What a jerk!

She'd been perfectly mature and what had it gotten her? She felt worse. Tim deserved to know what he did but telling him off was too easy.

The loser in her needed revenge for the humiliation. But how? Her genius IQ could solve this. Maddie'd gotten dumped, lost her friends and changed her life because of him. At the very least she wanted to see him dumped. Every action deserved an equal and opposite reaction. The world had laws. Right now nature was out of balance for her.

Who could she get to seduce him? He'd never go for her. He'd been Mr. Professional on the tour. Besides Maddie knew she wasn't the type to seduce men. She never got that sort of attention. She needed a plan.

Opening her file for the meeting, the answer slapped her in the face.

Her pheromone study!

Maddie left her chair for the workbench in her office. Her current study was adding pheromones to normal perfumes to track the results. The data weren't all in, however the informal input from her volunteers suggested it was worth a try. Maybe, just maybe, it'd work on Tim.

He was an attractive man. She'd get what all those girls in college wanted. That might actually help her confidence in the men department. Then she'd get to dump him herself. A little innocent revenge. For once in her life, Maddie wasn't going to be the loser. Ginny would think it was immature, but sometimes people had to go back and heal the past to move on. Maddie wasn't going to let this follow her throughout her thirties.

Chapter Two

Maddie steadied her nerves as she stood on Tim's porch. After five different outfit attempts, she'd settled on a wraparound plum skirt and clingy lace top to match. It was the sexiest outfit she had.

Somehow, Maddie hadn't allowed herself to back down. There was no guarantee anything would happen, she reminded herself as she rang the doorbell. She had to try. If she didn't, she'd regret it. And with the perfume on her side, she hoped tonight would be a success.

When the door opened, she felt herself breathing harder. She'd really regret it. Tim was in jeans and a T-shirt with a smile. Still sexy.

"Hi." Maddie felt her skin tingle as she took a step closer to him. There was no doubting the attraction she felt despite her lack of confidence in this area. Which made her plan perfect. She'd work through her immaturity issues with the help of the pheromones.

"Come in." His hand casually slid to the small of her back. Maddie's pulse picked up.

She could smell the pasta sauce cooking and his shampoo. His hair was still a little damp from the shower. It only made him sexier.

"You didn't have to cook." She tried to sound normal.

"I make a good sauce."

He was close and the warmth made her whole body tingle. She could barely focus on his words. "Make it?" How much trouble had he gone to?

"It was just me and my dad growing up, so one of us had to know how to cook." Tim guided her toward the kitchen.

Maddie wanted to ask about his mother. Maybe that was getting too personal. Instead she focused on the house. It was a smallish kitchen that screamed a man cooked here. Dark blue and lots of stainless steel—no decorations. Very functional. He had a bottle of wine breathing on the counter and sauce simmering on the stove. Not at all intimidating. Just dinner to start. She couldn't get ahead of herself. She wanted him.

She could get used to a man cooking for her.

"Wine?" He took a glass from the cabinet.

"Please." The small butcher-block table was set for two. Being alone with him felt real. They were truly alone. No Ginny or Bellows for her to find. No one would come around the corner.

He brought her the glass. She sampled it. "Thanks. It's excellent."

"I did a job for a winery in Northern California. They send me a bottle or two every year. Have a seat. It's ready." He pulled out her chair. Maddie sat and marveled at the change. She hadn't known Tim that well in college but he was the quiet, brooding type who didn't talk much. He'd always avoided her. It was grating on her that he didn't remember her.

Tim set a plate loaded with pasta in front of her and set another on his placemat. "Ever hear from Mark?"

"No." So he did remember her. Maddie refused to react. She had a plan to stick to. "You?"

He returned with a plate of garlic bread and sat. "No."

"I didn't think you remembered me." Maddie took a sip of wine.

"Business first. You had a busy day that I was interrupting. I understand a tight schedule." He dropped his napkin onto his lap.

Business. Two could play. At least he hadn't blanked on her. "How do things look at the tank?"

"Good. It needs a lot of work but it can be done." Tim began to eat.

Maddie dug in. The man could cook and he looked good. She had to stay strong and follow the plan. Another glass of wine and this wouldn't be hard at all. She was nervous but pushed it from her mind, falling into conversation about her office.

Forty-five minutes later Maddie helped Tim clear the table then followed him to his home office. Actually it was a second bedroom that looked like a top-secret government hideout complete with multiple computers.

"You do it all from here?" she asked.

"No, I have an office in downtown Vegas, but with this I can run it from home if I want." He moved some blueprints off an old sofa. "I only have a few questions."

"Sure. Whatever you need." Maddie sat and inhaled as he sat down next to her with the blueprints spread out on their laps. Time to start trying to be seductive.

"This room." He pointed to a center room not far from Maddie's office.

"The robot boys." Maddie tapped at the square with her hand brushing his warm rough skin.

"Who?" Tim cleared his throat and seemed to inch closer.

"They work on different things solo. As a group, they love to tinker with robotics and so on. Very advanced but they don't really have a direction. More like, what can the Frankenstein guys build today? What about them?" Maddie leaned closer.

Tim laughed. "The room seemed disorganized. I wanted to make sure what they did before I decided what to do with it. No one was there."

"The robot boys must've been on other projects. They're a fun group but there's no leader or assistant to keep them on task."

"Are you dating one of them?" he asked out of the blue.

"No. Why would you think that?" Maddie was already screwing this up. The last thing she needed was for him to think there was another man.

Tim looked her in the eye. "You seem fond of them."

Maddie felt his stare so intensely that she felt naked. "Like brothers. I was an only child so it's nice to have guys around all the time who look out for me. We're a close group of co-workers. I just know them too well. That's why the break-ins are so strange. No one wants to be there alone now. Before we all felt safe."

"I'll start on perimeter security tomorrow. No one will hurt you." He brushed a strand of hair behind her ear and rested his hand behind her. "I was an only child too. Must be nice to have those kinds of friends."

Maddie nodded shakily. His arm was warm behind her neck on the back on the sofa. "Do you have any half or stepsiblings?" She knew it was a dumb question but she didn't know what else to say. His touch turned off her brain. She hoped she didn't do or say anything else really stupid.

"I don't want to talk about that." He leaned closer.

Maddie knew it was now or never. She pressed across the few inches and kissed him softly. The scent of him overrode her brain as his arm wrapped around her shoulders. Her hands found his shoulders, the feel of his muscles made her nipples hard. She wasted no time in pulling him closer. She wasn't sure how it'd happened but he was seducing her! Apparently she just needed to be a little more confident. Wearing the perfume had done the work for her.

When she slid her tongue into his mouth, Tim pulled back. "Don't start something you don't want to finish."

She never expected him to be such a gentleman. The ball was in her court and Maddie wasn't going to back out. She'd never get this sort of courage again if she didn't do it this time. The perfume was on her side. Looking at Tim, she would regret it if she didn't take the chance now. Wrapping her fingers around the neckline of his T-shirt, she tugged him closer and kissed him so there was no mistake. He wasn't pushing but she couldn't resist.

Shutting out any doubts, Maddie tried to take her time and enjoy the intensity of the kiss. His hands caressed her upper arms. Maddie felt him guide her to her feet and lead them to his bedroom without breaking the kiss that had her moaning ever so slightly in her throat.

As she felt the bed against the back of her knees, something in the back of Maddie's mind flipped. Her hands stopped shaking as she tugged his shirt over his head, breaking the kiss just long enough to admire him. The man was a drug. She wanted more.

Tim reached to pull her back but she turned the tables. Her hands steered him to sit on the bed then slipped her own top off. A surge of sexual confidence filled her while Tim stared. Every other time Maddie'd had sex she'd let the man lead, not wanting to make a wrong move. This time it would be different—she could feel it.

She unwrapped her skirt and let it fall, rewarded with the sight of his erection growing under his jeans. Standing in her underwear and pumps, Maddie didn't let her hands stop for fear that she might feel self-conscious. Instead she unhooked her bra. She felt sexy and safe with Tim—it was an intoxicating first.

Tim reached for her again. She stepped back and out of her pumps as she let the lacey underwire bra fall. Not one to give up control, he slipped a finger between her lavender French-cut underwear and her hip and tugged until the panties joined the rest of her clothes on the floor.

Unable to wait anymore, she ran her hand up his arm while straddling his lap. Maddie let her hands mold over his chest. "You must work out."

"You want to discuss that now?" He cracked a subtle smile.

"You'll need the stamina." She licked her lips.

Tim reached for her again. Maddie knew she'd have to concentrate to keep her sanity. His hands were gentle but not tentative. They cupped her breasts, teasing her nipples until she arched her back for more. There was no doubt what she wanted. Maddie slipped her hand lower and opened his jeans.

She wasn't about to rush or act as eager as she felt. Instead she slowly ran one long mauve-painted nail up his hard cock. The idea that she'd aroused him so fully made her want him more.

Tim leaned back on his hands with a groan. "You're a tease."

Maddie smiled with growing confidence. She could do anything. Have anything with him. She'd doubted her plan? At the moment, she had no idea why. Tim would enjoy it as much as she would.

"Do I pass inspection?" His voice was raspy but made Maddie shiver.

"Definitely worth further study." From her somewhat limited hands-on research, she could tell his penis was roughly average length. Maybe a bit better. It was the thickness that had her getting wetter by the second.

She shifted off him and knelt down for a closer look. She slid his pants down and he quickly kicked off his shoes to make it easier for her to get them off. Then she softly tongued the head as he muttered something that sounded encouraging. The taste of him clouded her mind even more. She kissed her way up his chest letting her sensitive pussy press against his shaft. His body was just too good.

Tim pulled her flat against him, kissing her in bites and licks as she shifted her hips to separate her lips and ride him with the most sensitive parts of her. All the girls she knew in college would've killed to be where she was. Maddie felt powerful and vulnerable and loved it.

She wanted to really ride him, fuck him just like this. The feeling of him against her clit plus the taste of his devouring mouth made it hard to think at all. Tim's kisses messed with her mind. His strong hands kneading her ass didn't help either. Finally, she caught his lower lip in her teeth and pulled back slightly.

"We need a condom." No reason to play games. Maddie knew she couldn't take the foreplay much longer. More importantly, she didn't want to. She wanted him and didn't want to ruin it by getting cold feet. Why she was here suddenly didn't matter. Desire for Tim pounded through her body.

Tim tried to get up but she held him down. "Where?" She leaned down to tease his flat nipples with her teeth.

"Drawer." He nodded to the nightstand.

Maddie crawled up him. She opened the drawer and fished out a condom. Then she felt his tongue trace arousing patterns on her breasts.

She stalled there for a bit, letting them both enjoy the position. Eventually she sat back and opened the packet. It wasn't the time for patience.

Grabbing it, Tim wasted no time putting it on and then tried to lift her. Maddie had no intention of changing positions. "I told you not to move." She pushed him flat on his back and lifted herself onto his lean, hard body. Slowly she sank onto his cock, one hand anchored on his chest with the other teasing his balls and holding him steady. Maddie wanted this to be perfect. There was no way to know how many chances she'd get. It was even better than she'd ever imagined.

His hips eased up slightly and Maddie gasped at the reality of his width. Her body stretched and tightened around him until she had every inch. Maddie opened her eyes. Tim was watching her every breath. It felt like he could look right through her—all the way down to her soul.

His hands skimmed up her legs and grabbed her ass, tipping her forward to him. Maddie braced her hands on the bed and kissed him. Still mostly inside her, Tim's hips pumped again as she ground down more. His hands urged her back up. Maddie could get lost in the pace but didn't want it over too soon.

Pulling back from the kiss, she looked him in the eye and slowly eased up until only the tip of him had any contact with her. His hands tried to urge her down but she resisted. She could wait—but not long. Teasing him made it even better. Tim's hands relaxed and one slipped around to the pale brown hair between her legs, finding her clit.

Maddie groaned in approval. She wanted—needed—his cock. Of course, she wouldn't say no to his extra effort.

Her body had finally had enough of pleasure games and sank back down. Tim gasped at her quick change-up. She plunged relentlessly, while his fingers stayed on her clit, only driving her need harder toward release.

He was such a perfect fit—she wanted to mold a vibrator out of him. The odd thought evaporated as her pussy convulsed around him. The best orgasm of her life took over. She clawed at his shoulders, trying to brace herself for more as the waves of pleasure hit.

Tim held her as she came down. Talk about a natural high. Maddie wondered why anyone would bother with any other drug.

"You have a wild focus." He started to turn them over. Maddie shook her head. He was still hard inside her—the fun wasn't over.

"Don't you like this position?" she whispered.

"I love it, but you're done." He stroked her hair.

"I'm just starting." She tongued his neck while slowly moving her hips again. Her body was vibrating on its own. Still wanting the feel of his hard cock inside. It couldn't be over until she saw him go over. Maddie needed to finish what she had started. The simple idea of getting him off was turning her on again.

This time she leaned back, trying a more direct up and down motion that triggered what had to be her G-spot. She fucked him—hard. Tim kept his hands on her hips but made no move to stop her as his hips met hers. When his fingers dug into her flesh, she knew he was close and backed off. His hips pounded up at her from the bed. Her body tightened around him, not wanting to let go.

When she landed on him, she saw stars. This was how sex was supposed to be. The G-spot was no myth. Now she had first-hand evidence. Maybe she'd study that next. Then she heard her name escape Tim's lips and she opened her eyes.

Tim's orgasm was amazing to watch. In the midst of her own haze, Maddie held on as he gripped her and pumped, whispering something that she wanted to believe was her name again. Neither was left with an ounce of energy to even look for the covers.

Chapter Three

Maddie's eye snapped open as she felt Tim move beneath her in his sleep. Her body still hummed approvingly at her efforts. Her brain was in shock. Somehow she'd managed it. She'd spent the night with Tim on what was barely a first date. He'd seemed completely into her. Things like this never happened to her.

Now that the hormones had subsided, Maddie knew it was her pheromone perfume she had to thank for last night. It wasn't really about her. But it would serve the plan.

She'd never intended to stay the night. Glancing at the nightstand clock, she saw it was already three in the morning. Deep down she knew she should grab her things and leave. Being this intimate could mean getting attached to him. His body was warm and seductively strong. Hard to pass up.

Shifting so she wasn't completely on him, Maddie noticed that Tim didn't even move. A heavy sleeper, she concluded and gave herself a few more minutes of pleasure. Hadn't she gotten enough? Maddie was stunned at herself wanting more.

A man like this was one she couldn't really keep. Like all the non-academics she'd briefly dated, he'd grow tired of her talk of experiments at the think tank. Tim may have attended Princeton, but he'd made his life much too normal to take her seriously. Which was why Maddie knew she'd made the right choice. A little fun and a little payback. He'd learn a lesson, then they'd both go back to their lives. At least now, Maddie knew she could actually let go of her controlled side. There was passion in her.

Maddie decided to enjoy every second she could, especially if Tim didn't know about it. Her lips trailed down his throat while her nails softly dragged along the plane of his chest. There was time to take in the feel, scent and beauty of his naked body. Before she went too far, Maddie eased from the bed, shimmied into her clothes and grabbed her purse.

She crossed her fingers that he hadn't set the alarm when she wasn't looking. The green light on the panel looked harmless so she tried the back door. Luckily no sirens blared. She made it to her car with a sigh. The plan had sounded so simple but already it felt complicated.

As she drove, Maddie reminded herself of the big picture. She was dealing with her past and, as a bonus, had the best sex of her life! The pheromones worked.

* * * * *

Tim started the morning with some simple perimeter security. He had no intention of pushing Maddie too far, too fast. He missed her. Somehow things last night had moved at warp speed. In his defense, she'd been the one with her foot on the gas. Waking up without her had made him wonder. Did she regret it? He wasn't in a hurry to hear that news.

By midday, Tim was itching to see her again. He made his way to her office to find her bent over her laptop inputting data with an intent look on her face.

"I missed you this morning," he said instead of a standard greeting. He wanted to see how she reacted.

Maddie blushed a deep red, rolled her chair away from the desk and stood. Then she fidgeted. "Sorry about that. I woke up at three. I didn't have anything to wear or any of my stuff. I don't usually do that sort of thing."

"It's not an everyday experience for me either." He crossed the room and overrode her tension with an engulfing kiss. Relief filled him when she eagerly kissed him back.

"When I didn't see you here all morning, I thought you were upset." She pressed her lips to his collarbone, slowly working her way up.

Tim tightened his grip on her waist. Maddie mysteriously knew every button to press. The collected Dr. Simons could be vulnerable as well as passionate. "No, just got pulled into that robotics project down the hall." He leaned closer to inhale the scent of the lavender shampoo she used. It did anything but relax him.

Maddie abruptly lifted her head. Tim resisted the impulse to maneuver her back into action. Was he going to do her there on the desk? That might be pushing his luck.

"You were working with the robotics team?" She looked surprised.

"Nothing really." He shrugged. "They needed a second opinion."

"I thought you were a security expert."

"It's all the same. Circuits and programming. I used to rewire and fix everything in the trailer park my dad managed." Inwardly, he cursed himself. He hadn't meant to share that lovely bit about his father. It was too late. If she thought she was too good for him before, she'd know it for sure now. His tough exterior was slipping fast.

"Did you fix it?" she asked.

"I fix all sorts of things." He didn't want to talk about it. Maddie wasn't shutting him out and nothing else mattered. It was so rare he felt close to anyone, mostly because he didn't let them in. Nothing could keep her out.

"I meant the robot. They do some extremely advanced stuff. It's over my head." Her smile seemed to say that she was impressed.

"Sure, it works now." He wasn't interested in that topic but it was better than her asking about his family again. This woman had a power over him. Just like college, only worse because he'd had her now. On the other hand, it was better because he could have her again.

"Impressive. Be careful Dr. Bellows doesn't try to hire you on here. You'll become one of us." She gave him a tender kiss that hit him hard.

He could think of a lot worse things than seeing Maddie every day. Unfortunately he knew better than to believe he'd be invited. Tim didn't doubt he had the brains. He possessed the skills. However, he didn't have the degrees to back them up. Never earned anything beyond his bachelor's degree. Everyone here was post-graduate and overeducated all the way. It wasn't likely they'd turn over some big project to him.

"I like working for myself." He changed the subject. "What experiment are you working on?"

Maddie looked over her shoulder at a bench with several glass bottles. "Pheromone study. We're trying to determine how effective certain concentrations are when added to everyday commercial perfume."

"How do you study that?" He moved over to the bench to take a closer look.

"We get couples to volunteer. They chart their sexual activity and reactions for a month without any added pheromones. Then we add them to the wife's existing perfume and have them chart for the next month."

"They all get a real dose?"

"Of course not. Some get a placebo and some get a dose. It's all tracked, then the results compared anonymously."

"What about the men's cologne?" He turned to face her.

"That's next. One variable to test at a time."

She was so professional about her studies, even when they involved sex. "Got a lot of data back yet?" Tim wondered if she knew the power she had over him *without* any perfume additives.

"No, we just started the second phase with the pheromones so it'll be a few more weeks. Assuming no one breaks in and destroys my work. How's the security going?"

"Looks like someone got in the side door again. Nothing was missing or moved but I'm focused on perimeter right now. Internal security seems to be less of a problem." He had done some work today. There was a lot more ahead of him.

"Working late?" Her question sounded innocent.

"No. I'll have three guys working with me. I'll pull more on if I need them." He moved in closer.

"You could come over for dinner. I'm no cook but I order in very well."

"Sounds great." Tim leaned in and kissed her without restraint. Her response told him that she wasn't done with him.

Tim's brain did something it had never done until Maddie. It shut off. All he felt was Maddie plus his own desire. She was too good to be true. His instincts had been right all along. No wonder he couldn't get over her. His hands steadied her as she wrapped her arms around his neck, deepening their kiss.

In the distance, he heard the door open and wished he'd thought to lock it.

Maddie immediately pulled back. It was Ginny in the doorway but it didn't make her feel any better. She'd never been caught in the act of anything before. She'd never done anything to be caught at before.

It felt exactly like she'd imagined it would. Instead of doing what Maddie expected—apologizing and leaving, Ginny just stood there looking stunned.

"I'd better get back to work," Tim finally said.

Ginny grinned at him politely but her expression was hard to read. Once he was gone, she closed the door. "What's going on?"

"What were you doing, spying on us?" Maddie wiped off her smudged lipstick.

"I wasn't spying. I just wanted to see how you were dealing with his working at the tank. I didn't know he'd be here. I guess you've forgiven him." Ginny leaned on the door.

"I tried, but I couldn't." Maddie eased into her desk chair. "This is giving me a migraine."

Ginny came farther into the room. "What do you mean? If you haven't forgiven him why were you kissing him?"

Maddie knew Ginny wouldn't approve, yet she needed a sane voice. "I really tried to put it behind me, Ginny. He was just so distant and rude yesterday. I had to do something to get back at him. I felt like I was right back in college. I needed to take charge this time."

"So you dated him?"

"No, well yes. I have to get past this somehow so I decided to use the pheromone perfume to have some fun." Maddie knew she didn't truly hate Tim. If she did, she'd never have slept with him. There was just something in her that needed to take action. And now…sex had never been like that before. She wondered if her reaction was due to him or her own mental state mixed with the perfume. He'd still hurt her back in college. A big part of her was still mad. Tim needed to learn a lesson.

"Fun? Dating? Perfume?" Ginny sat in the guest chair. "Tell me what happened."

"Dinner was great. He's very smart. I can actually talk to him." Maddie didn't want to count how few men fit that list.

"You didn't bring up college?" Ginny lifted a pencil-drawn eyebrow.

"We talked a little about it but not much. I went to his place and we had dinner and wine…it all happened so fast. I don't know what came over me. It was so good." Maddie's headache faded at the thought.

"He was already here this morning wanting more? I'm very confused how this works if you're mad at him." Ginny frowned.

"He got me dumped so the most logical form of revenge to help me feel that we're even is to dump him. I left in the middle of the night. It just seemed too strange sleeping there." She shivered, remembering how she really didn't want to leave at all.

"Obviously you didn't dump him from what I saw just now." She lifted a finger at the door.

"No. Not after one night. I'm just not sure I can manage this. The sex is unbelievable! I don't want it to end but I feel terrible lying." Maddie wanted to talk to him about everything. She'd never met anyone so easy to talk with as Tim. She could tip her hand with too much talk about college or her perfume study though.

"The answer is simple. Tell him the truth. You'll only feel worse if you put it off. It's good you recognize you're not past this and want to get there. There simply has to be a better way." Maddie knew Ginny watched too many episodes of *Dr. Phil* and put her own spin on them every time.

Maddie also knew that Ginny had a point. The result of telling the truth was to dump him anyway. She didn't want that yet. Tim had brought out a passion she'd never experienced. If she confessed, then it'd be over. It was her own fault. She wanted more. Which meant she had to keep up the perfume. It was the only way.

"I don't think I can tell him the truth," Maddie admitted.

"Then you'll have no one to blame except yourself when it blows up." Ginny's tone was matter of fact.

"I know." The results would be bad, but would they be worse after some more amazing sex?

"You *can* tell him the truth and you'll feel better when it's done. Then you'll forget all about it except for being the bigger person. You're not in college anymore." Ginny's last remark hit home.

"But on this topic, I still feel like I am." Maddie gave a shrug as Ginny left.

Ginny was the complete opposite of Maddie's own mother and for that Maddie was grateful. Ginny didn't care how smart Maddie was or wasn't. She only cared if Maddie was happy. Since Maddie had come to work at the tank, Ginny had made it her personal job to get Maddie to stretch her personal skills a little more than her brain.

Deep down, Maddie knew she needed to resolve things with Tim. Everyone had humiliating stories about junior high or high school—that wasn't news. But to have college ruined and for her to have run away like that not so long ago—the wound was still fresh. Maddie was as mad at herself as she was at Tim. She'd beat herself up about it for months in England. Now she had a chance to share the blame. Tim might not be the same man who had hurt her back in college—she suspected he'd matured—but it wasn't like the plan was going to seriously hurt anyone.

People got dumped every day of the week. It was hardly criminal. Plus he was getting some fun sex out of it too. Most guys wouldn't complain. He probably wouldn't even be mad. It was a sound rationale. Maybe then Maddie could be more confident when she dealt with any man who crossed her path—or her bed. She'd keep a good supply of the perfume at the house just in case.

When the security job was done, Tim would be on to the next job—and for all she knew, the next woman. She'd feel better for being the dumper not the dumpee and that's what mattered. She'd be empowered. Her IQ was high enough. She needed some more notches on her bedpost with a man who could have any woman he wanted.

For now, he wanted her!

Chapter Four

Maddie had ordered all her usuals and a few extras from her favorite Chinese place. Mrs. Wong had sounded very stunned when she'd more than doubled her usual order. Luckily, the Golden Panda was too busy for Maddie to get questioned by the old Chinese lady who always sent her extra sweet and sour sauce. It was a relief because Mrs. Wong routinely wanted to know if she'd found a nice boy yet. Maddie wasn't sure what she'd have said this time.

Timing it just right, Mrs. Wong's youngest son had dropped off the food and collected the cash by quarter to seven. Then Maddie dabbed on the pheromone perfume to be ready for Tim.

Food spread out on her square glass kitchen table, Maddie found two fortune cookies at the bottom of the bag. She'd ordered almond cookies for dessert but couldn't resist cracking one open just to see her fortune. She didn't need a prediction for great sex—that was a certainty. She really needed a sign.

The little piece of paper mocked her with its words. *True love will knock at your door.*

Confusion rattled her. Maddie ate the cookie and stuck the fortune in the pocket of her black slacks. When had she begun taking advice from a cookie? That was desperate and not at all scientific. But Tim had a strong effect on her. *Love will knock at your door.* Sure, and a new car will fly out of the fireplace.

Then there was a knock at the door.

Maddie looked at her watch, seven sharp. Why couldn't Tim use the doorbell like normal people? The fortune had said nothing about bells.

The excitement wasn't something she could ignore. Maddie opened the door. It wasn't just Tim, it was Tim with flowers. He was making it hard to dislike him.

Maddie felt the heat rush to her face. Why had she gotten her mother's ultra-pale complexion and tendency to blush at the slightest thing? Men should bring flowers. Maybe it was just a second date habit for Tim. She felt a pang of guilt over it either way. She didn't deserve it.

"Hi." He took a step inside her newish little ranch house. "Nice place."

"Thanks. I bought the model when they were done with the subdivision. Saved me a lot of decorating." The automatic and very boring response gave away her distraction. Her eyes were on the flowers.

"These are for you." He extended the flowers.

"Thanks." Maddie hesitated but took the roses. "They're beautiful."

"Probably need some water," he suggested.

"Right." Maddie felt her feet become unstuck and headed into the kitchen. She found the one vase she had, set it in the sink and flipped on the water.

She wasn't being the world's best hostess and turned to find him inches away. His mouth was reassuring on her neck, making all of the uneasiness slip away.

"I hope you like Chinese." Her eyes eased shut as she leaned into him.

"Love it." He reached behind her, turning off the water that was overflowing the vase.

"Something to drink?" Maddie's hands slid up his arms in no hurry to move.

"Sure." He slowly stepped back and opened the fridge to their left.

Maddie put the flowers in the water. "There's some white wine if you want to open it." She set the vase on the table, still amazed she'd been given roses.

Tim brought two diet Cokes.

"Not in the mood for wine?" She went for glasses. Maddie wasn't a big drinker but it hadn't hurt last night to relax her.

"I don't really drink much. If you want wine, I'll open it. It's just my dad died of cirrhosis so I try to limit my alcohol."

"Oh, I'm sorry." Maddie set the glasses on the table and filled them.

"He did it to himself. The only thing he ever drank was beer. I try to avoid all of it." Tim stood like a statue, his eyes focused on some invisible spot in the distance.

Maddie moved closer. She wasn't great at emotional stuff but she understood parental issues. "I bet you've never touched a beer in your life."

Tim snapped back to look at her. "You'd lose that bet. I had a few in college before dad died. That stopped me cold. A glass of wine now and then is about all I do. To make sure I'm in control of it."

"I don't blame you." Maddie gently kissed his jaw. "Did your mother leave because of his drinking?"

Tim nodded. His eyes wandered back somewhere over her shoulder.

"And she left you with him?" Maddie tangled her fingers in his hair.

"Pretty much. Ready to eat?" He stepped away and pulled out a chair for her.

"I thought my parents were bad." Maddie didn't push the issue. That was too much intimacy for the plan. She sat and grabbed a carton of wontons.

Half an hour later, Tim had proven himself equally as skilled as Maddie at the use of chopsticks. Maddie cleared the table, leaving only the almond cookies and the lonely fortune cookie.

"They only gave us one. You don't want a fortune?" Tim held up the plastic-wrapped cookie.

"No, you take it. I only get fortunes that say, 'A friend is like sunshine' or something like that. I like the almond cookies." She grabbed one.

"Okay." Tim tore open the plastic and cracked the cookie. Popping the cookie into his mouth, he straightened the little piece of paper. "'Secrets will be revealed.' You're right. The fortunes are a bust. That's a great place for Chinese food."

"Thanks. I'm a frequent customer." She quickly finished off her diet Coke and set the glass in the sink with a clink. If she had anything to do with it, no secrets would come out. Not tonight at least.

"Speaking of secrets. You know about my family now. What's weird about yours?" he asked.

Maddie lifted one shoulder and wondered if she could divert his attention with sex. Moving back to the table, she eased into his lap. "Nothing really."

"Come on. I know mine are exceptional, weird and uncomfortable, but there's always something." He wrapped his arms around her waist.

His touch felt like a truth serum. "Mine were basically the opposite. Completely over-attentive. My parents were both teachers. I skipped grades because my mother had started me early on everything. They were convinced I was going to be brilliant and pushed and pushed." It was her turn to be tense.

"Aren't you brilliant?" Tim toyed with her hair.

Maddie pressed close, attempting to think more of Tim than her history. But her history was part of why she had to do this and he should know. "My IQ is good but it was more grade skipping. I had two full-time teachers at home. I had homework from them and tests and languages and classes all summer and every break. It was more boot camp than natural ability. You do that to any kid starting from birth and they'll either deal or freak out."

"So Vegas looked good compared to…?"

"Boston. They're still there. I go home at Christmas for one week. It's nice. I get a good dose of snow with a side dish of guilt and I'm ready to come back." She smiled and looked into his sympathetic eyes. "No one ever abandoned me or ignored me. I had it pretty good overall. I just didn't do exactly what they wanted. They're a bit disappointed in me."

Tim pulled her face down and kissed her slowly. She could put on a brave front all she wanted, but he could see the pain in her eyes. No wonder she was always on edge. He'd grown up wanting attention and she'd grown up trying to avoid it. To her, all attention had some grade or judgment behind it. The blushing and the jumpiness all added up. School had been his salvation—for her it was a prison.

She didn't seem on edge in his arms though. In his lap, Maddie was kissing him back with a need deeper than sex. He could feel it in her hands as they moved on his neck and up to his slight case of five o'clock shadow.

Tim couldn't resist. "How many PhDs do you have?"

Maddie pulled away, lips pressed into a smile, and smacked his shoulder. "Only one."

Tim rolled his eyes, deliberately unimpressed. "Anyone can do that." He tugged the pale-green blouse from her pants and undid the buttons slowly.

"That's what I like about the tank. I'm average there." She looked down at his hands as the blouse fell away. "Don't you think we should go into the bedroom?"

"Not as bossy tonight? Anywhere you want. Lead the way." He got up and followed her, studying the satin seafoam-green bra from the back. Not a man interested in fashion, even Tim could appreciate that the woman had sexy underwear.

Tim loved the fact that she wasn't shy or the type to play games. From behind, he undid her pants. Her soft skin made him wish he had more hands.

She turned and Tim's shirt was gone before he knew it and her lips were teasing his chest. This time things would go a little differently. He pulled her against him, kissing her while running his hands down her shoulders to her bra. It was gone in an instant. His hands slowly slipped down to her panties and then around, up to cup her perfect breasts. The dark pink color of her nipples contrasted with her pale skin to drive him crazy.

Tim dipped his head, licking and nipping until her peaks were hard while the rest of her skin flushed. "Lie back." He backed her up to the bed.

"No, you." Her hands didn't put up too much of a fight, though she managed to loosen his jeans and push them down before she sank down to the thick comforter. She gave in and Tim knew it'd be dangerously good.

Tim slipped off her panties and ran his hands from her pink painted toes up to her hips. His lips pressed into her curls, finding it more than erotic that she didn't shave or wax the area at all. The strong scent of her arousal made him instantly hard. It'd be even better with his self-control intact this time. She was an instigator.

Then Maddie slowly shifted, opening her legs. Self-control was obliterated. Tim sank to his knees at the side of the bed and let his tongue explore her warm folds.

She squirmed and moaned his name. Tim tongued her clit down to her core and pressed inside, following as her hips lifted.

Backing off slowly, he teased her outer lips and slid a thumb just inside her. He couldn't go too fast, no matter how badly he wanted to satisfy her.

"More." She grabbed the hand on her breast and pulled it to her mouth.

Tim held on to his control while removing his hand. The taste of her was what he needed and he was done playing. Both his hands braced her as his tongue dipped into her wetness and worked its way up the inner lips. He circled her clit and had her twisting her hips for more. No one had ever been more responsive. He'd never needed any woman more.

His taste buds took in every bit of her. Then he wanted to hear her, to taste her climax. The tip of his tongue pressed against her clit and her hips jerked. He took his time to find the perfect rhythm for her. It took only a few firm swirls to push her over the edge. He didn't want it to end.

His cock strained for attention but his mouth didn't want to stop. When her cries stopped, Tim kissed his way up her body and slid his tongue into her mouth. The drive to possess as much of her as possible was insanely strong.

Her hands worked down his back, eventually pushing his boxer-briefs and jeans off his hips. Tim broke contact long enough to get rid of his clothes. He wanted the focus between them. Clothes were just a distraction. Tim had to give in to her.

Maddie scooted back so she was fully on the bed. For a moment, he paused to admire her. Long limbs and a waist that flared to sexy hips made for his hands. But her breasts were to die for. Firm and full, they stood at attention for him. He had to have her again.

"My turn." She reached for his cock.

"Not now." Tim wanted to feel her mouth on him but there was only so much foreplay and teasing he could take. Her mouth wasn't enough for the need he had. He wanted more of her now.

Maddie didn't argue and pulled him down on top of her while her hand dug into a drawer and produced a condom. He made no protest, putting it on before he was too carried away. Her skin felt like warm velvet from lips to toes. Tim felt every inch pressed up against him. No way was he going to rush this. Every time he was with her, he wanted it to last forever.

Her legs wrapped around his and teased up his calves encouragingly. Not that her lips and hands were idle. He'd captured her mouth, teasing her tongue with his. Finally, she braced his head with her hands and deepened the kiss to a dizzying intensity. Tim had more than a weakness for her.

Patience gone, he sank into her. Maddie's body tightened around every part of him and her hips lifted. Pulling away for air, Maddie moaned. He found the right pace for them and reclaimed her mouth. Tim knew he'd never be satisfied unless he had all of her. All at once.

Her fingernails digging into his back, Maddie met his every move. Suddenly her body tightened. She orgasmed, mumbling inaudibly into his mouth.

One more thrust and he followed. Tim was completely in over his head with her. He never wanted to come up for air as he collapsed on top of her. This was the woman he was meant to have.

* * * * *

Tim felt a warm kiss on his neck, teasing him from sleep. Somehow he'd ended up on his back again. Then again, he always slept flat on his back. Maddie fit so nicely, curled up against him. Being in her bed meant she wasn't going to bolt this time. She'd invited him, so she didn't want to. He couldn't ask for anything more.

The fact that it was one o'clock in the morning and she was teasing him and kissing him sent his ego soaring. Wrapping his palm against the back of her neck, he pulled her gently to him. A soft and slow kiss to start, he wanted to keep her there all night and make out like teenagers. They'd gone beyond that already, but he wanted to sample her at every pace — not just overdrive.

Inevitably, she came up for air with a smile. "Sorry to wake you."

"Taking advantage of me in my sleep?" He ran his fingers through her hair as she leaned in for more contact. Maddie dazzled him with her shameless passion.

"Not yet." She pressed a hand against one shoulder and ran it down his chest, not pushing, but it felt like she was just admiring his form.

"We do have to work tomorrow." He folded his arms over his head, not about to stop whatever she had in mind. If she started it, he wasn't going to be blamed for her complete lack of sleep.

Her tongue teased his ribs and nipped at his stomach and hips. The woman wasn't wasting any time. Maddie wasn't the type to play around when she was after something.

When her lips touched the base of his cock, Tim tangled a hand in her hair. He had no intention of stopping her but it was a reflex.

Maddie smiled as she tongued the head of his cock dipping her head and taking him in until he felt the back of her throat.

Tim made no effort to stifle his groans as she continued to suck him. It wasn't enough—he wanted to feel her body. He tugged her hair slightly to get her attention.

Backing off, she looked up at him. "What's wrong?" she whispered.

"Come here." His hand was on the back of her neck, urging her up to him.

"No. I want this. Behave." She pushed his hand away and gently pressed her lips to his balls.

Tim didn't have the strength to argue. Maddie's mouth enveloped him again and he was happily at her mercy. Her mouth worked farther and farther down until again he was at the back of her throat. Tim knew he wouldn't last long.

Then he felt her press lower. The intense pleasure of his cock being completely surrounded by her mouth and throat to the point her lips were at his base blurred everything. She didn't even seem to be straining.

Maddie was amazing! No woman had ever done that to him. He was too big, or so he'd thought. She must have no gag reflex. He already knew she had intense focus. How she applied it was impressive.

Tim couldn't think until she finally eased back and picked up the speed. Her hand snug over his balls and anchoring him for her.

She clearly knew her power over him and was working him. He'd never been happier than that second when he came in her mouth. There'd been no time to warn her. She showed no interest in moving her mouth away, licking up every drop.

Through the haze, Tim heard a familiar tune. He knew it. How did he know it? Maddie's tongue was still licking at him. She was thorough and he'd never enjoyed it so much. Good sex had never put a ringing in his ears before but this was an actual tune.

"What *is* that?" Maddie sat back finally.

The ringing hadn't been in his head. Relieved, Tim got up on his elbows and with some blood back in his brain it was obvious. "Cell phone."

"Not mine." She wasn't interested.

Neither was he. "Don't you have any gag reflex?" He pulled her close to him.

"It's just a reflex. Mind over matter." She gave him a smug smile. Then the phone rang again.

"It's mine. It's in my pants pocket." Tim started to move but Maddie, being on top, got there first and leaned over grabbing his jeans. The view of her ass was worth any late night interruption. He moved to steady her in case she reached too far.

Back on solid bed, she handed him the cell phone. It'd stopped ringing by now but before Tim could go in for his messages it rang again. The caller I.D. said it was his monitoring station. In his experience, private contractors responded better than the bigger companies, so he'd created one himself. The added money was good and he could trust his work would be maintained.

He flipped open the phone and hit the speed dial. "Foxmor returning a call."

"There's an alarm at the Bellow's location. Back door. You asked to be notified," the operator supplied.

"Thanks. Send the cops. I'm on my way."

"Yes sir." The operator disconnected. Tim shook his head in disgust.

"What?" Maddie had tugged on a bra and panties during the call.

"Another break-in. Damn, the cameras aren't even up yet." Tim pulled on his pants and T-shirt before shoving the phone back in his pocket.

"The cops have been there before. They never find anything." Maddie dug in her drawer for a T-shirt and jeans.

"That's in the morning. The alarm just went off so we've got a better shot." Tim stepped into his shoes and found his keys. "You don't have to come if you don't want to."

"I won't sleep anyway now." She laced up her gym shoes then pulled her hair back into a ponytail.

She still looked incredible. Tim was now really pissed at whoever was breaking in. Not only was he endangering Maddie's work, but he was interrupting their time alone.

* * * * *

Fifteen minutes later they pulled in at the tank, both yawning and full of adrenaline at the same time. The squad car's flashing lights eased Tim's mind. He wasn't bringing Maddie into a dangerous situation. The cops wouldn't let anyone in, even him, until they'd cleared it.

Of course, Maddie headed straight for the front door as soon as they stopped.

"Sorry, ma'am, we need to talk to you first."

"Did you catch them?" she replied.

"No, it was empty. Whoever it was got in but we can't tell where." The cop nodded to Tim.

"Alarm monitor said back door. It isn't broken?" Tim thought that was strange. Someone must've left it unlocked.

They all went around back and found the door closed, no sign of break-in. "Maybe someone lost their key and someone else found it?" The cop shrugged. "We swept inside. No one. If you want to go in and let us know if anything is missing we can make out a report."

"That'll have to wait until morning. When everyone is in to inventory their things." Maddie said as she went in, heading straight for her office. The door was thrown open. Tim waited while she checked her computer, the experiment and her drawers for anything missing. "Nothing's gone."

"I'm going to check the robot room." Tim grabbed Maddie's hand. He hadn't intended to, but he didn't want her far from him right now. To his relief, she laced her fingers in his. Any robbery would be unsettling—more than one had her nerves shot. Tim could feel her anxiety.

The robot room proved as untouched as her office. The door was open. One of the prototypes was on the floor but not harmed. "Weirdest thing I've ever seen," Tim uttered.

The cop stood in the doorway. "I'd make sure no one has lost their key. Change the locks. Someone is getting in without breaking in."

"From what I've learned, the other break-ins were similar, correct?" Tim asked.

"The first one we assumed someone left the door open. I mean it happened all the time before. Whoever comes in first finds the door unlocked. We didn't notice until something was broken or moved around. That's when we started locking up.

One time there was a broken window. We thought it was just an accident, maybe some kids. It doesn't make sense." Maddie put the robot back where it belonged.

"An officer will be back in the morning to get your information. I'm going to take a final tour and make notes about anything that looks odd. You two okay?" the cop asked.

"Fine." Tim watched the cop stroll on. "I'll have the crew working on the cameras first thing tomorrow and change the locks to key cards like in the hotels. If someone breaks in or loses their key card, you reset all the key cards and the computer. You don't have to change out locks or swap keys. It's easier. It's all on order—I'll just have them rush the shipment now."

"Sounds good." Maddie seemed lost in thought. "Will there be cameras inside?"

"That's up to you guys. I'd recommend them at least in the main halls and by the entrances. Robot room is a toss-up but probably not in the offices. I don't want any of the security people watching us in your office." He slipped his arms around her from behind and felt her tense then relax. "Sorry, didn't mean to scare you."

"You didn't." She rested her head back against his shoulder. "I just hate the idea of someone else being in here. They could ruin months of research."

"Or worse." Research could be redone. Tim liked the people here. He'd grown very protective of Maddie in a matter of days. "Promise me you'll never be here alone."

"Tim." She started to pull away.

"At least until the break-in attempts stop and the system is fully in place." He'd settle for what he could get.

"Fine. I don't usually work that late anyway. I'm more of a morning person."

"As long as you're not alone."

"I *am* a grown woman," she countered.

"I know." He pulled her close. The protectiveness toward her grew stronger in him. "And you're passionate about your work. Just don't let that passion cloud your common sense."

"Common sense isn't my biggest asset." The corners of Maddie's mouth lifted slightly.

She could fight admitting it, but everyone wanted someone to care about them. Tim knew that more than anyone. She'd just had overprotective parents who didn't know the line. He wouldn't smother her but he cared. It was too late to deny it. She just had to accept it.

Beyond that, Tim could sympathize with her. The opposite of overprotective parents wasn't much better. How many times had he been left home alone all night at not even ten years old? Nothing had ever happened more than a drunk guy cutting through the yard or a weird phone call. But it'd begun his obsession with security.

"You okay?" She tugged on his arm.

"I bet your parents never left you home alone."

Maddie frowned. "I think when I was about fourteen I put my foot down and wanted to not feel like a third wheel when they went out to dinner. Before that I went everywhere with them. They thought I needed to learn how adults acted since I was moving up grades so fast."

"That's what I thought. There's no reason to take risks." He kissed her forehead. "Let's go. We can get a few hours sleep before coming back."

"I want to be here first thing in the morning. So no one touches anything." Maddie led the way out to the hall.

"We'll be here first. But we might have to cut out early to get a nap." He wrapped an arm around her shoulders. They headed off after the cop to secure the place before they left and then they could rearm the system. Tim was pretty sure the criminal wouldn't be back tonight after the loud alarms and instant lights had been triggered, but better to be safe than sorry.

Chapter Five

The next morning, Maddie felt the good sort of tired felt only after great sex, no sleep and plenty of adrenaline. Last night had been a wild ride and Tim was the ideal partner for it. Unfortunately, the night had to end. Her routine was back at the tank. She'd come in extra early and put out the word about the break-in. Everyone knew the drill by now.

Ginny's presence reminded her of what she was doing. Enjoying herself, yes. But part of her was getting attached! It'd been easier when Tim was just the hated guy from college. Now he was a person who didn't seem at all malicious. The confusion was giving her a headache as she avoided Ginny and made the rounds with the cop who'd arrived early.

The conclusion was just as she'd predicted. Nothing was stolen. A few things were broken. There was one odd thing though. Every door in the place had been opened, including closets and bathrooms.

After the cop left, Maddie stayed in her office. Thankfully she was meeting free with a quiet day planned. She wasn't much in the mood for anything today.

"It's so weird," Maddie muttered to herself as she reviewed her personal notes from each break-in.

"What is?" Tim was in her doorway.

Maddie jumped slightly. He didn't knock, didn't even make a sound. What was the point of having an assistant who didn't warn you about guests? Not that she wasn't looking forward to seeing Tim, but he'd seen her talking to herself. She shouldn't care. This was about revenge. She wasn't out to impress anyone. It didn't feel like it anymore. It felt wonderful and worthwhile. Ginny wouldn't approve. However, for now, Ginny didn't know.

"Something wrong?" Tim closed the door behind him and came closer.

"I didn't see you there." Maddie wanted him to stay despite his distracting influence.

"Sorry. What's weird?" He sat on the desk, only inches from her.

His leg brushed hers and she suppressed a shiver. No man had ever worked on her like he did. Tim didn't even seem to be trying all that hard. "You have ears like a dog. I was just thinking out loud that it's weird that every door in the place was opened. They were looking for something. A specific something."

"Anything stolen?"

"No. Nothing. Which only adds to it. What are they looking for?" Maddie leaned back in her chair and studied Tim. He was much more pleasant than the list in front of her. When she didn't have the answer, sometimes it helped to get her mind off a problem. Tim was too tempting a distraction.

"Maybe they're not after a thing but a person," Tim suggested.

"Like a stalker?" Maddie stifled a laugh.

"What? That's so impossible?" He tugged her chair closer.

"Not impossible but very unlikely." She thought about it and then shook her head dismissively. "No. Most of the younger staff doesn't have the most active social lives. We're research geeks not models or showgirls. Not exactly prime targets and Vegas is full of beautiful people. The older staff is all married. I guess it could be someone having an affair with someone. Or maybe some online romantic interest. But why here? Why not their home? Obviously whoever they're looking for isn't here when they come, so why keep coming back in the middle of the night?"

"Obsession." He took her hand softly and tugged at her until she got up out of the chair. "The right woman does that to a man."

"That's what restraining orders are for." She knew that look in his eye by now. Part protectiveness and part desire. "No one is after me. Trust me."

"I do." Tim wrapped his strong arms around her, pressing her to him. "But this guy doesn't know where he's going when he gets in if he's after one person. Which means he's not very familiar with the place. Or he's after anyone. Or he's just plain crazy and the randomness is just that."

"Always possible." Maddie rested her head on his shoulder and the tension eased. Then she remembered how Ginny had barged in on them. If she stayed this close to Tim, things wouldn't stay calm and innocent for long. Stepping back was hard but she managed. "I should get back to work."

"You okay?" He gave her a once over.

"Sure. Just sleep deprived, thank you very much. My work has been my life for so long I'm not sure how to manage this." She gave him a playful shove toward the door. "Your fault."

"I'm not the one who woke up and started things in the middle of the night," he reminded her.

"I didn't hear any complaints." Maddie tried not to blush. It only made her redder as she remembered. It was her instigating things. Tim was like a compulsion. It wasn't enough. She wanted more of him every time she saw him. She wanted more right now but knew they'd be interrupted. Getting caught kissing the security guy was one thing. Getting caught screwing him in her own office—that was a different issue.

Especially after a break-in, people would be in and out of each other's offices talking about it. She'd been hiding on purpose but today wasn't the day to risk sex in her office. "Bellows will probably want to know about your status."

"I've got two teams of three guys on the cameras right now. That'll be in by the end of the day. It'll take another day or two to get them up and connected to the monitoring service. I'll sit on them for it. I've got one team of three converting an abandoned office into a safe room."

"Safe room?"

"Also known as a panic room. If someone is here when the alarm goes off, it's a room where they can bolt themselves in and monitor the entire complex. You can see the cameras, contact the police and lock or unlock the outside doors."

"To let in the police?" Maddie saw the virtues of the panic room.

"Exactly. Plus it's fireproof, waterproof, bulletproof and has its own energy supply with an OnStar-type communication system that can't be disconnected from any outside place like your landline phones can. You make it there and bolt yourself in. Then you'll be safer than the Prez underground."

"Before last night, I'd say it was overkill but it's good to know there's somewhere to go inside the building." Maddie sat back in her chair so she wasn't tempted to get closer to Tim again. "What about the keys?"

"That's going to take a big longer. It's on order. I'm going to have the guys wire the doors so they're ready when we get the units, but until then we'll have to make do." Tim looked frustrated.

Maddie wondered if part of it had to do with her personal safety. No one had been attacked, nothing expensive stolen or even destroyed. "I'm sure it'll all be in place in no time. Besides, no one got hurt. It doesn't seem like this person is violent so there's no reason to push the panic button."

"Nothing is going to happen to you." He looked her in the eye and Maddie felt his gaze deep within her.

"No, and nothing better happen to you while you're rewiring or installing anything either. That's more real danger." Two could play the protective role.

"I do it all the time. My guys are all safe, certified and not stupid." He leaned down and kissed her hard. "I'm going to go check on their progress. But if you ever need to stay late, you let me know."

"I don't need a bodyguard." She rolled her eyes.

"I've seen your body. You're getting one." He left without another word.

Maddie knew she'd never smiled so hard in her life. Somehow Tim had crept into her heart. It was scary, thrilling and really threw a wrench in the whole revenge idea. Even those thoughts couldn't remove the smile.

* * * * *

Tim lay in a crawlspace above the ceiling, installing another heat sensor. His team was busy turning a vacant office into the safe room. Much as he liked the people at the tank, the construction and security were antiquated beyond belief. Of course he'd only taken this job because of Maddie. He had to make sure she was safe.

Part of him still didn't want to admit his luck. He'd never imagined she'd be the least bit interested in him. She'd showed no signs in college when she was dating his roommate. Now she was in his bed and while it wasn't exactly serious, it was still early. What a difference a few years made.

His luck was finally changing! A lousy childhood followed by struggling to pay off loans to start his own company were now behind him. His company was turning a solid profit, he had a good team and now he had the reputation to expand into higher-profile security jobs on the Vegas Strip.

The best part was Maddie lived in Vegas.

Tim scooted a few feet and knew he was over Maddie's office. He added an extra heat sensor. He wasn't going to let her be in any danger. Hearing voices, he pressed his ear flat to listen. It was Ginny and Maddie, as usual.

"Things aren't going well?" Ginny asked.

"They're fine. Too well." Maddie paced the room. Tim could hear her heels clicking against the floor.

Were they talking about him? Tim loved how Maddie's reserve disappeared in bed, but she didn't confess any emotions and never wanted to talk about what their relationship was or wasn't. He'd wanted her too long to pretend a fling would be enough. But he didn't want to scare her away either.

"It's just an experiment. I have to remember that. It'll be over and I'll start fresh."

Damn, not about him. Something about the perfume study.

"You don't believe that," Ginny said.

"I know. Tim is just so nice. I don't feel good about this." Maddie flopped in her chair, springs creaking. She was smart but not the most graceful. Now she had Tim's full attention.

It *was* about him.

"Isn't this what you wanted?" Ginny asked. "Using the perfume on him. Getting even?"

"It's not turning out how I expected."

Tim's blood pressure spiked. The pounding in his ears drowned out any more as he put it all together. She was using him in her study? The perfume? She was wearing the pheromones herself and seeing if it worked? No doubt Maddie had a detailed chart on him. If she wore this much, this was the response. No wonder she was eager in the bedroom and calm outside.

Before he lost his temper, Tim worked his way back to the empty office and fresh air. No wonder she wasn't getting emotional. She wasn't interested in him. The overeducated ice queen couldn't really want him. All she wanted was his body for research. Well he wasn't going to let her win.

In less than a week he'd be done. At least he wouldn't always wonder about her. But that wasn't quite enough. She needed to learn a lesson. Getting even was an excellent idea.

Stalking through the halls, he found Maddie's office. It was now empty and without Ginny as a lookout, Tim slipped in. He set a couple of tools on the desk. In case someone came in he could pretend to be working.

He went to her workbench. The full dose of pheromone and placebo were both clearly labeled. The pheromone perfume was being used. It was about half what the placebo tube held. Two could play at this game. Both liquids were clear and that gave Tim an idea.

Maddie might not care about him. She did, however, care deeply about her research. Taking the tubes, he dumped half of the placebo down the sink of the bathroom until it was level with the perfume. In under a minute, both tubes were back. Just in each other's spot. Labels properly traded.

And while Maddie would be wearing pheromone-free perfume, Tim knew exactly how he'd repay her for turning him into an experiment. If she thought things were hot before, she'd better brace herself. Her research was going to be extremely skewed.

* * * * *

"How are we supposed to get any work done with all these people around?" Bellows barged into Maddie's office in the late morning.

It wasn't a surprise. Maddie had expected he'd stop by to check on her progress sooner or later.

"The break-ins haven't stopped. We need the extra security." Maddie didn't even look up from the papers on her desk. It was classic Bellows. He hated change and ignored problems.

"I know, but so many?" He sat down in a huff.

"Tim can't get it all done by himself." Maddie finally accept that Bellows wasn't going to bluster and go away so she put the papers in their folder and sat back. He'd have to get used to the changes eventually.

"About Tim..." Bellows seemed lost in thought.

"What about him?" Maddie tried to be normal. Tim was a complicated piece of her life. When exactly had he become a part of her life? With Bellows, it was probably just business. The only one who knew anything was going on was Ginny, and she wouldn't say anything. Of course, Tim might've talked. He wouldn't do that again! Would he?

Had he told the robot boys? Maddie didn't want whatever this was with Tim to mess up her career like in her college years. She'd never forgive him. Not that she'd forgiven him for the first time yet.

"What do you think of him?" Bellows asked.

"He's good at what he does. You only hire the best. No one has said anything about him being rude or in the way. I think he's great at the security business. Completely professional." In bed it was a different story.

"I know that. The robot boys say he's been helping them. Know anything about that?"

"I might've heard something along those lines. I'm sure it's not causing any problems with the security."

"No. It's just unique to find someone at that skill level who I haven't heard of." Bellows frowned.

"He didn't do any graduate work." Maddie knew Bellows always recruited at the Masters level or higher. The think tank was as close to an academic life as possible without students and Bellows didn't want anyone not fitting in.

"That explains it." Bellows didn't get up to leave. "Smart man with lots of practical experience."

A knock on the door was followed by Billy's face peeking in. Bellows' son had been working there all summer but Maddie had barely seen him. Not really a surprise, the kid was a bit of a flake. Who wore long sleeves in the middle of the heat of a Vegas summer? And he always had a far-off look in his eyes that made Maddie wonder.

"Hey, Dad, ready for lunch?" Billy asked.

"In a minute. Come here, I want to ask you something." Bellows waved him in.

"What?" He walked in.

"What do you think of Tim?"

"The security guy? He's great. Fixed a robot with the guys. It was so cool. He wasn't even part of the design team. Why?"

"I'm thinking of hiring him on. What about you, Maddie? Think he'd be a good addition?"

Maddie felt her pulse pick up at the thought. Tim around all day. Every day. "He's really not related to my area. The robot boys would know better. But everyone seems to like him."

"Think he'd accept?" Bellows asked the next logical question.

"I don't know. He owns his own business. Freedom. Financial independence. Why would he give that up?"

"Can't hurt to ask." Bellows stood up and nodded for his son to follow. "See you after lunch."

"Bye." Maddie exhaled as they left. If it'd been about anyone else, this conversation would've been nothing but boring, but with Tim as a topic it put her on edge.

Did she want him around? Of course. But would they always be like this or would things blow up? How could she face him everyday then?

Chapter Six

෩

The next day, Tim was still pissed. It was hard to believe Maddie was that good a liar. Technically she hadn't really lied. She'd never said a word about a relationship but then again neither had he.

Tim hadn't been himself since he'd overheard that conversation. He'd completely avoided Maddie but this morning he felt like evening the score. It was all set and by now she'd be dabbing on pure placebo. All he had to do was go get her.

The sex worked—he knew he could get her there. If that was all she wanted, he might as well enjoy that while it lasted. He'd come in very early to work on the robot project before the guys got in. Few people had arrived yet and Tim suddenly lost his patience.

Putting down his robot, he headed down the hall. Maddie had to be here by now. She was always one of the first. He found her intently working in her office and slipped in without her noticing.

Tim locked the door behind him and saw Maddie's head pop up at the sound.

"Hi," she said.

He didn't say a word as he approached her desk. Maddie looked confused as he came close. Tim kissed her roughly and was rewarded with a moan. Her hands were on his chest, tempting him for more. This scientist was going to find out what happened when the lab rats fought back.

"Is everything okay?" she asked as his mouth traveled to her neck.

He ignored the question and devoured her perfect neck. Slowly his hand slid up her thigh to the hem of her charcoal gray skirt that was short enough to make him drool. His other hand positioned on her other thigh. He rocked her chair forward and lifted her out of it.

Maddie gasped as he hiked up her skirt and set her on the edge of her desk. "What are you doing?" Maddie didn't fight him. He knew she wouldn't.

Sitting in her chair, Tim took her right foot and removed her practical black heel then dropped it on the floor. He did the same with the left shoe and kissed his way up her right calf—through her stockings—that triggered something in his brain, or rather his cock. Maddie did that—without any stockings, without any clothes for that matter.

Not this time, he realized. This time was different. He was going to make it different for her. His mouth reached her red panties and Tim knew she was experimenting with him. Her underwear got sexier and sexier every time. Now *she* was going to be experimented on.

His hands slipped under her firm ass and lifted her, pulling the stockings and underwear down, slowly freeing one leg then the other. Roaming her bare legs, he licked and kissed random spots. She trembled and jumped as he nipped her soft flesh.

"Tim, say something," Maddie pleaded.

Starting at her toes, he looked up her body to her eyes and then back down to where her skirt bunched at her waist. Nothing in the world was more inviting to him. He needed to be with her but wasn't going to let himself have her—not this time. He was going to stay in control.

Tim rolled the chair closer and kissed her thighs, inhaling the scent that was hers alone. The pads of his fingers itched to touch her. Finally he gave in, tracing a pattern through her pale brown curls.

Maddie groaned and Tim saw her head tilt back. His thumb dragged up her pussy as her legs opened even farther. Already he could see her growing wet under his touch. He ran his index finger along her outer lips and then slipped between them just above her clit. Maddie's muscles flinched as her hips rocked forward.

The power he felt was almost as good as the taste of her but he was going to make her wait. Instead he dragged that finger down to the source of her wetness making slow circles until she moved her hips down trying to get him inside of her.

He smiled and pulled his finger back and dragged it to her clit, rubbing the moisture all over. Repeating the motion three times, he was amazed at how wet she got so fast. He had the woman of his dreams writhing on a desk from one finger. His head was spinning but he wasn't done with her. Like a dream, this time with her couldn't last so he took in every detail of her.

Slowly he gave her what she wanted, sliding his index finger inside her. Warm and wet she clamped down on his finger, moaning as her hips moved back and forth. He wanted to be inside her. Wanted to possess her.

"More," she whispered.

Tim was feeling generous. He'd teased her a lot, but now he slowly introduced another finger. He glanced up at her face and cursed the fact that this would likely be their last time. Her eyes were squeezed tight and her teeth dug into her bottom lip. The woman had picked the right man for her experiment. She was smart. He'd give her that. At the moment, her brain wasn't what he wanted.

With engineering precision, he stroked his fingers deep inside her. Pressing into her hot wall, he then turned his hand and repeated the act until he'd rotated completely around her circumference. If he was going to please her so she'd never forget it, he needed to be thorough.

Her squirming hips did nothing to change his pace as he introduced a third finger and was rewarded with a gasp. There was a momentary tightness within her body then she relaxed. His fingers eased in, pressing down and rotating until he got down to his third knuckle.

Tim picked up the pace, a few experimental thrusts and found her G-spot. His name was coming out of her mouth in quick gasps, but she hadn't seen anything yet. As one hand fucked her pussy steadily, his other hand traced her opening and massaged up until his thumb was circling her clit. The scent of her was arousing.

A groan escaped her throat as if she was in pain but he knew better. His fingers were swallowed up inside her, soaked as his other hand moved from circling to rubbing her clit. The pace was teasing at first but he soon matched the clit manipulation with the thrusts and felt her hips banging into his hands matching the rhythm until she screamed his name. Tim felt her body contract around his fingers.

Carefully he removed his fingers but didn't stop rubbing her pussy. Her body was now limp on her desk, occasionally twitching when he touched her clit again. He could let her come down or drive her over the edge one last time. Using the pads of his fingers he began making a slow figure eight down from her clit and back up. He kept the same slow pace even as she murmured objections or encouragement.

Maddie's breathing became faster and her hips began to move to him until her back arched and his name escaped her lips again. Tim watched her come down from the second sexual high he'd just given her. Maddie's eyes, finally able to focus, found his. "What was that?" she asked.

Tim grabbed a handful of tissues from her desk as he left. She might be a genius but Tim was pretty sure he'd just taught her a little something without saying a word.

* * * * *

Maddie's brain was fried. What the hell had gotten into him? It wasn't like the other times. It was weirder and more intense. Finally it was the end of the day and she could hopefully slip out unnoticed. She'd spent most of the day barely able to have a conversation but who could blame her? Tim had done things to her that morning she never knew would cause such a reaction.

He hadn't used his tongue or her favorite—his nicely built cock, to fuck her brains out. No, he hadn't used anything but his long fingers. That and the commanding presence he'd walked in with. It had disturbed her at first to have him not say a word but he had been so intent on getting what he wanted. Apparently what he wanted was to make her orgasm twice with just his fingers and walk away.

Their first night together had been sexy—the best of her life—but nothing like what she'd just experienced. She liked both.

Maddie never pretended to fully understand Tim. Why did that man do anything? He was so quiet and reserved, even in college he'd kept to himself. An island of mystery. So why had he gotten her dumped? None of it made sense.

His parents certainly weren't going to win any awards. Part of her suspected it all stemmed from his family. The way he'd talked about his parents, a father who ran things with a bottle of beer or the mother who left him behind made her feel sorry for him. Tim wasn't like either of them but he was brooding. Before tonight she'd suspected he kept to himself because that was all he could control.

This morning she'd seen a different side of him. If he needed a little control trip now and then, she didn't mind. The weirdest part was how it didn't feel weird at all. Letting him have his way and trusting him with her body when he wouldn't even speak hadn't bothered her at all. It only made it more intimate.

Burying her face in her hands, Maddie knew she'd fallen for him. It was against everything she'd planned but the past wasn't going to change and it wouldn't make her happy if it did. Tim made her happy. He could confuse her without saying a word but even that felt good with him!

She knew what she had to do. Getting up from her desk, Maddie hoped he hadn't left for the day. She headed for the robot room. The boys had left early for a conference at one of the hotels on the strip so she could corner Tim there. She found him alone twisting wires and adjusting parts.

His back to her, Tim was unaware as she undressed completely and walked closer. It was unlike her but Maddie didn't dwell on it. She thought too much at times. From behind him, she covered his hands with hers, urging him to put the robots down. He turned and his eyes betrayed what the rest of him pretended not to notice. "Finding clothes too confining around the tank?" he teased.

"You started it." She took a step closer.

"I finished it too." He didn't move.

"That was eight hours ago and I don't remember you finishing." Maddie needed to reciprocate.

"My choice."

"That's right. Your choice." Maddie took his left hand and sucked each finger until she saw his Adam's apple jump in his throat. "Let's just call today gentleman's choice. I think I know what else you want."

His eyebrow lifted as she stepped closer to kiss him. Maddie had been aching to kiss him all day. To touch him and get him naked. Getting off would never be enough. She needed the contact with his body. The taste of his lips. The feel of him against her.

"What are you saying, Maddie?" he asked against her mouth.

It was her turn to be silent as she smiled. Her fingers pried open his button-fly jeans and pushed them, along with his briefs, to the floor. Her body followed slowly as her hands grazed his hips, thighs and calves. Kneeling, she tugged off his boots and socks and cleared away the jeans and briefs completely.

She kissed her way up his legs, mirroring what he'd done to her. Mirroring his self-control was harder. She could feel her wet pussy reacting. How did he manage this without fucking her? Maddie didn't care. She'd do whatever he wanted and worry about it later.

Her fingers stroked his balls and she saw him already growing stiff. Not too fast, she decided. She stood letting a nipple graze his cock and feeling satisfied when she saw it twitch. Her body responded to the sight of him. Her mind was quickly overheating and she hoped she was having more of an effect on him than herself.

Maddie removed his T-shirt and let her nails scratch through his dark chest hair. She made sure to catch his flat nipples a few times. Suddenly his hands caught her wrists. Maddie's eyes met his. She wasn't sure what to do next. Luckily he wasn't short on ideas.

"You liked what I did to you this morning?" he asked.

"Yes." Maddie kissed him as he still held her wrists. She could feel his self-control slipping. He needed relief and she wanted to have that power over him too. His erection brushed her thigh and he released her wrists.

Carefully Maddie pushed Tim into a chair and knelt down. She wanted to kiss him, lick him, taste him and explore him in every way. He would get full points for self-control. She was weak and gave in. When it came to him, there was no other choice.

Her tongue brushed the head of his cock and she heard a growl from inside his chest that spurred her on. He tasted indescribably delicious as she began at the base and proceeded up one side and came down the other until she'd covered every centimeter with saliva.

Her left hand slowly tickled his balls as her right braced his cock. Kissing the tip, she engulfed the head and pulled back. Another kiss and she went a little farther. She was determined to go slower this time. Every time she was with him, it all went so fast. The passion took over.

Tim's muffled groans were growing louder as she took more and more of him in her mouth. Eventually pressing him down her throat. She'd never done this to anyone else, at least not this far. It was unexpectedly erotic. His hand was braced on the back of her head, not forcing her down but as though he were on the verge on something. Maddie liked him off balance.

She'd swallowed all of him but couldn't hold it too long this time. At a teasing pace, she released him and noticed a drop of precum at the tip. Her tongue darted to retrieve it as she glanced up to look him in the eye. There was no doubt she had him where she wanted him and vice versa. The fun had just begun, but to get anywhere she needed to relieve him first.

Her hand surrounded the shaft, pulling and twisting gently to keep him on his toes. Finally she licked her lips and sucked the head into her mouth. Her tongue toyed with the opening until she tasted more drops of his arousal. Her lips and hand found a pattern, milking him to get what she wanted and after a few brief minutes his body tensed.

A deep groan came from Tim's chest as he came in her mouth. A second stream was too much and her lips released him while her hand squeezed it out. She swallowed as the last few drops landed on her breast. Impulsively she wiped them up with her finger and licked them clean. Savoring the experience, Maddie knew there wouldn't be many more of them. She never wanted it to end.

Maddie kissed his spent cock and then kissed a trail up his stomach, chest and neck until she had his mouth. His body was limp under her touch but he deepened the kiss.

After only a few moments of recovery, Tim stood and pressed her back into the workbench, kissing her harder. Unexpectedly he picked her up and deposited her on the large flat surface, climbing up after her. Maddie had no idea what he was after now but happily played along and kept kissing him. The next thing she knew he was lying flat on his back, tugging her onto him so their bodies meshed.

She could've stayed like this forever but she felt his hands inching her up, little by little. There was more of the intimacy they'd enjoyed before but it felt amazing. His mouth was on her neck, her breasts where he nipped and licked until she moaned. Maddie began to feel the wetness in her pussy growing again. She now understood how he'd managed to do her so thoroughly this morning. Going down on him had become her total focus. She'd forgotten about herself for the time. Now he was reminding her and he'd better not be toying with her.

His tongue swirled in her bellybutton and moved her forward. Maddie was now on her hands and knees to keep from falling. His tongue traced the line of hair on her pussy. She moaned and got up on her knees to look down at him. His hands molded up her body and squeezed her breasts as he parted her lips with his tongue. A few muffled squeaks made it past her lips before Maddie had to brace herself on her hands.

But it was no good, sitting on his face she was in contact with no other part of him this way. She stood and he grabbed her but she didn't go far. With plans of her own, Maddie turned to face his masculine form laid out for her and let his hands pull her back to his eager tongue. She knew he wanted to eat her out this morning and admired his control. There was no need for control now that he could have anything. She wanted it just as badly.

His tongue was flicking her clit, Maddie moaned and kissed his hips before dropping kisses on his cock. She loved his body. Every warm masculine inch. Maddie got a warning grunt from him but didn't listen. Her tongue had a mind of its own and what he was doing to her only fueled her desire to get him hard and ready again. She didn't just want his tongue inside her, though it felt wonderful. That was not enough. She wanted him deep inside her body.

It wasn't long before he was hard again. Maddie knew she'd get exactly what she wanted. Tim's tongue was lapping at her clit as she rocked on his face. When he suddenly slipped two fingers just inside it sent her right over the edge. Her body shook as she muffled her screams in his stomach. Before she'd completely recovered, Maddie flipped herself around so she was facing him and straddling his hips.

The look of surprise on his face was even more arousing to her as she took hold of his cock and eased herself down on it. She had been fantasizing about this feeling all day. Stretched and filled to her limits, there was nothing better in the world than Tim's cock.

"Maddie," he said in a half gasp and half warning.

She flashed him a smile that said she was boss for this turn and flexed her hips to prove it. There was no doubt in her mind this would work just right. She planted her hands on his chest as she pumped up and down on his cock until her brain shut down. Her body took over. Tim's hands grasped her hips and she ground into him as her orgasm hit her hard. She felt him explode inside her as she collapsed onto his chest giggling and gasping for air.

"What is so funny?" he demanded.

"Nothing is funny. I've never felt this good in my life." Maddie kissed him softly. There was no other man she'd ever wanted this much—needed this much.

Chapter Seven
ಸಂ

This wasn't working.

Tim sat home alone, staring at the television without taking a word in. He didn't know what to do with himself. He'd intentionally avoided Maddie the entire next day. Ignored her messages on his cell phone asking him to hang around after work. He knew she wanted more *research*. She could hire someone. That's what he told himself anyway.

Now he missed her. One day without contact and he was missing her. But he couldn't stand being her lab rat any longer. Tim had his pride.

He'd tried to change things, to throw her off but it hadn't worked. She'd met him, loved it and joined in. The woman was insatiable.

Maddie hadn't even been turned off slightly by what he'd done. A little surprised, sure, but did she demand an explanation? Put a halt to it? Had she ever asked where this relationship was going like a normal woman?

No.

She'd done none of the normal-woman things to determine if he was in it for fun or open for more. Their relationship had never been normal. So his odd behavior hadn't freaked her out. The lack of intimacy wasn't even a real problem. It'd felt intimate. She'd let him do anything he wanted in her office.

Better yet, she'd reciprocated and then some. With any other woman that'd be fine, but he wanted more from Maddie. He wanted her to want more than great sex from him. He wanted to have the same effect on her that she did on him. Tim wanted her to be crazy in love with him.

Deep down, Tim knew that'd never happen. He was an average boring guy with a business and a Bachelor's degree. She was an academic egghead nightmare with no feelings. The woman was a nympho or a research maniac. Possibly both. But he wasn't going to let her use him for research. Sex was one thing…though he was already beyond that now. He just wanted *her*.

Tim was used to not getting what he wanted. As a child, he'd wanted his mom to stay and his dad not to drink. He'd lived without either ever happening. He'd live without Maddie in his life or in his bed. Survival was something he was good at.

This woman had to get out of his life or get off the research and into his life. Based on what he knew about Maddie Simons, there was only one way to get that kind of extreme reaction from her.

Cut her off.

Then tell her he'd screwed up her research.

At least now he couldn't say he'd never known what it'd be like to take a shot with Maddie. It was his biggest regret from college. Even if he'd tried and failed, he'd tried. It was best to cut his losses and move on now.

There were only a couple days left of work to do. The keys had to be swapped out for the cards and the new electronic locks put in, but that'd only take a day with the team he had on the tank. The equipment was finally due in tomorrow.

That would be it. He'd have his fun and then let the truth out on the last day. Let her pick up the pieces and redo the research on some other guy who didn't love her.

Tim was clear now that he had a plan.

He got up to order a pizza for dinner. Before he got to the kitchen drawer for his takeout menus, his cell phone rang.

Glancing at the number, he saw it was the security monitoring facility. A sense of dread filled him. Another break-in?

He flipped open the phone. "Foxmor."

"Alarm at the Bellows Think Tank."

"Anything on the cameras?" he asked.

"No. We've got the police on the way to check things. We do have someone in the panic room. Any other instructions?"

"No. Good. Thanks for calling. I'll get over there." Tim hung up and grabbed his keys.

Maddie had left him a message wanting him to hang around. He knew she'd be stubborn enough to stay behind, despite his strict rules not to stay late alone. She was the one in the panic room. His gut had no doubt.

It was his turn to panic now. A contained internal panic as he sped to the tank.

It was worse than he thought, finding her and the police in the panic room. Part of him was mad at her but he was furious with himself.

Ignoring the cop, he pulled her close and looked her up and down. "You okay?"

Maddie shakily rested her head on his shoulder. "I'm fine. I don't know who broke in but the room worked."

"We're searching the area but it doesn't look like they hung around. The back door was wide open."

"Let us know if you find anything. The cameras will be hooked up tomorrow." Tim held Maddie tighter.

"You're all right, ma'am?" the cop asked.

"I'll be fine." Maddie took a deep breath.

"Let's get you to your office." Tim steered her from the panic room.

"Make sure to lock up." The cop headed for the door.

Tim closed the door to Maddie's office and pressed her against it. Nothing bad had happened to her but he kissed her like she was going to disappear.

She was kissing him back, her fingers curling tightly around of his arms.

"I'm sorry." He kissed her forehead.

"What for?" She looked confused.

"I shouldn't have left you here alone." He looked deep in her eyes. "You could've been hurt."

"I'm a grown woman and your system worked just fine. You should be proud of your work." Maddie threaded her fingers through his hair.

"I'm not really worried about the system right now." He couldn't care about anything else.

Maddie's arms wrapped around his neck and she deepened the kiss, shifting gears in a way Tim hadn't intended. But he needed to possess her, to know things were back to normal…or as normal as things got between them.

Not letting her mouth free of his, Tim slid his hands under her skirt and pulled it to her waist.

Maddie's fingers trailed down his chest as she unbuttoned his fly. The feel of her hands made him hard. Her mouth worked on his neck while her leg slid up his thigh.

Tim gently lifted her leg up over his hip and pulled her closer. With his other hand, he pulled her lace underwear to one side. Slipping his fingers between her folds, he found her already wet. Her hips pressed closer as Tim slowly eased into her.

"Tim." She snaked her tongue into his mouth.

Tim had to take things slow. He never wanted to let her go. She belonged with him. The feel of her writhing between him and the door only drove his need. Tim let one hand wander, feeling the curve of her hip and the strain of her breasts against her blouse with her back arched to him.

"You're going to wear me out." He didn't mean only sexually. The worry wasn't going away.

There was nothing more important than her. Tim pulled her leg tighter up over his hip as he ground her into the door. Her head bobbed back against the door as his pace increased. Watching her, Tim saw her eyes pop open and meet his gaze.

Tim felt her body tightening around him and he lost control, pouring into her. His moan mixed with hers and Maddie's mouth sought his again.

"No arguments, you're coming home with me," he said firmly. One more night, he deserved it. He'd never be able to sleep if she wasn't safe next to him.

"You like it when I argue," she whispered. "But seeing as you're so determined you can have your way this time."

This woman held a power over him like no other. He would never have enough of her.

* * * * *

Maddie knew something was wrong in her life. Alone in her office, she couldn't concentrate on anything. She had to change things before it was too late.

Since her panic room incident, where evidence of entry was found but no theft again, she'd kept terribly routine hours to avoid being there alone. The problem was Tim. That night he'd not only believed her, but he was also worried about her. The intimacy between them had returned. Things had felt right and safe.

The past two days he'd been so busy putting in the finishing touches on the system, the cameras were now linked and the key cards were ready, that Tim hadn't had a moment to spare for her. That went against everything he'd said and done for the first week he was there. If he was just mad that she'd stayed late that night he'd be over it by now, she hoped. She hadn't known she was the last one there that night.

There was potential for tonight though. He'd answered one of her voicemails with a voicemail asking her to stay after work. It made Maddie hope and fear all at once. Today was his last day at the tank.

A knock on the door made her hopes soar but only Ginny entered.

"Hi." Maddie pretended to be lost in thought about the papers on her desk.

"So? It's his last day here. Have you done it yet?" Ginny had been tight-lipped about Maddie's little plan. Not mentioning it more than once in the couple of weeks since its inception.

"I can't." Maddie looked Ginny in the eye and saw the disapproval.

"This isn't good for you."

"Yes, it is. I can't give him up. Everyone loves him around here." Maddie knew she loved him too but wasn't ready to admit that to Ginny.

"Tell him the truth. It's the only way to deal with the past."

"It's just that. The past. He's not the same person. He's not mean or rude. I have to tell him the truth. Then he'll hate me and it's ruined."

"You set up it to be ruined. It was a lesson, remember?"

"He's the closest thing I've ever met to Mr. Right. I don't want to lose him." Maddie knew her odds were slim but she couldn't keep seeing him without confessing. Once she did, it'd be over. It was a stalemate in her mind.

"Tell him how you feel, but tell him the truth first," Ginny advised.

Maddie nodded. "It was one thing to try to get back at him. A childish attempt at healing, but not evil. However, if I want a real relationship, I can't keep this up. The truth is I want to know why. Why he did what he did back then.

Dumping him won't change anything. Knowing why might help me. Did he just think it wouldn't matter? We barely talked in college, it might not even have occurred to him. The way he acts, it didn't. But he knew that no one knew about me so why tell?"

"Then that's what you need to ask him. After you tell him the truth." Ginny looked hopeful.

"I know I'll probably lose him. But I'd rather lose him because of the truth than because I dumped him when I didn't want to." Maddie tried not to think too hard about the logical and probable outcome of her plan. No doubt Tim would be glad to be rid of her and all the troublemakers at the tank when he found out what she'd been planning.

But she had to try to do her best to keep him.

"You'll probably lose him. Voluntarily lose at the game you set up. Would you feel better going through with your original plan?" Ginny challenged.

"No, I couldn't do it. At least I'll feel I've matured since college. I wanted revenge so badly. That's how I felt when I saw him again. Like I was right back in college, living it again. I shouldn't have played the game but confronted him and got it over with like an adult."

"Then again, you might never have taken the chance to sleep with him. Get to know him. Fall in love with him." Ginny's pursed lips were half smiling.

"It's that obvious?" Maddie wanted to crawl under her desk.

"Yes. It wasn't part of your plan but love rarely follows plans."

"You're not saying my plan was right?" Maddie had expected a lecture of some type.

"Not right, but true to yourself. What you needed to do. It's your life." She smiled wider. "You're the only one who knows what'll make you happy. If he's it, grab him. Don't take no for an answer."

"Thanks." Maddie realized instead of gaining confidence from revenge, she'd gained the courage and maturity to go after what she wanted in life and in bed. Now she just had to get Tim to understand. He was exactly what she'd had no idea she wanted.

"I think I'll take off early. You'll be busy." Ginny left the office.

"Bye." Maddie began mentally rehearsing what she'd say. Not to make it sound less than bad, but she had to be able to get through it without babbling or going off on a tangent. She had a few hours to practice. Love probably wouldn't even matter. He'd be so angry with her it'd be over before she got that far but she had to try.

* * * * *

Tim had been focused on two things. Get this project done despite the delays. And get Maddie out of his head. Avoiding her hadn't helped but at least it kept him from indulging in her body. Some things he couldn't resist. His mind kept wandering as he walked Dr. Bellows repeatedly through the security codes and key card procedures.

Maddie was a menace. The woman was using him in her sex experiments. Still he wanted to protect her. He'd failed miserably at self-control the night she'd bolted herself in the panic room. It was fear and adrenaline, he told himself. He knew he was lying to himself. The woman had him. He loved her. But just like his parents, she was bad for him.

It wasn't her fault. Tim knew her parents pushing for overachievement and placing little value on her feelings had made her the detached scientist she was. For a while he'd found the loving and passionate woman underneath. Was it an act?

All the evidence said yes.

Dysfunctional parents and being too smart as kids—that they had in common. It wasn't enough. He'd have to walk away, love or not, for his own good. One day the research would be over and she'd say "thanks, but we're done".

Thoughts of that day made this day easier. He'd asked her to stay late so he could end it. Inform her he knew all about, and had screwed with her experiment. Saying it wouldn't be hard. It was the fact that she probably wouldn't care about anything *but* her experiment. Just like Dad — as long as there was beer, life was good.

"You know, we could use a smart guy like you around here." Bellows tried the card and had it backward, again.

"This way." Tim flipped the card and ignored the question.

"I'm offering you a job." Bellows stopped playing with the key card. "I don't let the bright ones get away."

"I've got a job." Tim demonstrated the key card then handed it to Bellows. The sooner he was free of this place the better.

"I've been thinking about that too. You've got a good-sized staff. Nothing says you can't own your company and let them do all the work. You collect the cash and only get involved when trouble comes up."

"Trouble always comes up." Tim watched Bellows finally get it right.

"We're flexible. No one says you have to put in eighty hours a week or even forty. Some people work from home — others like the lab environment. You can't tell me you haven't been having fun with the robot boys. That isn't part of the security job."

"I tinker." Tim didn't want to talk about a future here.

"Then this is the place for you." Bellows got it right again and smiled. "See. That's easy. You just think about the offer. Let me know."

"Thanks." Tim couldn't take it seriously. No way could he work with Maddie. Not in the same building, not a chance.

"I'll stick around tonight. Make sure we've got all our stuff out of your way and the place will be yours again."

"Take the weekend and think it over. Let me know on Monday." Bellows slapped him on the back and left.

"Sure." Tim knew the answer was unnecessary. Bellows wouldn't understand why anyone wouldn't take the job. All in all, Tim felt at home in the tank. The robot boys were great. Everyone else was nice, even with their quirks. Bellows was generous and easygoing, if a bit odd.

If it weren't for Maddie, he could hide away in a place like this and live out his dreams of creating and inventing. But with her at the tank he'd never be relaxed. Besides, it wasn't a practical life for him. Those were all dreams, Maddie included, dreams that didn't come true for guys like Tim.

Checking his watch, Tim knew most people would be leaving soon. Almost time for his talk with Maddie. He wanted it over with and at the same time didn't want to do it at all. That was life though. It wasn't easy, he'd gotten used to it. The question remained, would he ever get over Maddie?

* * * * *

Maddie's office door was open and he waited in the doorway for her to finish whatever she was typing. "Hi," he said.

"Hi." Her smile was strained.

Things hadn't been the same between them since that frightening night but she didn't seem to want affection. He wondered if tonight was the night she'd planned on ending things as well. Maybe it was too inconvenient to continue the research if he wasn't available to her twenty-four seven. "Busy?"

"Just cleaning up some notes and waiting for you. I'm glad you're finally free. I wanted to talk to you."

"Me too." He sat in a guest chair.

"Okay. First off, I wanted to bring up the fact that on the night of the last break-in, I didn't think I was the last one here. I had no way of knowing I was alone. We need to deal with that security issue. It's been a flaw from the beginning and I'm not sure it's entirely gone."

"I'm afraid the only way to fix it is a security guard who locks up and makes rounds. A computer system that would do that is quite a bit more money than hiring a rent-a-cop. But with the new security system it shouldn't be a problem. The doors lock automatically. No one without a key card can get in and anyone trying will be on cameras that are monitored by the security center."

Maddie made a note on her desk. "Sounds reasonable."

"Do the other security measures meet with your satisfaction?" Her calm demeanor annoyed him. This wasn't about business, but then again it was for her.

"Yes. I just didn't want you thinking I'd disregarded your advice before. People get caught up in their work, I'm as guilty as anyone. Experiments take concentration and time. We can all get isolated in our labs so it's not that easy." She put down the pen and looked up at him with a softer expression. "I also wanted to talk about us."

"So do I."

"I'd like to go first. I have a confession to make." She finished her sentence but Tim wasn't listening anymore. His head cocked in the direction of the door.

The chime of the outer door being opened caught his attention. Everyone was gone—he'd walked the place personally. Probably someone forgot something, but he wasn't going to take the chance. "We can talk later—someone's in here. Come on."

"What? That's not the alarm I heard." Maddie looked lost in her thoughts.

"It's just the door but I want to see who came back." Tim grabbed her wrist and tugged until she came around the desk.

He hustled them into the panic room, thankfully located close to Maddie's office.

Tim sat at the control center and pulled up the info. Bellows' card was used. However the scrawny young guy with his back to the camera wasn't Bellows.

"He's in this hallway," Maddie said.

Tim and Maddie looked at the door to the panic room. In their lack of panic, they hadn't closed it. Cursing himself, Tim made a grab for the door but it was too late.

Chapter Eight

ಙ

Maddie stared at the handgun pointed at her and Tim. Her eyes roamed from the gun up to the intruder's face. It couldn't be Billy Bellows. Not the owner's son. But it was. What was going on? When would the police get here? Why was Tim annoyed with her? Her mind raced on every topic at once but she didn't move a muscle. This felt like a movie but it was very real. Refusing to acknowledge Billy wouldn't make him go away.

"Where are they?" Billy demanded.

She had to deal with this. Tim might be a security expert but she was the one who knew the intruder better. "Billy? What are you talking about? Where are who?"

"I'm sick of you all hiding the truth from me. Now show them to me." His gun hand shook.

"Billy, please calm down. We're going to help you." Maddie took a step forward. Billy gripped the gun tighter so she stopped. "What's wrong?"

"My dad wants to send me away. He's going to put me in a place with crazy, messed-up people. He found my stash and needles." Billy's body shook and Maddie now worried as much about being accidentally shot as deliberately.

"What place?" Tim whispered in her ear.

"Rehab?" she asked Billy.

Billy gave a jerky nod. Scratching at his arms as the sweat beaded down his neck. Maddie hoped he wasn't trying to harm his father's co-workers and friends. There was no telling what was going through his mind.

"Billy, what do you want to see? Who are they?" Maddie asked. Right now she wanted to keep him from getting too upset. Keep him talking.

"I want to see the aliens." Billy had an arrogant tone.

"The aliens?" Her brain tried to process a response but distraction was her best bet. "Billy, you know me, right?"

"You work for Dad. You do chemistry to human behavior stuff." Billy waved his gun casually.

Maddie tensed and felt Tim's hand reach for hers. She took another step forward so he wouldn't do anything crazy like standing between her and the gun. Tim was just the sort of man to do it, but Billy was more likely to shoot someone he didn't trust as much as someone he'd known for years and who had been nice to him. She hoped.

"That's right. I work with your dad. I'm sure your dad is very worried about you. I'd like to talk to you. First can we put down the gun?"

"No. No one listens to me unless I do this stuff. Dad'll send me to rehab but it's a waste. I'll just run away or sign myself out. I'm over eighteen. I don't want to talk anyway. I want to free the aliens." The tension in his arms more clearly revealed track-marked, scarred veins.

Maddie quickly concluded he was heavily using and with his supply cut off—in massive withdrawal—Billy needed to be in a hospital.

"Billy, have you been coming to the tank at night to try to free them?" Maddie asked.

"Yeah." He nodded slowly. "I came a few times but no one was here. Nothing I could pawn either. Dad wouldn't give me any more money. You can show me the aliens now."

Maddie glanced back at Tim who looked ready to tackle Billy. Maddie wanted to avoid that. Tim might be angry with her but she couldn't stand to get him shot. She subtly waved him back with her fingers. Tim getting aggressive wouldn't help.

"There are no aliens here, Billy. We study science and society. Not UFOs. We solve problems." Maddie didn't know if convincing him was possible. Real aliens probably couldn't convince him. He'd be too strung out and think they were human. Somehow she had to get him to drop the gun.

"That's what you want people to think. You want everyone to think you're just a bunch of eggheads who do goofy experiments. I know the truth. You're hiding them. Experimenting on them."

"Billy, I'd never do that. You know me, I've worked here for years. You know I wouldn't lie to you. It's me, Maddie." She tried to lean toward him but he backed up and pointed the gun with a stiffer arm. Maddie inhaled sharply but stood her ground. "You don't want to hurt anyone. We won't hurt you or send you anywhere."

"I know the truth!" he yelled. "This is Area 51. It's all a government cover-up."

Maddie wanted to laugh but she knew the gun was real even if the story was insane. "The *X-Files* is just a television show. You need to watch something else." He probably had the entire series on DVD. He'd spent all of his high-school years addicted, according to his father.

"It's the truth," he insisted.

"This isn't Area 51. That place is a few miles away from here. It does exist but we're not it." Maddie rubbed her temples. It was beginning to make more sense. "Did you steal your dad's access codes and key card to the new system?"

"Don't tell him. He doesn't know I know about the aliens."

"How will aliens help you get high?" Tim asked. Maddie glared at him. She'd gotten Billy to talk rationally about reality and he was helping the fantasy.

"Ignore him, Billy. He's just the security guy. Now why don't you put down the gun and we'll see if we can get you back home. Your dad won't have to know anything."

"I don't want to go back. I want the aliens to take me with them. Home to another world where I can be high or drunk or whatever all the time. They can experiment on me—I don't care as long as I get high."

"You're kidding." Maddie murmured but tried to get closer.

"It's better than college or work. I need it. Help me, Maddie! Please!" Billy was somewhere between begging and yelling. His grip on the gun never wavered.

"I don't know about any aliens, Billy. If you put down the gun maybe we can find out where they are." Maddie got closer and hoped he'd give her the gun. Billy grabbed her first.

She felt the barrel of the gun pressed into her neck and looked at Tim. Later she'd be trying to figure out where she went wrong. For now all she could think about was that gun.

*****

Tim cursed himself for waiting too long. Maddie had been making progress with Billy but he wasn't going to trust anyone or give up the gun. He'd run into a few junkies as a kid. Some could be pacified into doing what you wanted and some needed a firmer hand. Now Billy had a hostage—the woman Tim loved. Tim pushed down his feelings to focus on the kid with the gun.

"Don't hurt her, Billy." Tim did his best to sound calm. "If you hurt anyone the police will lock you up. It'll be worse than rehab."

Billy's cheek twitched. "The aliens will take me away. Show me the aliens and I'll let her go."

"Please just let me go and we'll talk about this." Maddie's voice shook.

"No, you're my insurance policy now. I'll get to the aliens." Billy smiled.

"You're right, you will." Tim nodded. "The game is up, Maddie. Let's just give him to the aliens and everyone will be happy."

"I knew they were here!" Billy shook Maddie a bit and her eyes grew wide.

Tim hoped Maddie would get the message to play along and keep quiet.

"Now the aliens don't like Maddie because she's been trying to convince them they aren't really aliens. So you can't take her in there or they'll think you're on her side." Tim hoped Billy would buy it.

"Scientists." Billy hissed in Maddie's ear. "I can't blame the aliens. How do I know you'll go through with it if I let her go?"

"You've still got the gun," Tim reminded him.

Billy paused. Finally he pushed Maddie at Tim hard. Tim steadied her. Before Maddie could argue with him, he pulled her close behind him.

"Follow me to the alien sanctuary." Tim left the safety of the control room and headed for the pit. It was dark and empty with no way out once it was locked.

Tim entered the code and the door opened. He felt Maddie's fingers holding on to the tail of his T-shirt. All he could do now was hope it worked. "They don't like the light. You have to go in the dark." Tim pointed to the room.

As Billy looked in, Tim shoved him in and closed the door. Maddie entered the locking code.

They leaned against the door in relief and Tim pulled Maddie to him. Her ragged breath against his neck triggered all the fear he'd suppressed. Running his hands up her hips and back to her face and down, he made sure she was safe and real. Maddie held him tightly in return.

Tim wanted to never let her go but he had to cut the tension. "Don't tell me the unshakeable Maddie is scared by a kid on drugs with a little .22 and an alien fantasy."

Her head rested on his shoulder. "I thought I had him under control or at least was getting there. I really thought I could get him to trust me."

"I know. I was hoping you could too. He was just too out of it." Tim kissed her forehead. She was safe and the break-ins were solved. Tim could hear the police sirens outside.

"What I don't understand is how he's been doing this for weeks and his parents never realized." Maddie rubbed her neck and Tim held her tighter.

"His father needs to get medical custody. Billy has to be in an in-patient program or he'll end up in jail or dead." Tim finally felt his heart rate returning to normal.

Billy suddenly began to pound on the door swearing at both of them. Tim felt Maddie jump in his arms. His hands soothed her as he moved them away from the door.

"The police will be here in a minute. They'll deal with him." Tim walked them toward the front door.

Maddie stepped back from his grasp. "Thank you for saving me."

"Anytime." He leaned in for a soft kiss to her lips.

* * * * *

"The cops are taking Billy home. He needs to get checked in somewhere," Tim said as he closed to the door to Maddie's office behind him.

Maddie leaned back on her desk as her heart stopped pounding from the adrenaline rush. "At least no one was hurt."

"And?" He came closer.

"And?" she repeated.

"I think you owe me an apology for doubting my security talents." He planted both hands on either side of her on the desk. Caging her in.

"He still managed to break in," she countered.

"Because his father had a master passkey and the blueprints to where the cameras were going to be. With that info you could get into the best systems unseen." Tim leaned closer until Maddie almost flinched.

"So I should apologize because of who the burglar was? I don't think so." She fought the urge to inch back even as she wanted to lean forward. He'd always have this effect on her, no matter how annoyed she was with him.

"I really thought you were different." He shook his head.

"And to think, I wasn't going to dump you," she replied.

"Dump me? Honey, I already screwed up your research so be my guest."

"Research?" She frowned.

"Your little perfume sex experiment. Using me for a lab rat isn't very nice. Fun, but not nice. The joke's on you, though. I switched samples. You were wearing the placebo for the last week."

"I didn't use you for a lab rat." She sat back on the desk to get some breathing room. "This wasn't about the perfume."

"You didn't use the pheromone perfume?" he returned.

"I wore it, but not for research. How else was I going to seduce you? I needed it but not for the experiment."

"Then what?" He folded his arms. "I've played enough games."

"Games? This wasn't a game. You screwed up my life in college. Got me dumped by your roommate, remember? Outed me as a grad student passing as an undergrad so I lost my boyfriend, my friends and everything. I had no choice but to take that Rhodes Scholarship to get away."

"That's what you're mad about?" He took a step back.

"Of course you don't get it. Why would you even think about it? All I wanted was the real college experience. Not to feel too young or out of place for once in my life. But no, I couldn't have that thanks to you." Her lip quivered and she bit it to contain her emotion.

"So you were going to dump me because I got you dumped?" He turned away.

"Yes, as a matter of fact I thought it was a good plan. We had some fun and you get to know what it feels like to be discarded. It didn't work out the way I planned."

He studied her over his shoulder. "Want to know why?"

"Why? Why what?" she huffed.

"Why I told your boyfriend about you?" He turned and stared her straight in the eye.

"You probably thought he could do better. But yes, I really would like to know. Let's have it." She threw her arms open and then braced her hands on the desk. Maddie wanted yet didn't want to know.

"Because I wanted you for myself." Tim remained like a statue as the words sank in.

"What?" She shook her head as if she hadn't heard him right.

"You heard me. I wanted you. One night I had too many beers and he started talking about you, in detail. I couldn't take it anymore." The muscles in his jaw tensed.

"What about everyone else finding out?" Maddie stared at him in disbelief.

"That was your boyfriend. I knew he wouldn't stick with you when you were a brain. I couldn't ask you out while you were dating him. I found out the truth from a professor of one of your grad classes. It wasn't intentional. I wasn't going to tell anyone but that night I was weak. I didn't know that ass you were dating would go and tell the world. I also didn't know you'd bolt before I got the chance to talk to you."

Maddie was silent for a few seconds. Her thoughts were scattered from shock to emotions she couldn't even name. "Why didn't you talk to me first?"

He took a step closer. "It's a guy thing. You don't take a friend's girlfriend. Maybe he wasn't my friend but he was my roommate. I was a stupid college kid trying to have the decency my dad didn't."

"I had no idea," she admitted.

"I know."

"Why? Why me?" She wasn't the prettiest or the sexiest co-ed.

"I can't explain it exactly. I felt like you'd get me. At first I thought it was just hormones, but it never went away. I knew I wanted you. Just like I knew I could fix things when I was a kid. I thought I understood you somehow. Not well enough but I wanted more."

"You barely spoke to me in college. Maybe if we'd known each other better I'd have realized…" Maddie had a tingle of hope.

"Doesn't matter now. I had no idea I'd screw things up for you. I really didn't think it'd still bother you so much. I never meant it to hurt you."

"It felt nice to be part of a regular group. To fit in. You're brilliant but you were a regular guy. I was a freak all my life. I should've known it wouldn't last. Sorry about that revenge sex ploy. I've never been good at confrontation.. I just felt like such a loser and a doormat even after all those years. Getting even doesn't work but it sounded good." Maybe he'd understand. She wanted him to know why.

"It wasn't that bad." He smiled.

"I'm really not a mean person."

"So are you still going to dump me?" Tim's eyes held hers. "I won't take the job Bellows offered me here if you don't want me to."

He was giving her the option to walk away. Tim was still there, not running and not hating her. She didn't know how to react. Maddie leaned back and contemplated the situation.

That was a lot of information to get after a near-death experience.

Luckily her mind and heart already knew what to do. "Let's see. You've wanted me for years, which I still can't quite believe. You see me as a woman, not a brain. You're brilliant. You're unbelievably good in bed. And you pretty much saved my life tonight. How could I possibly be stupid enough to give you up?" Maddie pushed off the desk and wrapped her arms around his neck.

Tim held her tight, but she could feel the relief in his body as she kissed him in a soft and simple way she'd never done before. "I love you," she said against his mouth.

He responded by lifting her off her feet and putting her on the desk. "About time," he whispered in her ear.

VEGAS STYLE

Dedication

For my little sister who is getting married and loves Vegas. But is a much less problematic bride!

Acknowledgement

And to my supportive writer pals Shawnna and Joanna!

Trademarks Acknowledgement

The author acknowledges the trademarked status and trademark owners of the following wordmarks mentioned in this work of fiction:

Disney World: Disney Enterprises Inc.

Ferragamo: Salvatore Ferragamo Firenze S.P.A Corp.

Gucci: Gucci Shops Inc.

Harvard Law: President and Fellows of Harvard College Corp.

Hummer: General Motors Corp.

Siegfried & Roy: Ringling Bros.-Barnum and Bailey Combined Shows Inc. Corp.

Tiffany: Tiffany and Company Corp.

University of Nevada Las Vegas: University of Nevada, Las Vegas State Chartered Institution of Higher Education

Chapter One

Vegas was heaven.

To Vivian Montrose it was anyway. Her senses were soothed by the bold flashing colors, familiar sound of the slots and the luxurious feel of a place made for fun. Walking through the main floor of the Victoria Royale Hotel and Casino near the center of the Strip, Viv looked up at the model of London's Big Ben, chiming that she was early as usual. True to its name, the Royale showcased a host of British-themed shops, pubs and rooms.

Boarding the elevator to the offices, Viv had a big day ahead of her. She stepped off on the twenty-first floor and heard a lot of talking and squealing. Not at all normal for a Monday. As she approached the crowd, Viv could guess the source of excitement.

"Look, Viv, I'm engaged!" The department's administrative assistant, Morgan, thrust out a large diamond ring to prove it.

Viv gave it the requisite admiration. "Very nice. Congratulations. What finally made him propose?" Morgan had wanted to join the ranks of the other married women in the office since Viv had known her but the boyfriend had been dragging his heels.

"I followed your advice," Morgan said appreciatively.

"My advice?" Viv searched her brain. She'd never in her life given advice intended to encourage an engagement.

"Of course. Remember when we talked about him? You said men only want what they can't have. Like a little kid who only wants a toy because another kid is playing with it."

"That sounds like me," Viv admitted.

"I told him we should see other people and he freaked. One date with another guy and I got a ring. Thanks, Viv." Morgan hugged her tightly.

"Any time." Viv gave a half smile in return. "I've got to go. I've got a wedding today. A repeat customer, no less."

Viv took the chance to escape to her office, complete with Southwest décor and a collage of happy couples that displayed her track record on the far wall. Ready for another wedding, she sat at her desk and pulled out the day's agenda. It would be a busy one with a wedding at two o'clock and a meeting with the hotel manager and a VIP client before that. If she wanted to be promoted, Viv had to nail this one. Staying busy was good. Especially when Morgan's engagement meant one thing.

"Well, how does it feel to be the only single girl in the office?" Morgan closed the office door behind her.

Viv didn't look up from her calendar. "It feels fabulous. Someone has to stay sane."

"You know, you're going to turn the big three-zero in a few months. What are you waiting for? Prince Charming isn't going to find you in here. All we get are grooms."

"I picked the right hiding place then." Viv pulled out her checklist for the wedding that afternoon and reviewed it.

"Viv, this whole marriage-is-the-enemy thing was funny for a while, but I never expected it to last this long."

"It's not an act, trust me, Morgan. I'm not getting married ever."

"It's not all bad. You have regular sex and a date for everything. You deserve to be happy. Marriage makes people happy, Viv."

"Tell that to my aunt who just got rid of husband number nine. The only thing making her happy is the alimony. Besides, I am happy." Every time they had this discussion it went the same way but Morgan was pushing harder this time.

"Don't you want a husband, kids and a real house?" Morgan asked.

Couples always seemed to recruit singles but Viv wasn't interested. "Condos are easier. But I'm fully capable of buying a real house and, for the record, my mother raised me without a husband."

"Just because your mom never got married doesn't mean you can't."

"No one said I couldn't. This is Vegas. I could marry a complete stranger in under half an hour. It's a choice. I choose not to get married."

"Why would anyone choose that?" Morgan leaned on the back of Viv's guest chair with a confused expression.

"Because marriage still favors men. Women still do most of the housework and childcare. Then you turn fifty and they trade you in. I'm not going to be used. No marriage means I have the control. If I were about to become a thirty-year-old virgin I'd understand your concern. That is definitely not the case here." Viv kept the conversation as light as possible. A lifetime of seeing both sides firsthand had led Viv to the simple conclusion that marriage was more trouble than it was worth. Too big of a gamble.

How could she explain it to Morgan? Who could possibly understand that no man in Viv's life had ever loved her? There had been no permanent men in her life at all. Only the dream of a father. Viv didn't feel sorry for herself, but the idea of letting a man in her life now was a foreign concept.

"I guess if I haven't changed your mind in seven years then I won't now. If I see a man worthy of a fling with you, I'll send him your way."

"Great. I've been working so much lately I've forgotten what fun is." Viv had gone nearly six weeks without a date thanks to her boss's departure, but the work was paying off. Being adamantly single, she needed her priorities. Her career was number one.

Today was her first shot at a true VIP. She'd helped out with them before, but this one was all hers. The hotel manager, Mr. Lox, had made it clear that if she wanted the promotion, she'd better keep this VIP very happy and she intended to.

Morgan glanced out the window of Viv's office. "Wow."

"What is it?" Viv scrolled through her cell phone for recent calls.

"Mr. Lox is here and this client of yours is too hot and totally yummy." Morgan said.

Viv put the phone away and checked her desk for clutter—though it wasn't necessary. "They're early."

"Too bad he's the groom or you'd have your next fling all lined up. Maybe you can talk him out of it." She slipped from the office with a thumbs-up.

Viv rolled her eyes and ran a hand over her hair to make sure it was neat. As the door opened again, Morgan showed in Mr. Lox and a man who was even better than Morgan had described. Hot and yummy had been a gross understatement. He was all man. Viv found herself wondering what he would taste like. No doubt better than the most expensive wine.

Not classically handsome, he had strong features but was no pretty boy. His body was encased in an expensive suit that fit him so well it looked painted on. He was only about six feet tall but his broad shoulders gave him the illusion of dominating the room. His brown hair with subtle streaks of gold looked like the work of the sun and not a hairstylist.

His mist-green eyes were studying her, she realized. A man about to be married shouldn't be looking her over the way he was. But men would always be men, Viv reminded herself. The attraction was mutual. She'd need to keep that in mind around him. If he weren't the groom, he'd be just her type. One date and she'd have him naked.

Mr. Lox made the introductions and Viv recalled the name J.R. Haddery mentioned. Once the boss was gone, Viv took a deep breath and sat down. "Will your fiancée be joining us, Mr. Haddery?"

Why, oh why, did he have to be the groom? Morgan was right as usual. He'd be perfect for a lot of things. Viv was already fantasizing but forced those thoughts away for now. This was her job—her promotion.

"I don't have a fiancée," he replied with a sexy casualness that made her shiver.

Viv was sure she'd just imagined that he didn't have a fiancée. That would be too good to be true. She had to be hallucinating but her body already believed it.

The silence between them felt easy. Exterior professional manners firmly in place, while her interior burned. Viv let him study her. She wasn't about to pry into his private life no matter how much she wanted to. He could clarify his remark when he was ready.

"Aren't you going to ask me why I'm here if I'm not getting married?" he asked expectantly.

"Naturally." Viv played along and kept her tone professional. "Why are you here if you're not getting married?"

"My cousin is getting married," he replied.

"I'm glad someone is or you don't really need my services. Will the bride and groom be here soon?"

"Tomorrow," he said with an authoritative nod.

"Tomorrow," Viv repeated. "And you're here today to do what exactly?"

He looked her straight in the eye. "Make sure you're the one I want."

The innuendo in his voice made Viv wonder what he was thinking. With most men she could tell right away. J.R. was different. She felt the chemistry but also his self-control.

"My cousin is the closest thing to a little sister I have. I want everything to be perfect for her wedding. Lox said I could have you all to myself for as long as I need you. I want to make sure you're just what I need if we're going to be on top of each other for two weeks straight."

Business first. They could negotiate who'd be on top later. "Two weeks. Mr. Haddery—"

"It's J.R.," he cut in.

"Fine, J.R., I professionally coordinate weddings and you're my only client right now. My schedule is usually much more hectic. Trust me, it won't take that long to plan her wedding. No matter how elaborate or costly, I promise you I can cut that time in half without any less of a wedding."

"But you won't," J.R. stated.

"I won't, because…?"

"Because the family would like some time together. They travel a lot because of work."

"Understandable. You want time with the family. Makes my job easier." Viv was already plotting their positions. She definitely wouldn't mind more time with him. He was sexy and entertaining. The longer the wedding went on the better.

"My cousin will want the most elegant and expensive wedding you can dream up," he added.

"The Royale is an excellent choice in that case. Can I assume then that my budget is open?"

"Wide open. Money isn't a concern. Plus my construction company renovated the Grand Ballroom here when the old contractor fell through, so Lox owes me a favor. I want my cousin to enjoy everything. I have a few suites upstairs for them. It's all arranged. You may be asked to advise them on clubs or events in Vegas, but they're very adventurous and outgoing so they'll probably prefer to explore on their own. I understand you're a native of Nevada?"

"Las Vegas itself as a matter of fact, born and raised here. Where is your family coming in from?"

Vegas Style

"My aunt and uncle are from New York. They're in Europe right now. I grew up in New York but I live here. Family time together is hard. My aunt will throw a large society wedding out East when it's convenient. The essential people will come in for the ceremony here."

"I would hope so. It's a big day. As for making sure I'm what you want, if you'd like to see me in action then you're welcome to come by the Grand Ballroom today at two. I have a wedding this afternoon. After that, I'm all yours. I promise."

J.R. smiled and Viv knew he'd picked up on her word choice. His not-too-discreet glance at her left hand convinced her he was very interested. She checked him for a wedding ring and was relieved. Two could play this game. And neither was moving slowly. Viv appreciated a man who didn't waste time with false romance.

"Two it is."

"I hope that isn't an inconvenience. I'm sure you have a very busy schedule." Viv didn't want the meeting to end.

"Not right now. I've taken some time off. I've also taken a suite upstairs to be near my family. Today I only planned to meet with you and settle in. We'll go to the airport tomorrow to pick up the couple and a maid of honor. The bride's parents will arrive the day of the wedding."

"I'll arrange a limo," Viv informed him.

"Excellent."

"Will we need anything else for their arrival tomorrow?" Viv scribbled a note in her agenda book with a silver pen engraved with the hotel's name and logo.

Viv noticed J.R.'s eyes move from the pen to the tips of her fingers and he seemed to be lost in thought. Viv knew it was her nails. They were painted a teasing cherry red. For some reason that color sent men into heat. That was exactly why Viv loved it.

"J.R.?" Viv drew attention to his extended silence.

"I'm sorry, what?" He didn't even try to cover and Viv liked that.

"Anything else you would like to arrange while we're here?" she asked again.

"No, I'll meet you downstairs tomorrow at noon to go to the airport. I'm looking forward to your work this afternoon. You're sure the couple won't mind me crashing their wedding?"

"Not at all. The groom is a local businessman. He owns several very lucrative pawnshops. This is the second time he has used my services so it'll be no trouble. As long as you don't get drunk and hit on the bride, of course." Viv smiled.

"The bride is safe." J.R. looked her right in the eye until she got the sense that *she* might not be safe in a very good way. Finally he glanced away and Viv exhaled slowly. "Do you have many repeat customers?" he inquired.

"A few," she admitted. "I certainly don't want any of my couples to split up. But with the divorce rate what it is, it's inevitable I'll get some business back if I do my job well. I'm amazed people keep getting married again and again but at least I'll never run out of customers."

"Exactly how many times have you been married, Viv?" he asked.

That wasn't a question she normally got. Mentally she groped for an appropriate answer. "Me? Um. None. I'm not really right for marriage. Besides, I grew up in Vegas, remember. You never bet against those kinds of odds."

He lifted an eyebrow but Viv expected that reaction. Most men didn't understand the concept of a single woman who wasn't husband hunting. "A Vegas philosophy of life. I've never met anyone like you, Viv." J.R. stood and shook her hand, holding it longer than necessary.

"I'll take that as a compliment." Viv rewarded him with another smile. "I'll see you this afternoon?"

"Count on it." J.R. headed out of her office.

The chance at a promotion and more time with J.R. Viv couldn't wait for this wedding.

* * * * *

"He's not the groom?" Morgan asked in astonishment as she and Viv made a final tour of the Grand Ballroom before the guests arrived. The wedding party was being photographed, which gave Viv and Morgan a chance to do a final check.

"No, he's not." Viv was thrilled. He was free and clearly attracted to her. The zap she'd felt from the handshake alone made her need a cold shower. She still didn't feel she had a handle on him though. "His cousin is getting married. What kind of man can afford to pay for an open-budget wedding, bring the family in and it's not even his own wedding? Or his daughter's."

"A rich one. Who says dreams don't come true?" Morgan teased.

"He's a client. That isn't the best move I can make for my career." Viv knew that it was all too true. This situation had never come up before. J.R. was not some random guy who set her pulse on fire. He set her whole body on fire and could impact her career. Bad mix. One wrong move could cost her job or, at the very least, any chance at that promotion. But she still wanted him, against her better judgment.

"He's single and you're single. Just don't screw it up. You're the mistress of casual, no-strings-attached relationships. You can pull this one off. I have faith in you."

Viv didn't like what was at stake. Why did the first man in years who intensely sparked her mind and her body have to be the key to her promotion too? "It might work out but for now I'm only going to worry about keeping him happy."

"Men love that. I'm sure you can think of plenty of ways to keep him happy. It's usually all about them anyway," Morgan whispered.

"I mean professionally," Viv corrected. "This is a very hands-on project so there is no rush to make a mess of things. I'll get that promotion. But I do want to get my hands on him at some point." Guests began to filter in and Viv checked to make sure that the waiters were on hand and everything was ready. Perfect as always. She mentally patted herself on the back.

Viv spotted J.R. the instant he entered the Grand Ballroom. Her eyes locked on his and she nodded in recognition. J.R.'s response was a slow, easy smile that raised Viv's temperature.

"You've got nothing to worry about," Morgan piped up.

"What do you mean?" Viv slowly rubbed her lips together to make sure her lipstick hadn't worn off.

"I mean he can't take his eyes off you. I give it a few days on the outside before you two are ripping each other's clothes off."

"That long?" Viv acted insulted. "If I were really going to try, it'd be more like a few hours. But he's a client, not a piece of meat."

"Can't he be both?" Morgan asked.

"Thanks but I don't need advice from a boring, off-the-market, engaged woman like you." Viv saw the bride and groom enter on cue. She gestured to Morgan, who took the hint to get back to her duties. As usual, everything was in its place and running smoothly. Viv had the details down like clockwork. The staff knew her standards were the highest.

Normally she went unnoticed and unneeded at her weddings and that was a tribute to how well she did her job. J.R.'s presence made her feel on display. She checked her lavender-pastel skirt suit for wrinkles.

"You sure know how to show a man a good time." The voice behind her was unmistakable.

Viv knew if she let it, that voice alone could melt her in seconds. His suggestive comments convinced her that she wasn't the only one who felt the urge to be in close quarters. "I beg your pardon?" She pretended not to have heard him, keeping her back to J.R. as she glanced over her shoulder.

"You throw a flawless wedding. Everything is perfect. I've definitely found the answer to all of my needs," J.R. whispered in her ear.

"I'll do all I can to make sure your needs are satisfied." Viv turned and let her eyes linger on him a few seconds too long. What those needs were, Viv wished she knew, but letting her imagination run wild was fun. He pushed her buttons and she didn't mind a bit.

"Don't take on projects unless you're sure you've got the stamina to handle them," he said.

Reining in her thoughts, Viv knew if they had to keep this professional, they'd better stop flirting or she'd cave in no time with this level of raw desire. They needed ground rules or she'd be a mess.

Viv's attention snapped back to the reception when she heard the howling of children. Glancing in the direction of the noise, she saw the flower girl frantically trying to retrieve her basket of petals from a boy a few years older. The boy began to taunt her, running away from her outstretched hands and in Viv's direction.

As the boy passed, Viv snatched the basket from him. She returned it to the little girl and pointed her in a new direction. Crisis averted!

"Never a dull moment." Viv turned back to J.R.

"You're good with kids too. Is there no end to your talents?" He sounded impressed.

"No, I'm not good with kids," Viv corrected fast. "Children are a part of many weddings but I'm certainly no expert. That's just crisis control."

"You are an expert on weddings though?" He took a step closer.

She could tell the question was leading to something and she couldn't resist the bait. "Absolutely, ask me anything."

"Care to dance?" He extended a hand that looked so perfect Viv had to restrain herself. The chance to get toe-to-toe and body-to-body with him was playing dirty and she believed he knew it. She still wanted it.

"I'm not here to enjoy myself, J.R. This is my job." Viv tried to wiggle her way out of it but his eyes told her he wasn't going to let her off that easy.

His hand remained outstretched. "We're not sneaking off to the coatroom to screw around. You'll be right here in the middle of everything. That's hardly abandoning your post. If anyone needs you, I'll briefly let you go. Besides, it's bad luck not to dance at a wedding."

"I've heard most every nuptial superstition there is in the world but I've never heard that one." Viv took his hand anyway and was rewarded with a jolt of sexual energy from his touch. He got high marks for effort. She just hoped he put that much effort into everything he did.

J.R. led her onto the dance floor. In seconds, her mind boiled over and she was lost in the feel of him. Hard and muscled everywhere, he was an ideal specimen. Viv knew this sensation would be burned into her brain. He danced effortlessly but with complete control. Viv gave no thought to following him but had to concentrate on not letting her hands roam. She could feel his fingers at the small of her back toying with the strands of her hair. His subtle motions triggered tingling up and down her spine as he slowly inched her closer.

"You could be dangerous for my career," she whispered and instantly regretted it. How could he have this impact on her? Suddenly she had no control over her own mouth.

"Your career? That is definitely not what's on my mind," he whispered back. His husky tone made Viv literally feel weak in the knees for the first time in her life. That had always been some silly expression to her, until that moment.

"I generally don't get this close to my clients," she explained.

"Lucky me." His hand pressed the small of her back.

"Don't get ahead of yourself. You haven't gotten lucky yet." Viv expected him to correct her interpretation. Again he surprised her.

"It's early," he said in her ear.

Viv felt his hand slide up her back very slowly and she shivered involuntarily. Her growing arousal made her pussy tingle beneath her neat suit. "In that case, you should probably know something about me."

"I intend to know everything about you."

Viv felt a jolt from him. "I don't do relationships. Rule number one is nothing serious."

J.R.'s expression didn't change as he leaned in. The warmth of his breath caressed her neck and fogged her brain. But she caught his words. "I can work with that. See you tomorrow."

He left her on the dance floor, wondering what would happen tomorrow.

Chapter Two

∞

The next day, J.R. refused to give in and show up early like he wanted to. Something told him Viv could be scared away easily. The curvy blonde bombshell had her rules. But rules could be changed. Everything was a negotiation.

And he was very adaptable. After the death of his parents when he was young he'd stayed with an aunt and uncle who preferred New York and East Coast ideals. He'd had to adapt there. Fit in and play the game when necessary. But after college he'd moved back to Vegas where he understood the people and the game better.

Viv was a native and something in him understood her. Not all of her. There was a mystery to uncover but he knew he had to handle it just right. Viv was strong and if pushed too far, she'd cut her losses and be all business. He didn't want that.

But Viv enjoyed the verbal give and take too much to be in control all of the time. She was the type who knew her limits, her comfort zone and J.R. wanted to see that stretch.

The office was a safe place for her. It showed in every inch of her body yesterday as she sat at her desk. Nice suit, sexy hair and nails meant to dig into his back. She had the home field advantage there.

J.R. had wanted to end the meeting differently. The fantasy plagued him, replaying the walk to her office door very differently.

* * * * *

Instead of shaking her hand, he rounded the desk, reached for her waist and pulled her against him. Viv's eyes went to the windows. J.R. kissed her and her blue eyes closed as her arms tangled around his neck. Her warm curves fit to his body and J.R.'s cock pressed into her waist.

J.R. reached for the button on her jacket and unwrapped her. The sleeveless top beneath was white and the pink bra under it teased him. Deepening the kiss, J.R. unbuttoned her skirt and pushed it down her curvy hips. The lacy pink underwear was a texture tease next to her soft skin. He tugged the sleeveless top over her head, breaking the kiss. Then the reality hit her.

"We can't. Not here." Viv stood so J.R. blocked her from the windows.

"Here and now." He dropped the top and removed his own button-down shirt as he backed her away from the front windows near the door to the window ledge behind her desk. The sunlight streamed through her hair and J.R. knew no delays were possible. "Perfect spot."

"But if someone comes in." Viv's hands were on his chest as she argued with her body's desire.

"You won't notice." He reached around to unhook her bra and dropped it on her desk. Viv's large breasts moved as her breathing became heavier. Her pink nipples called to him.

J.R. leaned in, tonguing one firm nipple and he felt Viv press against his touch. A soft moan came from her chest as he pinched the other nipple.

"I can't believe I'm doing this." Viv raked her fingers through his hair.

"You're not doing anything yet. But you will." He pushed her panties to the floor before he lifted her onto the deep ledge with a perfect view of the desert.

Viv smiled at him and reached for his hard cock. Freeing it from the pants, she stroked it with a soft and skilled hand.

The feel of her palm one second and the gentle scoring of her red nails the next pushed him to full erection faster than planned.

"It's too late for playtime." He pulled her hand away and leaned her back so the sun glistened off her body. Licking his way over both gorgeous breasts, J.R. dipped lower over the valley of her belly button and then to the wet slit that demanded his attention.

Viv parted her legs invitingly. J.R. could smell the subtle arousal and dipped a finger into her core. She arched as he pushed a finger deep into her. Viv's body tightened around him. "No more foreplay," she moaned.

"Just had to make sure you're ready." He slowly slid his finger from her and massaged the wetness onto her inner folds, circling her hard clit.

She stiffened at the touch. "Fuck me or eat me. Do something." It was half order, half beg. The very contradictions that made him want her more.

J.R. lowered his head and tongued her clit with slow pressure. Her hips flexed and her fingers dug into his scalp. "More," she pleaded.

The taste of her was an intoxicating spice that betrayed the sweet pink flesh and innocent blonde curls. Eating her would be enough for him but her body wanted more. Cream oozed from her vagina. He took his time, tasting her but not pushing her to orgasm.

"Please, if you have to play I want to suck your cock," she insisted.

J.R. lifted his head with a grin. "Sex isn't fair." He leaned in and kissed her throat then continued higher until her mouth found his.

Pulling her hips to the edge of the ledge, he pressed his cock to her warm, wet pussy. Viv ground at him, eager for more friction. Leaning back, he pressed the head into her entrance and slowly filled her as she chewed off her sticky lip gloss.

Her muscles opened and closed on his cock, not missing an inch as her hips pressed down for as much as J.R. would let her have. When he was fully inside, he took a slow breath and kissed her forehead. "You are dangerous."

"You're playing again. It's too much. Fuck me and we'll play all you want." Her nails dug into his shoulders as her pussy tightened around his erection.

J.R. knew she was right—his control was almost gone. Grabbing her hips, he pulled back until she only had the tip. He drove in fast. Viv arched to him, her breasts firm against his chest. She fucked up to meet him with her whole body in every stroke.

"Harder." Her eyes were open, watching him as he fought for control.

He thumbed her clit to throw her off balance again and fucked her harder. One arm braced around her narrow waist. His thumb pressed hard as Viv went rigid against him. Her body tightened around him and didn't release as he fingered her clit again. "Oh God. J.R. Yes!" she cried into his shoulder.

Her warm pussy throbbed around him, eager and satisfied. Slowly he thrust into her again and she rewarded him with a low moan. "That's better," she muttered in his ear. "Your turn."

J.R. blocked out everything but the feel of her body. Her breasts teasing him and her pussy meeting him. The control slipped away as he took shorter strokes to fill her. Viv's legs around his waist, he fucked her until he felt the rush and came deep inside her. All he could hear was Viv's heartbeat as he planned what he'd do next with her.

* * * * *

J.R. shook away the fantasy and stared at the view from his suite, not unlike the view from Viv's office. He had plans for her. But he also had a family to meet today. A problem solver, J.R. knew he'd handle both. Viv was unexpected but very welcome. A tricky problem.

But he'd play the game. Calm and with strategy, he waited until the appropriate time before leaving his suite. J.R. met Viv in the lobby of the hotel where a white stretch limo waited for them. Her effect on him was exactly the same. Every bit of him wanted to take her to his suite, get that business suit off her and see her the way she was supposed to be.

Getting comfortable in the limo, J.R. felt Viv slide in next to him. Their attraction had only intensified and it was hard not to lean close against her soft curves. She was a perfect balance, attractive but not obvious. Clearly Vivian Montrose knew how to appear professional and stylish without letting too much of her sex appeal loose to tempt the grooms-to-be. None of it diminished the reaction she sparked in him though.

Just like the previous day, her suit was tailored to fit her perfectly but not cut too low or too high. Viv's hair was a mass of golden-blonde curls that spiraled down her back, tamed only by a couple of combs. Her crystal-blue eyes gave a hint of innocence that he didn't believe for a second. This woman had a seductive side he wanted to explore. He'd spent so much time at work that finding a woman who got his attention at a time when he didn't have the distractions of the office was good luck.

"Why aren't you married?" His arm slid along the back of the leather seat.

"I thought we covered that yesterday. I'm not right for marriage."

Not right for marriage? None of the women he'd met in his thirty-two years had ever said anything like that. To be honest, he had always felt odd wanting to get married and have a family. Most men were in no rush to be tied down. However, after the loss of his parents and growing up as a cousin, he wanted to feel part of a normal family. He felt a certain connection with Viv, as though both of them went a bit against their respective gender's expectations. Still, he wasn't going to let her get away with that pathetic answer. J.R. wanted the details. What made this woman tick?

"That's called dodging the question," he pressed. "I want the truth. You're gorgeous, smart and clearly don't lack confidence. Why hasn't some guy caught you already?"

Her eyes still straight ahead, Viv shrugged the shoulder close to him. The gesture caused her suit to gape slightly and J.R. got a glimpse of her generous cleavage. Glimpses of lace bra confirmed his fantasy and made it harder not to touch her. Then, as if she'd planned it, she turned to catch him looking. He immediately looked at her face and adjusted his tie that felt suddenly like it was cutting off his air supply.

"I don't want to be caught. Why aren't *you* married?" She dodged the question.

"Work. Since college I've put everything into my construction and real estate businesses. Recently I branched out into other areas. The real estate boom won't last forever in Nevada."

"Should have gone into weddings." Viv winked and studied his smile.

"People will always get married and Vegas is the place for weddings." J.R. couldn't fault her plan.

"Absolutely. Of course the only men I meet are the grooms. Consequently, I don't get dates through work. Not that I don't date but I've been focused more on my career. I've never had a client who wasn't a person in the wedding until now. You're definitely the exception."

"I've been told I'm exceptional at a lot of things." He leaned in closer and knew he wasn't going to have to wait much longer for a taste of the woman who was driving him crazy. It wasn't just the overall package either, he realized as he studied her tiny sapphire earrings. The details made him want her even more.

"But shaving isn't one of them." Viv leaned closer and pointed at a red mark where he'd skinned his jaw.

"Am I bleeding?"

"No, just a scratch." Viv rubbed the area just under it and pressed a soft kiss to the mark. "All better."

Her brief touch was torture. "Tease." She had a gift for stirring up a man with not-so-innocent acts. J.R. wondered if she'd gone to a special school for that skill or if it was a natural talent.

A wicked smile spread across her lips as she wrapped her fingers around his tie and pulled him down toward her. He wrapped one arm around her shoulders as the other gently caught her waist. He was sliding her the few short inches along the slippery leather to him as the unmistakable sound of screeching tires set off a warning in his head.

He felt them suddenly being pressed into the back of the seat and held on to her tightly while bracing them for the impact. They were jerked forward as their limo skidded to a stop but there was no crash. His heart continued to race as the cars behind them stopped just in time. Everything was silent for a few tense moments.

J.R. realized Viv still clutched onto his tie and shirtfront. She noticed as well and released him slowly, trying to smooth the wrinkled material. They hadn't hit anything but the mood was definitely ruined. Viv no longer looked poised for the kissing.

"You okay?" He rubbed her upper arms to get her attention.

"Thanks to you. I'd have been thrown across the limo. This skirt is so silky it slides. Not wearing seat belts in limos is a very bad habit. Are you okay?" She made no move to put distance between them and J.R. couldn't help but notice her hand rested on his thigh.

"Fine." J.R. had no intention of letting her go until she was ready. Viv's posture remained tense but her breathing had evened out. As they heard the driver hit the down button for the privacy glass, Viv scooted back a few inches just in time to avoid being caught.

"I'm sorry, Viv. A three-car fender-bender right in front of us. No one is hurt. They're all out of their cars and yelling at each other. I called the police but it could take a few minutes to get it settled and start up again. You both all right?" asked the driver.

"Thank you, Henry. We're fine," Viv said as the lights of police became visible outside the window. At least no one was hurt and the police were prompt. J.R. hoped they wouldn't be too late meeting his family.

Henry got out of the car to talk to the police and Viv slowly exhaled. Glancing at her watch, she nodded. "We should get there in time. If not, I'll call ahead. I know a woman who works for the airport's customer service and she'll arrange a team of skycaps and a guide to take care of them until we get there."

He should've known she'd have an answer for everything. Unable to resist, he slipped a hand under her chin. J.R. turned her to face him and pulled her into a blast furnace of a kiss. Caught off guard, Viv momentarily failed to react, but not for long. When her arms wrapped around him and her hands pressed to his shoulder blades J.R. knew his instincts had been right-on. Adrenaline from the near-crash still surged through them both and only made the kiss even more intense. Her breasts pressed firmly against his chest and her thigh pressed to his. He wanted to devour her.

After what seemed like no time, J.R. heard the car door open and pulled away reluctantly. She started to protest but soon realized they wouldn't be alone for long. Viv shifted back and faced front just as Henry entered the car. Wiping away the evidence of her smeared lipstick, she glanced over at him from the corner of her eye. "Now who's the tease?" she accused in a whisper.

"You made the rules." He couldn't stop looking at her slightly swollen lips. It was his handiwork and he liked the way it looked on her.

She shrugged with a smile. They both knew he was right. Viv had made it clear she didn't want the driver to catch them. If he'd continued, she'd have been embarrassed. He was a man who knew how far he could go without blowing it. There was no way he was about to risk messing this up. Rare was the woman who had his full attention.

"I'll have a few more rules for you later but we have some business to handle first." Viv gave him a knowing look.

* * * * *

J.R. led the way to the baggage claim doors. His cousin Dawn, her fiancé Bruce and a tall, skinny redhead who lit up a cigarette as soon as she stepped into the open air emerged.

"Hey there, cuz." He leaned down and gave Dawn a hug and got an air kiss in return.

J.R. turned to the groom and shook his hand hard. "Bruce, good to see you." They'd been in college together and while Bruce had gone on to Harvard Law, J.R. had preferred to go west where his parents had left him land.

"This is my maid of honor, Ginger Regan. Ginger, my cousin J.R. Haddery." Dawn made the introduction with a lack of energy.

"A great pleasure." Ginger extended a hand and squeezed J.R.'s tightly.

J.R. knew a vulture when he met one. And he knew just the defense to throw in her way. "Nice to meet you. Everyone, this is Vivian Montrose, our wedding coordinator at the Victoria Royale."

"A pleasure. You must be exhausted from the flight. We have a limo waiting." Viv shook hands with each of them.

"Why don't you get our bags first?" Ginger lit up another cigarette.

"Our limo driver and a skycap are already seeing to that. This way please." Viv showed no reaction to the clear insult.

J.R. bit his tongue from correcting a guest. It was Dawn's wedding. This was the least he could do to repay the family who raised him after his parents' death. They didn't need his money but he wanted to do something and it was his friend marrying his cousin. Still, Dawn needed better taste in friends. It was possible Ginger was from old East Coast money and treated everyone without a fortune like a servant. That excused nothing as far as J.R. was concerned but he'd experienced the attitude himself.

They piled into the limo as the driver put the rest of the luggage securely in the trunk.

J.R. found himself between Ginger and Viv.

"How's business, J.R.?" Bruce cheerfully filled the silence.

"Steady. I've diversified to be safe." J.R. inched a bit closer to Viv and felt Ginger follow.

"You need to come back to New York. Vegas is for tourists and gamblers. It's all about the party." Dawn looked out the window.

"There's plenty of money to be made off that party." Viv smiled.

"Of course Vegas businesses are a great investment. It's just that New York has so much more to offer. Culture, society and family." Bruce put an arm around Dawn. "Your uncle wants you to come to work for him."

"I'm not moving east." J.R. stood firm.

"Do you have a lot of ideas for the wedding, Dawn?" Viv chimed in.

J.R. was grateful for the subject change.

"Not really. Something simple but elegant. I just want to get married. A nice quiet and private ceremony before the Broadway show Mom has planned." She rolled her eyes.

"Just because it's small doesn't mean you can't have it exactly how you want it. If your mother is putting on a large-scale wedding, then this is your chance to do it any way you like it," Viv encouraged.

Dawn gave a half nod. "I'll think about it."

J.R. leaned forward. "Anything you want, Dawn. You're like my little sister. I know how Aunt Irene gets. Do this wedding your way. Your parents aren't due in until the day of the wedding so it'll be too late for them to change anything."

"Sure, thanks, J.R. And there will be plenty of time for fun too." Dawn shared a look with Ginger.

"Definitely." Ginger blew her smoke across J.R.'s lap as she looked him over.

"Fun we've got in Vegas. Twenty-four/seven. Anything money can buy." Viv took a small bottle of air freshener from a compartment of the limo and sprayed it in Ginger's direction.

J.R. liked Viv's bold personality as much as he craved her body. She was unique and not getting away from him.

Chapter Three

ဢ

Viv led the bride and her friend down the hallway to their suite. The chatter of two twenty-one-year-olds made Viv long for some adult conversation. Turning thirty looked better and better. She opened the door to the multi-room suite. "Here we are." Viv stood back and let the girls go in first.

They strolled in and inspected the connected suites and the stocked minibar. Catty murmurs made Viv jealous of J.R., who was currently pointing the groom in the right direction. Bruce was the only one in the wedding with the right attitude. Viv thought it was odd that the couple wanted separate rooms but she'd seen some couples get very traditional right before the wedding. "Like it?" Viv asked.

"Excellent," Dawn admitted.

"What's excellent is J.R.'s ass," insisted Ginger. "Glad I brought my collection of thong bikinis."

"Yuck." Dawn sifted through the flyers and ads in the binder on the marble desk.

"You have to say that. He's like your big brother." Ginger ignored her friend and turned to Viv. "Don't you think J.R. is hot piece of ass and a perfect catch?"

"I think he's a little old for you." Viv tried to dodge the question but knew Ginger wouldn't be put off that easily. Ginger was a snob. Viv had met plenty of VIPs before and some didn't know how to treat people like humans.

"Oh come on, I'm legal and he's single. That's all that matters. I dated men his age when I was sixteen. Of course they weren't as good-looking."

"True," Dawn said. "You have dated less-hot, less-successful men. This is an improvement on your standards."

"Does he have a girlfriend, Dawn?" Ginger demanded with hands on hips.

"How should I know? Mom would be all over him to get married if he told her something like that. J.R. is too smart to admit it. I seriously doubt it anyway."

"Why?" Ginger pressed.

"He's always working and completely obsessed with his businesses. Some woman will have to hit him over the head to catch him." Dawn threw open the drapes to look at the view.

"That could be arranged. What do you think, Viv? Is J.R. taken by anyone seriously? Because I can scratch her eyes out fast." Ginger's insistence to get her opinion made Viv uneasy but she didn't let it show. It'd only been one kiss. Could the chemistry between her and J.R. be that obvious? The upside was if he was as much of a workaholic as Dawn made it sound, he might not be after anything serious either. Things might work for them.

"I think he's certainly successful and attractive. He hasn't mentioned a girlfriend but I only work here. If I hear something I'll let you know." Viv played off the employee angle and Ginger seemed content to believe Viv wasn't a threat or interested in anything but doing her job.

Now to change the subject. "Mr. Haddery has made plans for dinner. The reservations are for seven tonight at the Windsor Room. It's our best restaurant on the top floor. The view of the Strip is fabulous. There is no formal dress code but no shorts or jeans please."

"The Windsor Room? Good. I'm in the mood for steak and lobster," Dawn said.

"You don't want to go overboard," Viv reminded. "You have to fit into your dresses."

"I wouldn't worry about that. We haven't picked out any dresses. Plus, our metabolisms haven't started to go downhill yet." Ginger gave her a smile that made Viv want to smack the girl.

Not that Viv was afraid of a little competition, but she wasn't about to lower herself to the level of a gold-digging rich bitch barely out of her teens. However, something else Ginger said was more critical to the situation at hand. "You don't have dresses?"

"No, J.R. said you'd take care of it all," Dawn replied, unconcerned.

"For the wedding. Renting tuxedos for the men will be easy enough but choosing dresses and getting them fitted takes time. Most weddings in this price range don't buy off the rack." Viv stopped herself before she started to lecture. "Of course, it's no problem. I'll arrange for you to go to the best bridal studio in Vegas tomorrow morning. We'll find you both dresses. After that we can meet about the other wedding arrangements."

"All day tomorrow with the wedding plans?" Dawn whined. "This was supposed to be a vacation. My mother is going to kill me with wedding work for months after this. Bride is my new job."

"I know these plans can be stressful but once you decide the essentials of food and music and you pick a dress it'll practically be over. If you'd prefer, we could postpone the wedding meeting until the next day but I really think you need to get the dresses picked out as soon as possible. The color of the bridesmaids' dresses must blend with the colors we use to decorate for the wedding."

"Fine, but *just* the dresses tomorrow." Dawn relented with the attitude of a spoiled princess.

"Come on, Dawn. You're always up for shopping and this is the ultimate dress." Ginger sounded more interested in the wedding than the bride.

Viv wished someone in the bridal party cared. She didn't have a good feeling about this.

"I guess," Dawn said.

"And tonight we'll hit the Strip and go to the clubs." Ginger kicked off her sandals in the direction of the closet.

"Sounds like you have a plan. Be ready for dinner at seven. That should give you some time to rest. There will be time for you to see the hotel and hit the clubs after dinner. If you have any questions or want anything arranged just let me know." Viv wanted to get out of there before Ginger started hinting about J.R. again.

"Tell J.R. we'll be ready," Ginger called after Viv.

Viv took a deep breath in the peace and quiet of the hallway. How would she make it through dinner and a wedding with those two?

* * * * *

"Mr. Haddery is in your office," Morgan said as Viv retrieved her messages at the administration desk. The unexpected thrill the news gave her caught Viv off guard. So far so good with him but to have the mere mention of his name cause that kind of response was odd.

"Thanks." She did her best to hide any external reaction. Viv walked quietly down the hall and saw J.R. leaning back in her desk chair, facing the window. Even from the back he looked good. His interest turned from the view to the pictures on the ledge in front of the window. He picked one up.

Viv cringed internally but she wasn't about to make a scene over pictures. One was a woman standing proudly in front of the All the Days of Our Lives Wedding Chapel. The other photo was of a woman in a showgirl outfit perfectly posed in front of a hotel that didn't exist anymore. Why did that have to catch his attention?

Viv licked her lips and entered with the plan to distract him. "Am I interrupting?"

"I was admiring your pictures. Who are they?" He put the pictures back where he found them and turned to her.

"My aunt owns the wedding chapel and the other picture is my mother." Viv's reply was quick and without commentary as she propped a hip on her desk. Viv wasn't normally at a loss for words but she usually didn't care what men thought about her family. She was proud of her mother's career and no one raised an eyebrow in Vegas. J.R. was different. Viv wasn't sure how he'd react. What puzzled her more was why she cared.

"Was your mom dressed up for a Halloween party or something? I bet she won first prize. She looks great." He grinned but Viv kept her poker face.

He had to be kidding. She had no choice but to correct him. "That's not a Halloween costume. My mother was one of the best topless showgirls in Las Vegas history. She covered up in that shot. Thankfully I'm too short to follow in that particular family business."

"Really?" J.R. seemed genuinely surprised by the revelation. "Your mom's a topless showgirl? She's beautiful but I never thought of showgirls as mothers."

"Yes, well, she retired ten years ago and moved to Arizona. She still looks great for nearly fifty but that's the last picture she had taken and it's old. So, now that you've met my family, can we talk about yours?" Flirting hadn't worked so it was time to use business to distract him. Viv had a job to do and her family wasn't what he was paying her for.

"Sure." J.R. exited her chair and moved to a guest seat. "Are the girls settled in?"

"They definitely like their accommodations. We do have one critical problem however."

"What do they want?" J.R. was studying her and Viv had no doubt he was fantasizing about her in one of those showgirl outfits. Men had a thing for that costume.

"It's not so much a request as an oversight. I had no idea the bride didn't have dresses picked out. I'm going to schedule an appointment at the best local bridal studio for the girls tomorrow."

"Dawn's young, I'm afraid you'll have to hold her hand through a lot of this. Especially with my aunt not arriving until the day of the wedding."

"No problem, it'll take a little more time to get the dresses settled but we'll get it done. I'll make an appointment for the groom to pick a tuxedo style. They'll measure you guys and it'll be snap."

"Excellent. I assume you've made a plan to meet with Dawn about the wedding decisions."

"The day after tomorrow. I suggested tomorrow afternoon but they want a break from wedding plans. The dresses are the most time-consuming decision so that'll be the first thing we need to tackle." She made a note on her calendar.

"You're the expert. I think we should both go get changed before dinner." J.R. glanced at his watch.

"Changed? The Windsor Room doesn't have a specific dress code. It's not like we're in jeans," Viv pointed out.

"Exactly, both of us are in business suits. With everyone else dressed like the tourists they are and we'll look odd. We need to blend in. We look like we work here."

"I do work here." Viv reminded him. "And there are plenty of people here on business."

"We don't want to give ourselves away as people who live their jobs. Let's dress it up a bit," J.R. suggested.

"If you like, I'll change into something more formal. Before I do, is there anything else the groom needs? I left the girls to rest and unpack."

"No, I think the groom is fine for now. We do have one piece of unfinished business though." J.R. walked to the door and Viv joined him.

"Unfinished business? I'm not aware of any." Viv paused by the closed office door. The glint in his eyes gave her a clue but she didn't let it show. She'd made the first move. The next was his.

"We never got to finish this." J.R. pulled her to him and Viv was quickly pinned to her office door. His mouth adhered to hers and Viv appreciated his direct technique.

Her arms wrapped around his neck as she moaned. Viv had been as tormented by this attraction as he clearly was. She could feel it in every part of him, as she pressed closer. When his fingers laced through her hair, Viv thought she'd have to clear her desk and put them both out of their misery right there or she might not make it through dinner. If it weren't for the excessive number of windows in her office, she might have. The girls in the office didn't need a show from their future boss.

Coming up for air, Viv wondered how they were going to keep their hands off each other in front of people. Especially his family. For now all Viv could feel was the passion.

"What?" he asked.

Viv realized she was smiling as she looked over his shoulder. "Ginger won't like this."

"Who?"

"Dawn's maid of honor. She has her eye on you, even asked if you had a girlfriend. I'm not blind." Viv's fingers dug into his shoulders as if she could claim him for herself.

"And how did you reply to that question?"

"I didn't. Dawn did. She said you'd never admit it if you did, but she doubted it anyway."

"I should be offended. Why would she think that?"

"Because you work too much. I got the feeling they think we're over-the-hill workaholics, or at least you are. I'm no competition of course. Just a servant in Ginger's world. You don't have a girlfriend, do you?" she asked with confidence. Before he could answer, Viv pulled him into another kiss. J.R.'s hands roamed down her back, past her waist and pulled her up against him.

"No, I don't have a girlfriend and I don't think you're over the hill. You're definitely not a servant." J.R. nuzzled her neck and she shivered in response. "And I'm not about to go after a girl ten years younger when I have an actual woman right here."

"Sure, men hate sexy and barely legal girls hitting on them." Viv didn't buy it for a minute.

"You think I'm the type of man who chases twenty-one-year-olds?" J.R. pressed.

"No, I don't think you're a dirty old man," Viv admitted. "But I know she's going to chase you. Men love their egos stroked. Among other things."

"I have an idea." He softly kissed her from one angle and then changed to another, teasing her until her hands braced his head for a deeper kiss. The feel of his tongue on hers was like a full-body massage in a matter of seconds. Everything warmed and she clung to what was left of her self-control as she grew warm and wet.

"What's this idea of yours?" Viv continued to kiss him between their conversation.

"After dinner, why don't you come to my suite for dessert and we can discuss some of the wedding plans in private?"

"Not that I'm complaining, but don't you want to spend time with your cousin and her future husband?" Viv had found a man who triggered every urge in her and seemed as casual about it as she wanted him to be. There had to be a catch.

"I think they'll be busy with Vegas and since I live here, I've already done that. Besides, I need someone to protect me from that mean maid of honor, Maryann."

"Not Maryann. Ginger. I'm sure you can take care of yourself, J.R." Viv had no sympathy for him. He wanted her to be jealous.

"Is that a *no* to my invitation?" He squeezed her insistently.

Vegas Style

"I'm not saying no. I'm just not sure of your motives. Are you after me or a way to keep a gold-digging fetus nymphomaniac at bay?" Viv got the feeling few women told J.R. no. She wanted him but there could be no confusion over the terms.

"I think I've proven my intentions are very single-minded. If you scare off Maryann, it'll just be an added bonus." His eyes held hers and Viv believed him or at least very much wanted to. This man mixed up her radar. She liked it.

"Her name is Ginger," Viv corrected.

"Whatever." J.R. kissed her again, quick and hard, as he left her in the office wanting more. Viv prepared to enjoy the anticipation through dinner. This man knew what he was doing and she couldn't wait to find out what else he knew how to do well.

* * * * *

The steakhouse had a view of downtown Vegas and Viv had timed it so the party could see the beauty of the desert and the display of lights on the Strip come to life during cocktails.

"More wine?" J.R. offered.

"No thanks. I'm still technically working." Viv had changed into a little black dress with a slit up the side, but without a plunging neckline. It stayed at work for just such events.

"You're not dressed for work." J.R. looked powerful in a dark-gray suit but without a tie.

"No, that knock-off Gucci is hardly worthy." Ginger stirred her third vodka on the rocks with a lemon twist.

"Maryann," J.R. warned.

"Ginger. A knock-off yes, but I paid for it and I have the natural assets to fill it out." Viv glanced pointedly at Ginger's barely A-cup. She shouldn't have and knew it but couldn't resist. No man would fight her battles.

"I can buy those too. You're really not a guest here so why not keep your opinions to yourself unless it's wedding-related?"

"Then let me do my job. Let's talk wedding." Viv held back what she really wanted to say. VIPs were usually spoiled, demanding and superior. Dealing with it was one thing. But it was hard to smile and swallow it in front of J.R. She wanted him to see the real her. The woman in charge of her life. No one was going to push her around.

"No. That's so boring," Dawn whined. "I want to know where we're partying afterward."

"The Naughty Wench is on the roof. Very popular with celebrities in town. Of course there are others. Depends on the crowd you're after." Viv took her glass of water. Having done her job and supplied the info, she took a long drink of water to avoid more talking.

The waiter arrived for their orders and all seemed to go for the lobster. Viv went for the chicken.

"No, you should get the lobster," J.R. whispered.

"No, really," Viv insisted.

"The waiter said the lobster is the best." J.R.'s knee nudged her under the table.

"I'm allergic to shellfish. So unless you want to take me to the hospital tonight, I'll go with the chicken." Viv didn't usually share personal details like that. She wasn't one to object to spending J.R.'s money on a dinner. The man could afford it. Of course Ginger would run with it.

"Definitely don't want you all puffy." J.R. backed off.

"I don't know. Might give that pale skin some color. Don't you tan?" Ginger cut in.

"No. SPF 45 every day. Skin cancer is bad for you and this is the desert." Viv wondered how she'd survive since no one wanted to talk about the wedding.

* * * * *

His suite was one of their best and Viv felt like she could finally relax. Free from Ginger and alone with J.R. She noticed the room service tray ready for them. Strawberry cheesecake, her favorite, and coffee waited. "I doubt that's a coincidence."

J.R. smiled. "Your assistant is a wealth of information. Want a slice?"

"After all the food I ate tonight? I don't think I could even manage a bite but thank you. Maybe later. Dawn and Ginger sure can eat."

"They'll burn it off at the nightclub. You'll have to find another way." He poured the coffee and Viv accepted a cup as she sat on the leather sofa.

"Any suggestions?" Viv sipped.

"The tease is back." J.R. removed his jacket and sat next to her. "I thought we were beyond that."

"We are. But I warned you that there would be some ground rules."

"Shoot." He settled back in the couch, ready for negotiations.

Viv set her china coffee cup on the granite and glass coffee table. "I told you marriage and I don't exactly get along."

"I don't remember proposing." His fingers traced the collar of her dress, distracting her. She could feel her breathing growing heavy and her self-control slipping. J.R. wasn't making this easy but she had to get these words out before anything happened.

"You're funny but it's not a joke. Whatever happens between us, it can never be anything serious. I'm not cut out for that. I'm not saying that you want anything permanent but I need you to know what my terms are. I don't want this to backfire with my career involved."

"I don't see your job involved at all. Separate business and pleasure is *my* first rule. But you're right. We should be clear on the terms. That's a unique way to put it. What exactly are these terms?"

"I just told you." Viv felt off balance. He didn't seem upset or overly relieved about it either. In fact it seemed as though the terms had no effect on him.

"You told me what you wouldn't do. No marriage, kids or minivan for you. So what will you do?"

"I think it's pretty clear what we both want." Viv sidestepped the issue.

"Spell it out for me." He tempted her, his lips only inches from hers.

"Sex." Viv looked him in the eye. "Clearly we are both attracted to one another, neither of us is attached and there is no reason to deny this. Don't you agree?" Her voice shook as his thumb traced slow and soft circles behind her left ear.

"How could I disagree with such a concise argument in favor of sex?" His lips followed his thumb, caressing that sensitive spot until Viv thought she'd scream.

"So no strings for fun and consenting adults." Viv knew she was rambling and silenced herself by turning and kissing him with all of her pent-up desire. His less than perfect shaving created a scratchy sensation that made her crazy. To hell with a clean, close shave. This was much better. His groan fueled her on as she slid onto his lap. Viv could feel his hard cock and pressed closer as his hands slipped under the edge of her skirt and up her thighs to the skin just below her black lace underwear.

Pulling his shirt free from his pants, Viv vaguely heard a commotion in the hallway. Her hands now on his firmly muscled stomach and sliding up his ribs to his strong chest, she dismissed it. Her mouth moved to his neck, sampling the taste of him while a few layers of clothes still separated them.

Viv felt his hand on her back, finding the zipper on her dress. In return, she moved her hand to his belt buckle.

Someone pounded on the door.

Both J.R. and Viv groaned. They reluctantly untangled and got up from the couch. J.R. answered the door, looking ready to strangle the party crasher. Viv was frustrated with all of the interruptions. Her body ached for a ride on J.R.

"Dawn fell in the nightclub," said the maid of honor, who made a point of glancing past J.R. into the room and glared at Viv.

"Is she all right, Maryann?" he asked.

"Ginger," Viv corrected as she joined him at the door. She hid her smile behind J.R.'s shoulder.

"It's only a sprained ankle but Bruce wanted me to get you. He's got Dawn's ankle propped up with pillows and on ice in our suite."

"I'll be right there." J.R. closed the door.

Viv was disappointed at the disruption but it was only a matter of time. They would get to be alone soon. The most important thing was that J.R. had agreed to the terms. The fun was on. She just couldn't let it get too complicated. Things with J.R. felt like they could get out of hand.

Chapter Four

He'd almost had Viv. The idea still sizzled in his brain as J.R. sat at breakfast the next morning with the family chatting around him. J.R. was oblivious to the conversation. The clatter of dishes and noise from the casino both seemed distant. The places his mind had gone last night haunted him. Viv needed to become more than a fantasy.

J.R. couldn't get over the fact that he'd been a few minutes from sleeping with Viv last night. After the commotion about Dawn's ankle had died down, J.R. spent a lonely night. He chose fantasy over a cold shower, which only escalated his desire. It was a good thing he didn't know Viv's home address or he might have tracked her down like a madman.

He didn't treat women like that, J.R. reminded himself. Before Viv, all J.R. ever wanted out of life was to prove he could make it. The orphan made good and no one had to take care of him. He'd achieved that long ago but there was nothing else competing for his time or attention. So he'd continued to succeed in business. A family would come in time. One that was his, not one he was adopted into. Viv wasn't volunteering for the job but she was a fun detour.

It was Viv, J.R. decided, she had some chemistry he couldn't resist. He'd kissed her after only knowing her twenty-four hours. It felt like he'd known her forever. This desire wasn't going to go away, not that he wanted it to. Viv might not have a problem with just sex but part of him did. At first the idea seemed like every guy's dream but she was just a little too eager for the casual side of things. No way was he going to let Viv treat him like every other man in her life.

He wanted her, hell yes—more than any other woman on earth—but not on her terms alone. She would get her life turned upside down like he had. The bridal studio might be just the place to catch her off guard. She'd be in one of her ultra-professional modes and not expecting it. He wanted her in every imaginable way and had dreamed clearly of those long, spiral sunshine strands over her naked body, over his naked body. He wanted as much of her as he could get and he'd come so close last night.

"Good morning, Hadderys," Viv said.

J.R. was jolted from his fantasy as the family murmured responses. She just got sexier every time he saw her.

"How is the bride?" Viv asked.

"My ankle still hurts." Dawn winced. "I don't think I'll be able to stand to try on wedding dresses today. Maybe we should forget it for today."

"Well, we can get the dress for the bridesmaids picked out and the men's tuxes and you can look at some of the dresses for styles you like. As soon as your ankle is feeling better we can try on the styles then."

"It can't hurt to go and approve the bridesmaid dress," Ginger encouraged. "You can sit the whole time."

"Fine, but I don't think I should be on my feet too much," Dawn warned. "I still have to get to and from the limo."

"We can get you a wheelchair or some crutches if you like," Viv offered.

"No, I'll be fine," Dawn replied with a huff.

"Good, we'll leave in an hour." Viv headed for the huge coffee machine that dispensed every imaginable flavor.

A few minutes later, J.R. headed after Viv with the excuse of more coffee. "How are you this morning?" he asked.

"Fine and you?"

"I could be better. Dawn finally got to sleep about three this morning. She was always accident-prone as a kid. With the shoes she wore last night it's no wonder she fell down."

"Her ankle didn't seem too swollen last night. I had hoped she'd be better today. We really can't afford to waste time where the dress is concerned."

"Maybe she can find the style, like you said. We don't want her in pain or making it worse walking on it too much." He wondered if Viv was more concerned about Dawn or the wedding plans.

"Of course not, we're just on a tight schedule. If we have to order the dress or needed a lot of alterations it could take time. Brides are very particular about their dresses. If her ankle isn't better by tomorrow we'll call a doctor. She's walking on it so it can't be broken but she could have a very bad sprain." Viv filled her coffee mug with Italian Roast while J.R. sneaked a look at the table to see if he'd been missed. No one seemed to mind.

"Too bad her timing was off. I'm sorry it ruined our evening."

"Me too."

J.R. could see her face soften from critical business thoughts to more pleasant memories. "You are here to spend time with your family though."

"And I know you'll be very busy because this is your job but hopefully we can spend some time alone."

"I hope so too. What are your plans for the evening?" she asked.

"Probably spend time with Dawn while she's injured."

Her smile became more faint but she added sugar to her coffee. "At least I'll get to see you in your tux today. Looks like your birthday suit will have to wait." She gave him a seductive smile and turned to walk back to the table.

J.R. hung back a few moments and grabbed a fresh mug. What he needed was a cold shower. She was imagining him naked? And bold enough to tell him that to his face in public. This woman was one in a million and she wasn't going to make it easy to resist her. Viv knew her power and J.R. knew he'd give her exactly what she wanted.

"Too many choices?" Bruce's voice made J.R. turn.

He was near the coffee machine and pretended to be casually pondering the flavor choices. J.R. chuckled. "I'm not much of a coffee drinker but I need a jump-start today."

"She'd wake me up." Bruce grinned.

"She who?" J.R. played dumb.

"She, the hot wedding planner, who'd be in my dreams if it weren't for Dawn. Good to know you're getting out there. You'll have to tell me all about it."

"Don't talk about her like that, Bruce," J.R. warned so coldly that Bruce's head jerked to look at him. "Viv isn't like that."

"Sorry, J.R. Dawn said that Ginger said that you and Viv were more than friendly last night. I didn't think it was a secret or serious." Bruce shrugged. "My mistake."

"Make sure your fiancée stops gossiping."

"Easier said than done," Bruce agreed. "Dawn always blabs at the wrong time. You really like Viv?"

"She's different." J.R. knew he'd gotten overly defensive. He tried to lighten the conversation since he knew Bruce never liked a confrontation with his friends. "I've never met anyone like her and no one is going to badmouth her."

"Does she have a sister?" Bruce teased.

"No idea. But she's one of a kind."

"You have all the luck." Bruce punched him in the shoulder and grabbed a doughnut.

"The harder you work, the luckier you get," J.R. repeated his dad's motto.

"You must have worked really hard to get a girl that pretty." Bruce grinned.

"I don't have her yet thanks to Dawn's dancing act last night. But you don't get lucky without the effort. I think she's worth it."

"I'll say. From the sparks between you two, I don't think she'll put up much of a fight. Just reel her in, buddy."

"She's not a fish, Bruce, but she has a tough exterior. You've got to remove the needles before you can handle a cactus."

"So she's not a fish but she's a cactus?" Bruce teased. "I won't even ask for details. How's business?"

J.R. was glad for the change in subject. "Business is good. You could always come to work for me."

"No thanks. Dawn likes the society scene." Bruce looked over at the women. "So I really have to pick out a penguin suit to wear in one-hundred-and-fourteen-degree heat?"

"It's your wedding." J.R. just wanted more time with Viv.

* * * * *

The studio was a bride's dream and complete intimidation for any man. A sea of white, puffy dresses and a rainbow of bridesmaid gowns lined the walls. J.R. watched as Viv chatted with the owner. Ginger dove into the racks while Dawn leaned on Bruce until they got her settled in a chair.

The men stayed together. J.R. saw Viv nod in their direction and one of the employees approached them.

"Hello, I'm Gwen. If you'll follow me, gentlemen, I'll show you the latest styles of tuxedos and we'll get your measurements."

J.R. followed along and supplied his opinion to Bruce when asked but never lost sight of Viv. She sorted through a handful of lavender dresses with Ginger. He caught Viv's eye once or twice and swore she blushed a little. It appeared, after some debate, that they narrowed it down to three dresses and Ginger disappeared into the dressing rooms to model them for the bride. Soon Viv disappeared with them and J.R. was handed a tux to try on.

He followed the groom into the hall of rooms the women had just entered and found an empty one. As he slipped into the tux, J.R. heard a familiar voice in the hallway. "No, that dress isn't right either," Viv said.

"It's awful. The waist cuts me in half," Ginger agreed.

"Try the A-line. That style looks best on most people," Viv suggested.

"Why is Dawn making this so hard?" Ginger huffed.

"Because it's her wedding. You can't outshine the bride." Viv sounded unconcerned. "When she tries on a dress she'll get into the spirit."

J.R. listened to Viv's heels and heard the steps coming near him. This was too good to be true. Patiently he waited by the door. As she passed, J.R. silently swung the door opened and pulled her in, pinning her against the wall. But it wasn't the blonde dream he'd planned.

"I knew you'd come around," Ginger purred as she wrapped her arms around him.

J.R. froze and cursed himself. "No." He tried to dislodge Ginger's claws from him as he backed away.

"Come on. Why settle for an old thing like Viv when I'm right here." Her hands grew bolder as she turned the tables and pressed him to the wall. J.R. finally stopped playing the true gentleman and caught both of her wrists in one of his hands.

"Viv isn't old. You need a babysitter." He knew trying to push her away would mean letting go of her hands and he'd be right back where he started. There was no good way to handle this.

"Are you volunteering?" Ginger licked her lips. J.R. extended his arm as far as he could to keep her away but the woman wasn't about to give up.

Suddenly, the door swung open. Viv entered the dressing room without hesitation. Her weight was shifted to one hip and her arms crossed against her chest. "Is there a problem?"

"I thought she was you." J.R. moved as far away from Ginger as the small room would allow.

"You made a blind grab for anything female and thought you'd get lucky?" Viv smiled as Ginger left, glaring at both of them. "Must be getting desperate. At least you were dressed."

"I wanted to surprise you." J.R. closed the door and finally they were alone.

"You accomplished that without a doubt. Are you sure you didn't mean to pull Ginger in here?"

"Why would I want to do that?" He pulled her close to him. "She's an octopus."

"I knew that the first moment I saw her. Maybe you did it to get my attention. Trying to make me jealous?" She wrapped her arms around his neck. J.R. wished they didn't have to worry about an interruption. Whenever Viv got close his brain stopped working and another part of his body took over. However, he was determined that their first real time wasn't going to be a quickie in a dressing room.

"I'm not the insecure type of man who needs to make a woman jealous. I haven't mastered impulsive and romantic moves like this. I'll have to practice more." J.R. lowered his mouth to hers and felt Viv's hands tighten around him as she kissed him back.

"I'm supposed to be working," she whispered against his lips.

"That's right and you haven't said a thing about my tux." He wasn't going to let her slip away that fast.

"Let me see." Viv stepped back slowly to study him. "You clean up nice. Is this Bruce's choice?"

"No good?" he asked.

"It's fine. Not my first choice but it'll work. You'll look better in it than the groom."

"Is that your personal opinion?" J.R. closed in on her again.

"And my professional one." She adjusted his tie and smoothed her hands over his vest. "Bruce doesn't have the shoulders to fill it out. All men look good in tuxes but having the right build adds to the effect you have on women."

"Maybe I should buy it rather than rent it." He kissed her neck and felt her press closer for better contact as her fingers slid into his hair.

"No," Viv insisted quickly. "I mean if you really want to buy a tux I'll help you pick out a better one for you. I'd still rather see you out of everything but it appears circumstances are against us for now. I have to work with this establishment and can't get caught in the act."

"So it crossed your mind too." J.R. dropped another kiss on her mouth.

"Of course, but I don't want Dawn or Ginger walking in on us." Viv sounded very serious.

J.R. didn't care. He slid a hand up her thigh and under her tailored skirt.

Her fingers braced on his shoulder. "What are you doing?"

"What I can until you find a way to be alone with me." J.R.'s fingers slid under her lace panties and teased her outer lips. Slick and bare, no curls like in his fantasy. The reality of her wet pussy made him hard.

"We couldn't be alone last night thanks to your family," she gasped.

"I'll make it up to you now." Kissing her mouth, J.R. eased two fingers into her folds and her warm dampness enveloped him.

Viv leaned against the wall, opening herself as she tugged her skirt higher. Then her fingers went in search of him. She fumbled with his zipper until he grabbed her hand.

"One at a time," he whispered in her ear.

She groaned and leaned up, kissing him more intensely.

J.R.'s fingers eased to her entrance and stroked her pussy as it grew wetter and wetter. Viv did her best to fuck his fingers but he controlled it, he wanted to play and watch her come. Massaging her wet inner folds, he felt her hard clit. Viv tensed against him as he circled and pressed the pleasure point. Her hips bucked for more contact and he pinched the clit between his thumb and index finger.

Viv went rigid and clutched him. He watched her come as her eyes glazed over and she bit her lower lip to keep quiet. After a few moments, she rocked her hips, letting her clit graze his finger as she wound down from her orgasm.

The pleasure was written on her face as J.R. gently removed his fingers and Viv's eyes closed and opened. J.R. licked his fingers, spicy and warm like her. "Feel better?"

"Much. Now it's your turn." She started to slide to her knees but J.R. stopped her. Every piece of him wanted to let her demonstrate her blowjob skills but he knew they'd been alone too long. Someone would come for them.

"What?" she asked.

"Someone will be looking for you soon. We can't do that now. You should go."

"Your loss." Viv stroked his erection through his pants. "And mine."

"Too bad I don't get to see you in a tight little strapless bridesmaid's dress either." He tried to think of anything but Viv the way he really wanted her.

"And I thought you wanted me naked." Viv slipped out of the room.

J.R. controlled his urge to pull her back in.

Vegas Style

Soon. Very soon.

Chapter Five

They hadn't needed her services for the rest of the evening. The family had planned to spend time together. So Viv came home and did the normal routine she'd neglected for the past few days.

The evening seemed to drag on as she paid bills, did her laundry and pretended to do some light cleaning. Viv had the uneasy sense that a member of the Haddery family would knock on her door any moment. The thoughts of J.R. refused to be ignored. Viv's mind wandered to him again and again through the course of the evening.

Her work had never been so all-consuming. It must be the attitude of people, Viv concluded. Dawn and Ginger were trouble. Still, she had left her cell phone on just in case J.R. needed her. Or any of them, she quickly corrected her own thoughts. J.R. had hired her. There was clearly more than business between them but she had to keep perspective on her life.

J.R. filled her mind too much. That had to be due to their interrupted evening. Viv needed to completely satisfy that sexual urge soon or she was sure she'd go crazy. She'd done everything she could think of to distract herself but self-gratification was not enough. Even his dressing room antics only fueled the fire. She wanted J.R. and nothing less was going to do the trick.

Finally Viv called her mother to force her mind onto another subject. There was no answer at her mom's home. Just like Mom. She was probably out on another date. It was good to know that life, particularly the sex part, didn't end at age fifty. However, the fact that her mother had more of a social life than Viv did wasn't good for her ego.

Viv finally decided that only work would be interesting enough to put J.R. out of her mind. She spent the time on notes for the meeting with the bride the next day. Then Viv found herself inspired to improve it, she revamped her old system completely. Plus it would look good and might help with that promotion. Viv wanted to have solid recommendations and alternatives so Dawn couldn't squirm her way out of making a decision yet again.

At first Viv hadn't questioned Dawn's accident but after seeing her milking the injury at the bridal studio, Viv had to admit she had her doubts as to the severity of Dawn's pain. The bride would have to make some decisions eventually. A wedding coordinator could only do so much.

Viv hoped her over-organized plan would make the decisions easier. It might prove to be a useful new model to implement if she got the promotion. A format to help the planners be more organized and consistent. Everyone she worked with was very good but they all had their own systems and some were more abstract than hers.

Work seemed to be effective in keeping her mind off J.R. She planned the perfect wedding in her notes. All the items she picked were as if it were her own wedding. Not that she ever thought she'd have one, but they were her favorites. Now the entire plan was contained in one simple setup with suggestions and alternatives. Viv had done all she could without a decision from the bride.

* * * * *

The next morning, with notes firmly in hand, Viv emerged from the elevator to the lobby floor of the hotel. She hoped to catch the Hadderys at breakfast. Better that than having to chase down the bride for their meeting. Dawn hopefully would be in a better mood about the wedding plans but Viv wasn't about to take any chances.

As she approached the lobby, Viv saw Ginger and Dawn climbing into a limo. Glancing back, Dawn's gaze met Viv's and the runaway bride gave her a slight smile. Viv felt stood up. Most brides didn't do this. The bride could walk just fine now and continued to avoid any decision-making on her wedding.

Twisted ankle. Viv shook her head at the faker. For all of yesterday's fussing, to have such a miraculous and complete recovery seemed remarkable. The bride had interrupted her and J.R.'s night over a twisted ankle. Now she blew off their appointment for the wedding plans. That wasn't a good sign.

"Where is she going?" Viv asked aloud, sure she was quiet enough not to be overheard.

"That's my girl. Always going somewhere." Bruce popped up from a group of video poker machines.

Viv tried not to appear startled. "Sorry, I didn't mean to interrupt. I didn't see you there."

"Don't worry. Dawn has been flighty since we got engaged. Ginger wanted to go shopping and Dawn can't say no. I'm sure she'll be back this afternoon."

"I hope so. The wedding will have to be pulled together fast if we continue to have delays. I'm good but there are limits." Viv tucked her notes under her arm. This new system of hers better work.

"I wouldn't worry. It'll fall into place."

"Thanks, I'll see you later." Viv walked away before she said any more. Viv hoped that Dawn would shop for the wedding dress or at least be ready to work on the plans when she returned. Deep down Viv knew she was in for a struggle but there was little she could do now. Vegas had a lot of distractions and Dawn seemed easily drawn to them.

* * * * *

Viv sat in her office and inputted the notes into her computer with a nice font complete with wedding bells and tiny hearts. For some reason brides seemed to be more drawn to things that looked pretty rather than professional. As the new forms printed, Viv's cell phone rang.

"Hello," she answered.

"How are the plans going?" J.R. asked.

His voice made Viv smile but J.R. clearly had no idea what his cousin was up to today. "They aren't. Dawn and Ginger went shopping."

"You changed the meeting?"

"No, Dawn apparently elected to change our meeting. Bruce told me a few minutes ago. Did you need something?" She tried to sound professional.

"I don't need anything." He matched her professional tone and she wanted to laugh.

Viv felt a sudden unease about what else to say. As much as she wanted to talk with J.R. about Dawn avoiding her meetings about the wedding plans, this was his cousin's wedding. Having it go well obviously meant a lot to him. She had to handle the bad bride and make it work.

Viv had no idea why she had the desire to share her professional frustrations with J.R. This was not his problem. He paid her to handle the wedding problems. He'd asked about the plans and she'd answered him honestly. Enough said on that topic.

"Viv?" J.R. seemed concerned at the extended silence. "Everything okay?"

"Fine. It's not normal for me to have only one wedding at a time. I'm not quite sure what to do with myself." It was the truth. Not the whole truth but if Viv shared her concerns with J.R. she'd have to do it carefully. He was very protective of his family.

"If you're free now, why don't you come up to my suite?" He sounded casual but Viv felt a tingle over every inch of her skin.

"I thought you said you didn't need anything." Viv's voice dropped to a slightly seductive tone.

"I don't but if you're not busy I certainly wouldn't mind the company."

Viv knew she couldn't resist. "I'm just finishing up a little project. I'll be up as soon as I can." Hanging up the phone, she couldn't help but wonder why he was still in his room rather than enjoying another sunny and beautiful one hundred and ten degree day in Las Vegas.

First Viv applied an extra layer of her favorite lip gloss. Then, with her new creation in a red binder, Viv headed out of her office. She wanted to see him and it was pointless to deny herself.

Within minutes she was at his room and found he'd left the door ajar for her. Pushing it open a little, she saw him bent over what looked like a financial report. Business on vacation? Viv had to put a stop to this. "What are you doing in here? There is a whole casino, not to mention a city that never closes waiting for you."

"I had a little business to sift through. If I went down for breakfast I'd have been dragged into something else. Plus I thought you and the girls would be huddled over wedding cake and flower pictures. They decided to do some shopping without you?"

"That's what Bruce said. I got there just in time to see Dawn jump into a limo and drive away."

"Maybe she wants to do the wedding-dress shopping on her own," he suggested.

"I hope you're right." Viv didn't believe it for a second.

"But you don't think so?"

How could he read her so well? Viv had a good poker face—no taste for gambling with her money—but she could hide her feelings when she wanted to. "I don't see why she wouldn't want a professional's opinion. I'm here to coordinate, not dictate. If she never makes use of me you'll simply be out a lot of money. Anyway, this will be one unusual wedding."

"You're worth it." He lounged back in his chair and smiled. Viv felt a rush of heat and wondered if he'd asked her up her for the reason she wanted.

"Let's hope my boss agrees with you."

"Why wouldn't he?" J.R. asked.

"I have a promotion riding on this wedding."

"And I thought you were after me for my body." J.R.'s grin made it hard for Viv not to laugh.

"I am after you for your body. Luckily we both want Dawn to have a perfect wedding. I'll admit that your family event is important to my future position here. You're getting more personal attention because you're my only wedding at the moment. I'm so used to multiple weddings that having one bride who seems barely interested in my only wedding leaves me with too much time on my hands." Viv dropped her masterpiece on the table and turned to face the view rather than pace as she felt the need to do.

"Dawn is young. She wants to have fun and explore Vegas." J.R. slipped his arms around her waist from behind and Viv instantly felt her stress level drop. "You remember what it was like to be twenty-one, don't you?"

"Sure, graduating from college and picking life plans. Fun or not, we all have to make decisions in life." Viv let her head tip back to rest on his shoulder.

"I'll bet the summers in college you were wild. Your mother couldn't keep you in the house, right?"

"I had my share of fun." Viv pressed her body back firmly against him. "But I still had to pick a college and a major and classes and find a job. I did those first and then enjoyed the summers with some friends. Business first and then pleasure. Your cousin just doesn't seem interested in getting the decisions out of the way so she can have fun."

"At least her ankle is better. She walked fine last night." J.R.'s lips brushed her neck and Viv locked her knees to keep from putting her full weight against him.

"Her ankle's all better. That's good." Viv cleared her throat in an attempt to sound professional. "I'd make an appointment at the bridal studio but I'm afraid she'll ditch me again."

She felt his warm breath on her neck as he laughed. "Make it for the day after tomorrow, in the morning. I'll make sure she's there if I have to drag her myself."

"This is not normal." Viv had begun to doubt Dawn's desire to get married at all. She told herself not to worry about that right now. Enjoying the moment and where it seemed to be going was more important. Any attempt to figure out Dawn with her senses overloaded by J.R. was pointless.

"What isn't normal? Us or Dawn?" J.R. sank his teeth in her neck so gently that Viv's knees gave way. He caught her and turned her around. "Why don't we stop this talk about Dawn?"

"What was the question?" Viv pressed closer, not wanting to answer as her hands dug into his shoulders. The power of his muscles and heat of his skin made the dress shirt he wore seem invisible.

"Will anyone miss you if I keep you here for a few hours?" He changed the question and pulled her flush against him but didn't kiss her. Viv stifled a groan, he hadn't kissed her once on the mouth since she'd entered the room and it was driving her crazy. But she felt his erection against her hip.

Kissing had never been so intoxicating. She would readily admit he was the best kisser she'd ever had but he made her wait. Viv wasn't used to waiting for a man she wanted.

"Miss me? You're my only client right now. Unless your family needs anything, no one will be looking for me at all. But what could possibly keep me here for a few hours?" Viv could only hope it wasn't a classic male exaggeration.

"You grossly underestimate my talents," he warned.

"Prove it," she challenged and was immediately taken over by the kiss. She'd been waiting for this since the previous day in that dressing room. She would enjoy every second of being alone with J.R.

As her tongue darted across his lower lip, she heard the beep of the room phone. Her head fell back in defeat. "If that's Ginger, I'll have to have her banned for life from the hotel."

J.R. smiled and rather than rush to the phone, he cradled the back of her head in his palm. He pulled her in for a gentle kiss. "One second."

Likely story. Viv had dated men with big businesses and careers before. For some reason their job always seemed to come first. Viv understood, her career meant a lot to her too. However, men had never understood when her job interfered with plans. The classic double standard. This may be just the black mark Viv needed against J.R. to get him out of her constant thoughts. So far, he was very good.

"Hello." J.R. answered the phone but kept his eyes on her. She suddenly felt on display and ran a hand under her hair so it hung nicely. The move had the added advantage of cooling her off slightly as air hit the back of her neck.

"No, we have to reschedule," he said.

Viv's eyebrow went up but she tried her best to not appear nosy. He wouldn't really cancel plans.

"This afternoon at three." He made a note and hung up the phone.

"Am I disrupting your workday?" she asked.

"No, I had a conference call this morning but I moved it. Now where were we?" His hands were on her hips pulling her close as Viv let her arms wrap around his neck.

"I could leave so you can have your meeting." She didn't want to be blamed for a lost deal.

"Not a chance." He held her tighter and dropped slow, seductive kisses down her face and neck until she shivered. "This afternoon you can go over wedding plans with Dawn and I'll have my conference call. Right now is our time. It isn't easy coordinating the schedule of two busy people. We have to take advantage of it when we can."

"You are definitely unique." Her lips caught his as her fingers dug into his hair. It was her turn to lead and she wanted a slow, deep kiss that went on forever. He had changed his business plans for her. Viv felt unbelievably wonderful and for the first time really special. If she weren't so completely turned on, she'd be a little afraid of how he was making her feel. No wonder she needed to be in his bed.

His hands slid under her jacket and undid the buttons. With no effort he tugged it off her and his hands returned to her body as she felt him increase the heat of their kiss to unimaginable levels. Was it possible to be this aroused and still be fully clothed? Viv had never experienced this kind of desire before. The need built and had to be relieved before she lost her mind. What he'd done in the dressing room only made it worse. She needed him naked.

One by one, Viv undid the buttons on his dress shirt to reveal his magnificent chest. Every muscle was defined and ready for her. Slowly she let her fingers glide over them up to his collarbone. As his hands tugged her blouse from her skirt, Viv leaned forward and left a perfect imprint of her lips in the form of her creamy pink lip gloss above his right nipple.

Rather than bothering with the tiny buttons on her blouse, she shimmied it over her head and tossed it aside as J.R. groaned in appreciation.

"You're perfect." His strong and warm hands took hold of her sides and slid up to the edge of her satin bra.

Much as she adored the frilly things other women wore, her breasts required underwire for support. The silvery-blue color set off her eyes and was Viv's favorite choice. "You haven't seen everything yet."

"You're sure about this?" he asked.

"Are you suggesting I'm a tease?" She kissed his mouth and let her tongue explore every inch until he crushed her to him, his teeth tugging at her lips.

"Not at all." J.R. undid her skirt and let it fall to the floor. He pressed his forehead to hers. "You're too damn sexy."

Viv expertly undid the button on his expensive dress pants. Taking a half step closer, she pressed her lips to the other side of his chest but this time let her lipstick smear as she pushed his boxers off his hips and looked down. "You're the one who's sexy." His erection was as impressive as the rest of him. She wanted to dive in but rushing things was not called for here.

"Now you're overdressed." J.R. reached behind her and took off her bra like a pro. By the way his hands stroked and teased her breasts, Viv got the impression he approved of her form. Slowly he eased her back and Viv landed on the bed with a smile. J.R.'s mouth nibbled down her neck and finally engulfed her left nipple. Viv gasped in pleasure as the feel of his tongue triggered an intense throbbing of her clit and wetness between her legs.

His attention to her breasts drove Viv to near insanity. She had to keep her hands occupied or she'd take over and have her way with him this second. She didn't want to do that yet and let one hand slip into his hair. Her fingernails dug into his scalp while her other hand slid down his nicely defined chest and stroked his cock, careful not to be too rough as he groaned against her now incredibly sensitive skin.

"I'm still overdressed," she insisted.

He smiled up at her and trailed kisses down her stomach and continued over the satin. Viv knew her arousal was probably obvious. Taking a deep breath, she tried not to squirm in anticipation. Finally he eased off the material and his expression was priceless. He quickly returned the surprise as he traced his index finger up her bare slit and Viv shivered in response. Her waxing was definitely worth the pain and expense. "Glad you like it."

"I don't know what to say about this. I felt it yesterday—but seeing it. You are full of surprises." He stroked her, spreading her juices over her swollen pussy and exploring her slowly as she arched her back and spread her legs wider. Slowly his two fingers eased into her.

Her mind cut out and her body took over. "Your fingers are perfect," she moaned.

"Then you'll love this."

Viv bit back a scream as his tongue stroked from her clit all the way down and slowly, teasingly entered her and flicked expertly. Her hand clutched his hair, holding him to her. "More," she gasped.

J.R. lifted his head with a grin and eased three fingers into her while his thumb tormented her clit further.

"I can't take much more of this!" she demanded.

"Relax." He dragged his fingers through her folds, causing ripples of pleasure to radiate through every inch of her. His fingers continued up her stomach and deposited a pool of liquid on each nipple.

The cool feel of air and wetness on her tight nipple made it more intense. Her eyes were shut tight at the feeling. When his tongue lapped up every drop she couldn't stand it a moment longer.

Rolling to reverse their positions, Viv stroked his now-larger cock and watched as his hips lifted in response. He was as near to the edge as she was. Slowly she licked the tip and resisted the urge to do much more.

He dug a condom from the nightstand and slipped it on. Impatience overtook her as she straddled him. Viv smiled at his quick thinking. With any other man she'd have come prepared but he blurred her mind. Carefully she lowered herself and both groaned in the mutual need. J.R.'s hands pulled her forward and his mouth savaged hers as their bodies found their own rhythm. He filled her like no other man had. She was acutely aware of every nerve ending in her body and it was perfect.

J.R. flipped her beneath him and set a new pace that was better than anything she'd ever experienced. His rough, hard body rubbing against every inch of her only made it more intense. Even that spotty shaving she'd grown so fond of added a new element to sex as he kissed her neck.

Viv knew they couldn't keep this up much longer. Any moment his large cock would hit just the right spot. As he hit his mark, J.R.'s hand slipped from her hip down to her clit and triggered the orgasm she'd fantasized about for days now. Her voice rasped his name but it was muffled in his mouth as he came right after her. The feel of his body trembling and thrusting in her gave Viv a glorious sense of power and pleasure. Much as she tried, she couldn't resist his continued kiss even though they were both completely exhausted.

Finally she rested her head on his shoulder. His hot breath blew a few tendrils of her hair up in the air repeatedly. J.R.'s fingers finally caught the curls and Viv kissed his wrist since it was so attractively within reach. "That was worth the wait," she mumbled.

"And that was just the first time." J.R. rolled onto his back, removed the condom and then wrapped her close. Viv settled in, letting her eyes close and enjoying the warmth of him. No man had ever fit this well. She could get used to this kind of sex. J.R. was in a class by himself.

Chapter Six

ഔ

J.R. woke to find Viv still curled up with him. Glancing at his watch, the only thing either of them was still wearing, J.R. was relieved that it was only noon. His conference call wasn't for a few hours and then he'd let Viv go find his cousin. They could both get back to their work. Until then she wasn't going anywhere. For a woman so hell-bent on independence and control, she'd certainly allowed him to have the upper hand for a while.

Viv stretched against him and he couldn't resist pulling her closer. Her lips made contact with his shoulder and J.R. groaned. The smeared lipstick was still on his chest from her earlier antics. "You wore me out, lady, don't start that again." He pushed her mass of blonde curls out of the way so he could see her blue eyes finally open. The content smile on her face made him want Viv even more.

"Hi," she whispered.

"You fell asleep." His fingers trailed down her neck where the lipstick had rubbed off on her as well. That such a strong woman could also be so receptive made him want to know every detail of her.

"So did you." Viv shifted her weight so she was directly on top of him. J.R. thought nothing could feel better until she began kissing his neck. "You certainly lived up to your bragging."

"You doubted me?"

"Men have a tendency to exaggerate their talents in that area. I figure it can't hurt to stroke your ego if I want more. Enjoy it, I don't tell a man he's right very often."

Her honesty only added to her charm. J.R. wanted more. He felt a warm hand curl around his cock and groaned. "You wore me out."

"Hardly. But don't worry. You just lie back and relax." Viv crawled lower, kissing a path down his stomach and hips before kissing each ball, and then the base of his cock.

J.R. watched those red nails against his growing flesh. "You're insatiable."

"You'll have to prove that theory." She let her tongue glide over the head of his shaft.

J.R. groaned as she took the head into her mouth, sucking and licking him to full length. The beads of salvia ran down his cock. Viv thoroughly coated him balls to tip with the wetness of her tongue.

Kissing the tip, she studied the large cock. "It's too big. I'll never get it all."

"You don't have to. Take what you want." His hand went to the back of her neck.

Viv went down on him again. Taking as much as she could and slowly backing off. Her hand wrapped around the rest of his cock. Bobbing her head on the top half, Viv's tongue worked the head with singular focus until J.R. felt his balls tighten. The hand on her neck fisted in her hair.

J.R. strained for control as Viv's tongue pressed into the tip of his cock. "Viv." He groaned a warning.

Viv backed off but didn't release his cock from her mouth. Her hand worked him faster, milking what she wanted as he came in her mouth.

He felt her tongue lap at his spent cock. Slowly J.R. lifted his head to watch her. "You are too good."

"I've been thinking about that since the limo." She moved up and kissed his lips.

"Took you that long?" He reached for her hip. In the heat of passion, he'd noticed something there but hadn't had a chance to look at it. "What's this?"

"A tattoo." She lifted an eyebrow, but didn't say any more.

"I see you're determined to be difficult." He slid out from under her but didn't let Viv roll over onto her back. "I'll have to handle this personally."

"What are you doing?" She tried to move but J.R. pressed her into the bed with half of his body on hers leaving the tattoo revealed.

"Inspecting you." He traced the one-inch crystal ball with a green dragon perched like a guardian. "When did you get this?"

"When I was sixteen." Viv propped her chin in her hand and watched over her shoulder.

J.R. felt a stab of desire. She looked like a seductive goddess to him. A slightly bad girl with a tattoo. Who knew what other surprises were in store for him.

"It's my only one," Viv whispered.

"You got a tattoo when you were sixteen? Your mother allowed that?" His aunt would've killed him. "I have to meet this woman."

"Don't count on it. My mother lives in Arizona now. Besides, I don't want to scare her."

"I don't scare mothers." He pretended to be offended. "Mothers love me."

"I'll bet they do. I meant I don't want to give her the idea I'm serious about a man. Any man. That would upset her. If she shows up in the next week for a visit I'll introduce you. Mom didn't care when I came home with the tattoo. It's just on my hip. No one sees it unless I'm naked."

"Who did it? It's too good to be an amateur but don't most places require you to be eighteen?" J.R. didn't like the idea of some old guy with his hands on Viv's underage bare hip. Any man except him touching her wasn't a thought he wanted to entertain.

"Uncle Number Five did it. He had a tattoo parlor and came up with this design because I really like dragons. It was so perfect I had him do it. It was my birthday present. I really wanted a car but we weren't that well-off. Unfortunately, a year later my aunt caught him cheating and divorced him. He was a terrible husband but a good tattoo artist."

"So it's a happy story." He laughed.

"My aunt recently got rid of Uncle Number Nine and I still like the tattoo. So I guess it is happy. You don't like it?" Viv gave him a pouty frown.

"Actually it's growing on me, never dated a woman with a tattoo before. You're full of surprises." He couldn't resist leaning down to nip the tattoo and continued a trail up to her neck. "So when is your birthday?" After the lead in, he couldn't help but ask.

"June 1, and that's all I'm telling," she giggled.

"Nine uncles, really?" He nibbled her ear. No wonder Viv didn't want anything serious. All she expected was for a man to want to screw her and leave. But another would come along.

"Yeah, nine. My bet is she'll make an even dozen before she hits sixty. If you like the tattoo then you'll really love my scar." She pushed back the watch on her left wrist.

He examined two small puncture wounds. "What happened to you?"

"Rattlesnake." She stretched casually against his body.

"You were bitten by a rattlesnake?" J.R. felt a rush of concern and protectiveness. He knew Viv wanted to keep it light but he was already a bit attached to her curves and that wild side.

"It's the desert. They're not exactly rare. This happened when I was seven." Viv arched her back to kiss him.

"Were you hospitalized?" he asked.

"No. It was no big deal." Viv waved it off and didn't continue with the story. Instead she kissed his neck.

"Not good enough. A seven-year-old gets bitten by a rattlesnake. I want more," J.R. prodded.

"You really want the whole dull story?" She seemed surprised but J.R. wasn't letting up.

"I won't let you up until I hear it. How did you get bitten by a rattlesnake?" His arm pinned her more firmly.

"You big bully." Viv pushed back against him but J.R. wasn't about to give. Finally she relented. "It's not exactly a rare occurrence. My aunt runs a small wedding chapel. During the summers, while my mother worked, I'd help my aunt there. One day I went to the back room to dig out a weird goth tiara some client wanted to wear. I reached in a corner where the box was and surprised a rattlesnake."

"Did it hurt?" He traced the scar with his thumb and then folded her arm closer to kiss the mark.

"Sure it hurt. They have sharp fangs that look big to a kid. Luckily, it was a dry bite. No venom. My aunt washed the bite out until my skin was raw and bandaged it really tight. They watched me like a hawk for a day. It bled for a while but it was fine. Uncle Number Three said no venom got in my system because there were no symptoms, no swelling and no intense pain. He went in and trapped the snake."

"Did he kill it?"

"No, that uncle owned an exotic pet store. People keep some weird things as pets. Rats, spiders, snakes, lizards and even scorpions. He found a whole nest back there. He raised the babies and sold them all. Paid me a fifty-dollar finder's fee."

"So you're a snake charmer. What pets do you have now?" He wanted to know more about this woman. Anything. Everything. If she was talking he intended to keep her talking.

"None. I prefer furry types of pets but I don't have any. I work too much and such odd hours that it wouldn't be fair. Your turn." Viv pushed him over onto his back and slowly straddled his waist. J.R. felt less blood getting to his brain already.

"I don't have any pets." He enjoyed her takeover. There was no doubt Viv had a deep strain of independence in her and J.R. liked it.

"No, I'm going to check you for tattoos and scars." Viv ran her hands over his arms and chest.

"Actually, I have a question about this first." J.R. traced a finger along her inner thigh to the faint tan line of her bikini area. He'd had his share of women but the totally bare thing was new.

"The miracle of modern waxing techniques." Viv smiled. "I thought you liked it."

"Oh, I do. But why go through that?" he asked. "Doesn't it hurt?"

"I'm used to it by now and the reaction is worth it. Besides, I didn't really know any different." Viv's fingers toyed with his chest hair.

"I don't understand," he admitted.

"My mother was a showgirl. I hung out backstage a lot. Those are some really skimpy outfits, even in her day. Most of the women shaved or waxed it all off so there was no chance of a bit of bush revealed if the costume shifted. Appearance is critical. There were plenty of girls ready to take their jobs. Anyway, when I got old enough I started waxing too. My mom took me to the woman who did hers and she's an expert. Now it's just part of good grooming. Like brushing my teeth."

"At least it's a woman." J.R. rubbed her outer lips and ignored the possessive feeling.

Viv pinched his chest playfully. "You think I'd pay a guy to go down there. That's free. Now back to my scar inspection if you don't mind. I think you've gotten a full tour of my body."

Clean on his upper body, she scooted down his body until she saw the long scar on his calf. "That's no rattlesnake bite. What happened to you?"

"That's from the car wreck. I was lucky. Both of my parents were killed instantly. I needed sixty stitches in that leg and broke my right arm. That did require a trip to the hospital but I got this cool scar."

"I'm sorry. I didn't mean to bring up bad memories." Viv tensed, she clearly felt uncomfortable getting so personal. She'd crossed the invisible line that she had created and was in full retreat of the subject. The mood in the room shifted drastically.

"Scars aren't normally happy memories. Don't worry about it. I started the conversation. Not talking about it doesn't change what happened." He tried to get her to look at him but she turned her head. "My parents were killed and I was thrown from the car. The twisted metal gashed my leg and I landed on my arm. It's no one's fault." J.R. ran his hands up and down her upper arms trying to relax her tense posture.

"I'm still sorry." Viv was obviously not referring to the accident but something between them. "This was supposed to be strictly a fun time for the two of us. We shouldn't go into such serious stuff."

"You only want to have sex? No conversation? Come on, Viv, we have too much chemistry and too much in common to pretend it's nothing but sex. I agreed not to have this turn into anything serious but I'm not going to be treated like a sex toy. At least not all the time." J.R. gently pulled her into a kiss but Viv braced her hands on his chest.

"I like your conversation, J.R., but you're only here for a short time. There's a difference between acting like there is nothing between us and getting into some of our most difficult pieces of personal history. Neither makes sense. It's not just sex but I don't want us to spend the rest of our time together depressing each other." She kissed his chin and then moved down to kiss the hollow of his throat. Her lips dropped kisses slowly, swirled around his Adam's apple and returned to his lips for a final kiss.

"If you really feel bad then you should make an effort to take my mind off that tragedy." J.R. settled back in the pillows. It was clear Viv was more comfortable with the physical than any intimate conversation right now. "Any ideas?"

"Men." Viv rolled her eyes. "Sex fixes everything, doesn't it?" Viv settled her body against his and planted a kiss on his mouth as her hands roamed.

"Not everything, but most things." He saw the sparkle return to her eye.

J.R. rolled Viv underneath him and moved down her body until his mouth captured a hard pink nipple. Viv arched as her fingers grasped the headboard.

Running his tongue along the underside of her breasts, he felt her shiver. He bit each nipple until she moaned and then moved lower. There was no question in his mind how he wanted to end their morning together.

His tongue ran over her bare mound and dipped between her legs. "Open up." He lifted one knee and then the other until she was fully exposed. Wet already, J.R. could see her clit, hard for him.

A hand on each thigh, he tongued her center until her hips lifted. Not willing to let this go too fast, he licked every fold of her pussy—teasing with his tongue and going back to her core for more juice.

"You're playing." She groaned.

"You like it." He tugged her outer lips with his teeth.

"My clit," she insisted.

"What about it?" he asked against her pussy.

"Lick it, bite it, something." She arched but he moved before she got additional friction. "Please."

J.R. licked his lips. "Since you asked so nicely." He tongued her clit, teasingly at first but increased the pressure until she gasped one second and moaned the next. Her body tensed and he felt her thighs trying to close in on him. Slowly he let his teeth tease her sensitive clit and she came against his mouth.

Cream gushed and her hips jerked. "Yes, J.R."

J.R. kept licking her pussy until she came back down from her release and pulled his face up to hers. Kissing him, she let her tongue tangle deep with his. She pressed a kiss to his shoulder. "That was unbelievable."

"I'd have to agree." J.R. knelt up on the bed.

Viv gave him a naughty smile.

"What?" he asked.

Her hand reached out to his full erection. "We did have fun. I should go but I can't leave you like this."

"We'll just keep working each other up." He could do her all day and night but neither could ignore their work responsibilities for too long.

"One more little thing. It'll be quick, I promise." Viv stayed flat on her back and tugged J.R. by the cock to come closer.

He watched her dip three fingers between her legs and rubbed the wetness on his cock. A few fingers full and she worked his cock in her hand steadily. The pressure was perfect and J.R. knew it wouldn't be long—especially when she licked the head. But his eyes drifted past his cock to her beautiful breasts. The thought of fucking her breasts pushed him closer.

"You want to fuck my breasts." She pulled his erection between her mounds and pressed them together.

J.R. nodded. The feel of the soft but firm flesh was irresistible. He thrust slowly, watching her breasts surround him and then her mouth suck the tip of his shaft. The teasing of her mouth and warmth of her skin broke his restraint and he pulled back. Thrusting once more, he came on her breasts.

Viv licked his cum off one breast and leaned up, kissing him. "I'm not boring in the bedroom. Don't be shy." She turned his wrist and looked at his watch. "Damn. It'll have to wait until next time. You have a conference call in an hour."

J.R. checked the time but Viv was out of bed and pulling on her clothes. "Stay. Have lunch," J.R. offered.

"Lunch lunch or sex lunch?" she asked.

"You can order anything from room service. Just lunch." J.R. reluctantly looked for his pants.

"I definitely need food." Viv pulled out the menu.

* * * * *

J.R.'s brain couldn't get away from his morning activities. Viv had finally left after a room service lunch. Dawn had not yet returned but Viv's friends at the front desk were on the lookout. While she'd arranged that, he'd left a message for Bruce to come to his room for the conference call.

During lunch, the conversation had veered off to safer topics like their love of the desert. He was surprised to find that she liked to hop in her blue convertible and drive for hours just to be alone with nature. J.R. thought he was the only one who liked the feel of being alone in the world. He'd built his house in the middle of the desert and enjoyed it. Not another person for miles.

He'd resisted offering to show his home to her. Much as he wanted to share it with someone who could appreciate it, J.R. knew Viv would take that as too serious a move for them. Clearly Viv wouldn't be comfortable getting more personal or detailed. At least not yet.

He wasn't sure what it was. What happened to her? J.R. didn't know but he suspected there was something in her life she was holding back. J.R. didn't normally share the details of his accident but with Viv he wanted to. This woman was different and made him feel completely at ease. The little disagreement they'd avoided about Dawn nagged at him. Viv was worried Dawn wouldn't meet about the wedding plans. The novelty of Vegas would wear off for Dawn. It was just jitters, J.R. was sure of it.

A knock on the door made J.R. remember he had business to do. Opening the door, J.R. was glad to see Bruce. "Win anything?" he asked.

Bruce laughed. "Not me, I don't have the touch. I thought you had that conference call first thing this morning."

"I moved it. Something came up this morning." J.R. wasn't one to talk about details of his personal life but he knew Bruce wasn't stupid.

"Viv disappeared this morning too." Bruce took a seat at the desk and shook his head. "And you're grinning like an idiot. Any connection between those events?"

J.R. realized Bruce was on to him. "We've had trouble coinciding our schedules. When Dawn had other plans and Viv was free I decided to take advantage of the opportunity."

"You moved the conference call to be with Viv?" Bruce sounded surprised.

"Is there a problem?" J.R. asked.

"Problem? No, I didn't mean anything. Viv's great. She took Dawn's scatterbrained attitude and didn't miss a beat. I'm a little surprised that you moved business plans for her. She's not exactly the wife and mother type. You always said you wanted a family."

"I'm interested in her. Have the girls said anything about her?" Viv wasn't the type J.R. expected to want but he didn't like others finding fault with her. He liked Viv precisely because she was different.

"I think you've graduated beyond interested there, J.R. To answer the question, no. They haven't said a thing against Viv. Ginger is pretty jealous but Dawn thinks that's funny. Finally, a man Ginger can't sink her teeth into first. Viv can out-sexy and out-flirt Ginger in her sleep. She's on the short side but she's got the looks and confidence. I don't see why you wouldn't go after Viv."

"I intend to."

"So I guess we're going to see a lot of Viv even after the wedding?"

"I don't know, Bruce." J.R. was very interested in keeping Viv around. It was too early to make any definite statements but J.R. knew two weeks would not be enough. But would Viv cooperate?

"You moved a meeting to be with her but you're not sure she'll stick around. Don't tell me she's married or has a boyfriend or something." Bruce frowned.

"No, Viv is free and single. She'd never do something like that."

"Did you piss her off already?"

"No, she's pretty happy with me right now." J.R. was normally good at analyzing a situation and coming up with alternatives but this was not a new business venture or a family crisis. Viv was a completely different kind of puzzle and there wasn't enough information yet. He needed more time with her. "I'm just not sure about what Viv wants. It's still new."

"Good. If you want my opinion, I think she's good for you."

"Why?" J.R. was intrigued.

"You've always been very focused on your work. Trying to prove something. That's great and all. You just need something more in your life than work. Any woman who can get you to move a business meeting is one you should hold on to."

J.R. rolled Bruce's logic around in his mind. Solid reasoning and good observation. "You'd make a good salesman, Bruce." J.R. playfully punched Bruce's shoulder.

However, Viv's insistent comments about Dawn still nagged at him. "Did Dawn say anything when she left this morning?"

"Just that they were going to the high-end stores. Told me not to go near any wedding plans without her. Viv didn't look too happy about that."

"She wasn't. She seems to think Dawn is avoiding the plans." J.R. was sure that Dawn's reluctance was a mixture of wedding nerves and youthful distractions in a new environment.

Bruce waved it off. "I'll bet it's all the distractions."

"That's what I thought." J.R. felt reassured. "Vegas has so much to do and see that Dawn has never experienced. She's never been here before and she's newly legal to gamble and drink. I want her to take advantage of that fun."

"Absolutely, I'm having a great time. Give Dawn a chance to get it out of her system. I don't know if Dawn's back yet but Viv'll pin her down and I'm sure they'll work it out."

The phone rang and J.R. hit the speaker button for the conference call. Viv could be out of his life shortly. Before he knew it, Dawn would be married and Viv would be gone. The clock was ticking but J.R. was excellent with deadlines.

Chapter Seven

Sitting in her office and staring out the window, Viv had to admit J.R. was on her mind. She'd thought she could get him out of her system but two rounds of the best sex she'd ever had wasn't enough. Luckily their time wasn't up yet. They would have more, a lot more if she could swing it.

Of course, she had to go and bring up how his parents died. How stupid could she be? At least he wasn't bothered by it or it didn't appear that he was. J.R. was so laid-back it made Viv want to let her guard down. She had to be more careful or she'd get in over her head.

"Viv," her assistant said from the doorway.

"What is it?" She turned her chair. "Did Dawn finally get back yet?"

"No, not yet." Morgan entered the office and closed the door. "Are you okay?"

"Fine. The bride is hiding from me, the groom doesn't care and everyone in the family thinks it'll all work out like magic. How can this be the worst wedding I've ever done? I need it to be the best."

"I know this bride isn't exactly the down-to-business type but I don't think that's it."

"Then what could it be?" Viv tried not to sound too defensive. The wedding was frustrating her. J.R. took her mind off it.

"I think you're worrying because the promotion is riding on this wedding. You've handled brides like her before. You'll pull it off. You always do." Morgan was more confident than

Viv felt. Morgan sat in the guest chair in Viv's office, clearly wanting more information.

"I hope you're right." Viv meant it. She needed it to all come together with fabulous results. She'd worked very hard to get here and that promotion meant everything to her. Morgan did have an excellent point. Her promotion meant a lot to her, consequently Viv wanted Dawn to be a dream client so Viv could really shine.

"You were all smiles when you came in this afternoon and now you're down about the wedding. What made you so happy?" Morgan asked.

"That's personal." Viv remembered that morning. J.R. was excellent stress relief.

"Since when did we become so professional?" Morgan demanded. "What are friends for if I don't get to hear the good stuff?"

"I spent the morning with J.R.," Viv confessed. "In his suite."

"I knew it." Morgan was on the edge of her seat. "Was it as good as you thought?"

Viv blushed deeply and couldn't control her smile. "It was amazing. Better than I imagined."

"Glad to hear it. Everyone here just adores J.R. and they go on and on about how nice he is and handsome. He doesn't treat people like staff. If you didn't grab him the cocktail waitresses were prepared to shoot dice for him."

"The handsome thing is a given but he looks even better without his clothes." Viv leaned back in her chair with a grin that almost hurt.

"I knew it. What a way to spend the morning. The best part is he lives in Vegas."

Viv's smile went flat at the remark. "Why is that the best part?" His skill in bed was the best part. J.R. was the best sex she'd ever had.

"Come on, Viv. You always get in these situations with men who don't live here. Businessmen, tourists and professional athletes. Eventually they have to go, which is the reason it never lasts."

"Hence their appeal. No breakups or expectations beyond their stay here. I can completely be myself and it doesn't matter. J.R. doesn't seem to mind my rules or quirks. I knew J.R. lived in Nevada but I just couldn't resist him," Viv admitted.

"Exactly and even after he isn't at the hotel anymore you two can still see each other. Maybe you have finally found a man you can't get rid of so easily."

"Don't ruin this for me, Morgan." Viv tapped her nails on her desk in frustration. "I don't need that. I need to focus on the wedding. And believe me, when it ends so will my fun with J.R."

"What would be so terrible about finding a great guy who likes you exactly as you are?" Morgan asked.

"Nothing. I wouldn't mind that at all." Viv would like to find a man who could accept that she just wanted fun without the marital responsibilities or hassles. J.R. wouldn't settle for that. "I don't think he exists."

"Maybe I'm not completely convinced that you've explored your options. You know your way is safe but the other way isn't bad."

"I've never fallen asleep under the hot Vegas sun and burned to a crisp but I know I wouldn't enjoy that either."

"You're impossible."

"You never give up," Viv shot back.

"I hope someday some man proves you wrong. Someday you'll fall so madly in love that you get married, have twins and eat your words."

"And give my mother a stroke?" Viv asked. "Never." Her mother would wear black and object to any wedding that involved her daughter. "I really don't think J.R. Haddery is going to change any of this. He's nice but you should just be happy I have a great sex life right now. I've already stuck my foot in my mouth with him."

"Fine. I'm happy for you. How did you stick your foot in your mouth? Or did you mean his mouth and your foot?" She teased.

Viv wanted to sink into a hole rather than admit it. "I asked about a scar on his leg and it was from the car accident that killed his parents."

She shrugged. "You didn't know."

"I knew his parents were dead."

"Confiding in you already. How sweet. Viv, you didn't know the scar was connected. I'm sure he didn't take offense."

"You're probably right." Viv hoped she was.

"If it's just sex then why would you care?" Morgan pointed out.

Viv gave her friend a look that asked her not to push the issue.

Morgan took the hint. "Okay. I'll go check to see if Dawn is in the hotel yet. You've had your fun for the day so you should do some work."

"Thanks." Viv knew Morgan was just trying to help but Viv really wanted to enjoy the simple pleasure of good sex and no expectations. If only the bride would cooperate with her goals for the wedding. Realistically she needed to get started or she'd be in trouble before she knew it. Promotion or not, some things had to be planned in sufficient time or the bride might not be able to have everything. Viv's mission was clear. Get the wedding plans jumpstarted tonight.

* * * * *

Viv entered the Windsor Room on the top floor of the Victoria Royale. As she spotted J.R., Viv noticed that Dawn and Ginger had returned. Dawn refused to make eye contact but Viv wasn't going to let that stop her. Viv had a few tricks left up her sleeve to persuade a difficult bride. "Sorry I missed you this morning, Dawn. Did you have a nice day of shopping?"

"Um, yeah. I got a ton of clothes. Vegas has the best shopping. Tiffany and Ferragamo." Dawn seemed relieved that she didn't appear to be in real trouble.

"Obviously some wires got crossed. But I'm free this evening. We can get a lot done in just a couple of hours."

"I really hoped to go to the club tonight." Dawn pushed her luck and Viv forced herself not to react.

"You have to face wedding plans eventually," Bruce pointed out.

"Fine, ruin all my fun." Dawn glared at him.

"I'm sure the wedding plans could wait until the morning." J.R. the peacemaker chimed in.

Viv shot him a look but held her tongue and counted to ten. "I think that Dawn and Ginger could use a quiet evening after such a long day. Plus if you want to book our top entertainment for the bachelorette party we'll have to act tonight. Preview the male strippers." Her ace in the hole always worked and she hoped it would work with the girls.

Viv saw Ginger's eyes perk up. Naked men were a great incentive.

"Oh, we are so planning this wedding tonight!" Ginger confirmed.

"If we get done by ten o'clock we can catch a preview of them. There is a private room for parties in the club and we'll be able to watch a sample just for you. It's all arranged." Viv noticed the bride was no longer objecting so loudly and actually had a smile on her face.

"I suppose if I want the best I should book early. We can eat first, right?" Dawn asked.

"Of course, you don't want to see the Fantastic Five on an empty stomach. I've had women faint." Viv played her trump card expertly and it worked.

Viv smiled at J.R. in triumph and he shook his head with a slight grin. He should be impressed. She knew how to get the reluctant bride into action. The temptation of a free tease preview was too much to resist.

"Faint? Really, women have fainted?" Ginger was clearly ready for the show now.

"Oh yes. They are the best male forms in Vegas so eat up and don't drink too much. I want you to fully appreciate their talents. You'll only be getting the preview. The real party, we'll have to schedule."

"Isn't that party traditionally the night before?" Ginger asked.

"Yes but some brides and grooms prefer to do it a day or two ahead of tradition. Largely to avoid arriving at the altar hung over from the party. We can discuss all of that later." Viv opened her menu and smiled to herself. It worked. Willing participants, finally.

* * * * *

Viv survived Dawn's terrible choices and the preview of the male strip show. Now the girls were off to have more fun. She emerged in the hallway from backstage and was surprised that J.R. had waited for her.

"Are you lost?" she teased.

"I'm not the one coming out of the men's dressing room," he pointed out.

"True, but I'm an employee. All-access." Viv walked with him toward the elevators.

"Long show." He glanced down at his watch.

"It was only half an hour. Just a sample. You'll get a good show. I promise. So will the girls. You might even be rid of Ginger."

"Really?" J.R. perked up at that thought.

"She was all over one of the dancers and it was the straight, single one." Viv soon realized he'd hit the button for his floor. "Where are we going?"

"I thought you might like a drink."

"I've had enough." Viv didn't need the drink but kept walking with him. Hotel rooms were the only place they'd have any privacy from the casino cameras.

She followed him into his suite. As the door closed, Viv felt his arm around her waist. Seconds later she was pinned against the door being kissed like the world was coming to an end.

Viv couldn't help but respond. It had been a long afternoon and now that she knew how amazing J.R. was and how well they fit together, it was even harder to keep her hands to herself. But as J.R. tried to peel off her jacket, Viv pushed him away. "Not tonight."

"And what part of the morning's activities wasn't to your liking?" He continued to kiss her neck.

She was close to surrender but if she wanted things ready for Dawn first thing in the morning she had to act. "I enjoyed every bit but I have to get these plans going."

J.R.'s hand slid under her suit jacket and cupped her right breast. "They can wait for the morning."

"Dawn's has to try on dresses in the morning. I want them pulled and ready for her so she has no excuses. On my way home I'm going to stop off at the bridal studio." Viv let her fingers sink into his shoulders but didn't really hold him back.

"Can't you call it in?" J.R. removed her jacket and his hands molded over her hips, up her waist to roll her hard nipples through the fabric.

Viv groaned. "Okay, you win. Sit down." She pointed to a high-back chair by the large table.

Pulling out her cell phone, Viv made two quick calls to get things on a roll for tomorrow. He waited patiently for her business to be complete. She put her phone on the table and looked at J.R.

"Come here," he said.

"One second." Viv slipped her underwear down and set them on the table.

"I get a striptease?"

"No." Viv left her clothes on and straddled J.R.'s lap. Carefully she tugged her skirt up enough so she could maneuver but she revealed nothing.

"We're still dressed." J.R. sucked his breath in as Viv fingered his erection through his pants.

"We can access everything we need." Viv freed his growing cock and moved her hips in closer so she could rub him against her wet pussy lips.

His hands went to her waist as she rode him. "Take off your top."

"No. I don't have time for all that." Viv moaned at the feel of his cock on her clit.

"Make time," he insisted.

"Can't tonight. Business before pleasure." She caught his mouth with hers and kissed him. The focus made Viv want him more. When he was naked she wanted all of him. Now she wanted his cock inside her and his mouth kissing her.

J.R.'s hands moved to her hips and pulled her up. He slid on a condom and lined his cock to her body then pulled her down with a groan.

She lifted her hips only a few inches and went back down. She didn't want to lose contact with his mouth or his erection. Her fingers wrapped around the back of the chair for leverage. But when J.R.'s hands went from her hips to her hair, Viv pressed herself flush against him to kiss her harder until her pussy was only grinding him. She knew this sex was as intense as any they'd had. Maybe more because of the clothes. She knew how beautiful he was naked—the warmth of his skin—but now it was denied.

Her orgasm caught her by surprise as she rotated her hips on his cock. Viv pulled her mouth from his as her body shook. He held her as she came silently—watching her eyes.

The pleasure spread through every part of her until she gasped for air and relaxed her muscles. Just as she felt even again, Viv felt J.R.'s hips push into her as he came.

When he leaned his head back, Viv kissed him softly. "That was fun."

J.R. looked him in the eye. "I want you naked."

"Not tonight." Viv eased off him, stifling her groan at the loss. "I have to deal with the wedding stuff."

"What kind of bridal studio is open at eleven o'clock at night?" J.R. looked satisfied but pissed that she'd actually leave.

"In Vegas, anything related to weddings is open late. Even the marriage license bureau keeps Vegas hours. I'm not on vacation. Dawn's wedding has to be my first priority." Viv grabbed her jacket, panties and cell phone. "I'll see you tomorrow."

"Tomorrow night we're having dinner alone in my room," he said firmly.

"I'll try to pencil you into my schedule." Viv reached for the doorknob as he got up.

"This is official wedding business. I want to look over the honeymoon options that you can arrange. You do have some things through the hotel, right?" He'd make it about the wedding to have her and it thrilled her.

"Sure." Viv felt the word catch in her throat. J.R. wanted time—not just sex. "Tomorrow night. Dinner."

J.R. kept his distance. "Okay."

"Bye." She wanted to stay but didn't. She couldn't. The cool air of the hallway helped her get her back in control. The wedding plans were underway and J.R. was a great sexual adventure. She just couldn't get too attached.

Chapter Eight

J.R. watched as Viv and Dawn debated dress after dress. He'd promised Viv he'd supervise this in case Dawn tried to get out of it again. J.R. was content to watch Viv in action. His cousin was currently in a white thing that looked more like a floor-length nightgown than a wedding dress. It was the first dress she'd had on an hour ago and J.R. knew this was going to be a long morning.

He had chosen a seat away from the action but in Viv's path to the counter with supplies. "Is that for the wedding night?" he asked as she approached him.

Viv playfully pinched his shoulder. "No, that's your cousin's choice for a wedding gown. It's better than the layers and layers of material and hoops that would be my worst nightmare, but I had a different vision. Don't worry, we'll set her up with great lingerie for the wedding night but you don't need to see that."

"As long as she's happy with the dress, that's all that matters." J.R. definitely didn't want to see lingerie on Dawn.

"We'll see. She's going to try on the rest. I got Ginger to talk her into that much." Viv reached behind where J.R. sat and he did his best not to jump when he saw a display of garters not a foot behind him.

"Okay." He mindlessly stared at the thin piece of satin and lace.

"What? It's only a garter." She had picked up on the fact that it bugged him.

"Viv, she's like my little sister. I don't need to be reminded she has thighs." J.R. put the image of that around

Dawn's thigh out of his head. He replaced it with a vision of Viv in thigh-high stockings topped with those satin things.

"Then you might not want to line up to catch it when we do the garter toss." Viv patted his shoulder and disappeared into the dressing rooms.

That hadn't even entered his mind. Not that the superstition about being the next to get married bothered him. He wanted to get married and have a family of his own. If the other single men were trying catch a piece of satin, however, he'd have less men to fight off for Viv's attention. They could have every other single woman in the room but Viv was all his and that was not negotiable.

J.R. wondered if Viv had ever caught a bridal bouquet. Knowing Viv, he doubted it. She probably never went out to try at any of her aunt's weddings. That or she ran the other way if it came anywhere near her. He knew of no other woman who had such an aversion to matrimony. So why wasn't that stopping him?

Dawn appeared in another dress cut far too low and fit way too tight for J.R.'s taste. As Viv passed by he grabbed her hand. "No, she isn't going to walk down the aisle like that. My uncle would kill her."

Viv glared at him. "Men. It's her day, not yours. She's going to be a bride, so she can look as sexy or elegant or virginal as she wants on her wedding day. Trust me, that's modest compared to some of the gowns I've seen. This is Vegas not a convent. Just relax."

"I like the nightgown better," J.R. grumbled.

"Just picture me in the sexy ones," Viv whispered.

"I have been." J.R. shifted in the chair to see her better. All night he'd pictured her. It wasn't enough. He had to have her. They both needed it. The chair thing had been kinky but it only fueled the fire—it didn't quench it. "We're still on for dinner?"

"Of course. I have a bunch of brochures for honeymoons the hotel can arrange." Viv was in business mode.

"It's a casual dinner. No business suits," J.R. insisted. They looked great on her but a change would be nice. He wore jeans around his home office most days and he was itching to be casual again.

"Okay. That sounds nice. Don't worry, this won't last all morning."

"Good because I wouldn't go through this for my own wedding." J.R. instantly regretted that statement. Talk of marriage could easily freak Viv out. He didn't want her to end things over something that stupid. As jumpy as she was about the subject, she might think he'd meant their wedding. Did he? J.R. suddenly felt confused. All this wedding stuff and being crazy about Viv had him all mixed up.

Viv gave him a weird look but smiled. "If you were the groom you shouldn't be here when the bride is picking out her dress. It's bad luck to see it. One of those silly superstitions."

"I know, you're right. Make sure my cousin looks gorgeous. But please don't let her look like a hooker." J.R. winked as Viv went back to the pack of women. Marriage. Why was his brain stuck on that idea? He wasn't thinking about Dawn's wedding. Viv had managed to scatter his thoughts again.

J.R. always knew he wanted to get married but Bruce had been right. The women he'd always dated before were more like the women in his family, money-minded and snobby. Viv was nothing like them and she was stuck in his head. None of the women he'd dated before compared to Viv in the sexy and seductive department.

Was it possible she had everything he wanted? Why couldn't he stop thinking about her in that garter? The parade of dresses went on but J.R. paid little attention. Viv was in charge and she was sexy in action. J.R. sat back and watched contently.

* * * * *

J.R. opened the door to his suite and found Viv right on time and casually dressed in perfectly fitting jeans and a slightly snug, blue V-neck T-shirt. Her hair was softly pulled back except for a few tendrils that clung down her neck. She walked in, toting her folder.

"Couldn't wait to see me?" he joked.

"After how I had to leave last night, I figured if I were even a few seconds late you'd hunt me down and drag me up here." Viv smiled as she entered.

"I was the only one with roaming hands last night? I don't think so. You're not innocent." J.R. pulled the chair out for her as Viv sat at the table loaded with food and candles for their private dinner.

"My hands have nothing to feel guilty about. You started it." Viv pointed at him. "You asked me to dance the first day we met and then you kissed me in my office."

"I finished what you started and chickened out on in the limo," he argued. "If the driver hadn't had to hit his brakes when he did you'd have been all over me."

"We couldn't get caught by the driver. I work for the hotel. I have to stay professional if I want to be management." Viv sipped the champagne he'd poured.

"I'm not the groom. I don't see our relationship as a problem." He lifted the cover off the food to reveal two huge filets. "I hope you're hungry."

"How did you know the filet is my favorite?" Viv asked.

"At that dinner you said you were allergic to lobster. I did a little research. Your assistant really does like to talk," J.R. said.

"But I ordered the chicken that night," she cut in.

"I thought I owed you a fancy dinner."

"You don't owe me anything." Slowly she savored the first bite. "But you are very observant. Thank you."

"Glad you approve." J.R. started eating. "So you don't want our evening together to become common knowledge around the hotel?"

"Just because you're not the groom doesn't mean it wouldn't look bad for me to get involved with a client. Especially on this wedding."

"This wedding?" J.R. needed clarification.

"Any wedding of course, but you're my only client. I'm up for this promotion and Lox told me this wedding is pretty much the deciding factor. You are a wealthy and influential Vegas resident. This wedding is high-profile and high budget. If I screw this up my career will go nowhere fast. I've worked too hard to screw it up now."

J.R. was a bit confused. "So sleeping with me could get you in trouble?"

"It doesn't help anything except my stress level," she admitted. "But you're too much of a temptation so why bother to resist?"

His ego now stroked, J.R. knew her interest in him wasn't to improve her career. "Then you'll just have to spend a lot of time here."

"Definitely," Viv agreed. "There are no security cameras in the rooms. Every other inch of the casino and hotel, but not in the rooms."

"The amount of people and money that it takes to make this place run." J.R. shook his head. "I remember when we redid the Grand Ballroom. I had to triple my teams to get it done on time."

"The Grand Ballroom was only redone two years ago. I'm surprised we didn't meet then." Viv took another bite and groaned appreciatively.

J.R. was so glad Viv wasn't the type who never ate. She was bold in everything she did and J.R. loved it. Why hadn't they met years ago? "The construction guys weren't allowed in the offices. And I'm sure you would have distracted me and my men so it's best you steered clear."

"Much as I'd have liked to meet your construction workers, there were restrictions on who could go into those areas for safety purposes. It's not like you would have been down there personally sweating with your shirt off. That might have been worth violating security for."

"If we had visitors like you I might have worked down there." J.R. clinked his champagne flute against hers.

"You're so normal." Viv sounded amazed.

"I'm normal?" J.R. wasn't sure if he should be offended or not by that statement.

"I meant for someone with so much money. You don't act like manual labor or a buffet lunch is beneath you. My former boss used to tell me how a lot of her clients were impossible snobs. You're really refreshing."

"How can I be a snob? My parents weren't that way. You've only met this family. My cousin was spoiled and ran with it." J.R. knew the temptation to let money go to your head but he would never let that happen.

"Your family is very interesting. So where do you think the bride and groom want to go on their honeymoon?" Viv had smoothly transitioned from personal to work.

Apparently the excuse to get her into his room wasn't going to be ignored. J.R. admired her work ethic. He was incredibly turned on by the fact that she'd worn the same sticky pink lip gloss. Tonight wouldn't be a quickie in a hard chair.

"I'm not sure. The rest of the family might stay here in Vegas a little longer. I told Dawn she should pick somewhere far away for a change." J.R. wiped his mouth with a napkin and watched Viv spread out the brochures.

"Have you ever been to Hawaii?" she asked.

"No, but everything I've heard about it indicates that Hawaii is the ideal place for a honeymoon."

"You've done your research." Viv sounded impressed. "It is very popular. Lots of beauty and privacy there. Disney World is also very popular."

"Isn't that for kids?"

"Dawn's only twenty-one. But it is popular with couples of all ages. Lots of people go there. I agree Hawaii is a great choice. Cruises are also popular. Of course some couples spend their honeymoon in Vegas."

"They've already had a nice vacation here so I think Vegas is out. And Dawn is afraid of the water. She refuses to go on a boat."

"So no cruises." Viv rearranged her brochures. "I have travel packages for all of the major cities in the U.S. and abroad."

"Any personal recommendations?" J.R. asked.

"Not really. I've only been to New York, Chicago and Los Angeles for business conferences. Other than that I usually stay around here, visit Mom in Arizona or some friends from college who moved to California. That sounds kind of sad but I do love Vegas. I've always wanted to see Hawaii and Alaska. I love the desert but to see tropical islands and icebergs would be impressive."

"Alaska? Really?" J.R. was surprised, but with Viv nothing should surprise him.

"Why not? It's not like I want to climb an iceberg or ride a moose. I just want to see that raw natural landscape while it's still there. Like driving into the desert and seeing a cactus and nothing else for miles. I imagine that's like standing on the coast of Alaska or the beach in Hawaii and seeing nothing but ocean."

"You are a complete contradiction," he observed.

"Me? Why?" Viv demanded.

"You love nature and work in a city that is all neon and concrete."

"So? Every desert needs an oasis. I love civilization. I'd never want to be marooned in the wilderness without air-conditioning or filtered water. I enjoy nature but couldn't live without the excitement of Las Vegas either. We have the best of both worlds right here." Viv seemed to be daydreaming. His eyes caught hers and Viv snapped her attention back to him. "But it's not my honeymoon. Dawn and Bruce can pick when they're ready."

"Must be a relief to have Dawn's wedding dress chosen." J.R. changed the subject.

"Yes, a big relief. The alterations are underway and the basics of the wedding are all decided. So Dawn should have a few days of quiet before fittings and other details come up." Viv seemed very relaxed.

"Then there will be no running off tonight for wedding plans?" J.R. teased.

"No, all the wheels are in motion. I am free for the evening. What did you have in mind?" Viv leaned forward with her chin resting in the palm of her hand and her elbow on the table.

He'd thought of nothing else all day. Getting up from his chair, J.R. moved to tower over her. "I'll bet you can guess."

Viv leaned back in her chair and then stood slowly. Her hands slid up his arms and down his chest. "You know J.R., you haven't kissed me once this entire evening." Viv pressed her fingernails into his chest to get his attention.

"Your lips are broken? Or are you suddenly so old-fashioned that the man has to make the first move?" he taunted.

After a few seconds, Viv gave him a very wicked smile. "You're absolutely right." Her mouth captured his and J.R. felt something different in her kiss. Pulling off his shirt, she only let a few seconds lapse before her mouth was on his again. Viv undid his button-fly jeans as she walked him backward to the bed like a woman with a plan.

In one swift motion she pushed his jeans and boxers to the floor. Now he was completely naked and she still had her faded blue shirt and dark low-cut jeans on. The sexy, silver-chain belt she had on begged to be removed. Her little silver sandals showed off the matching polish on her toes and the color on her fingernails. How could those details be so sexy? he wondered. His cock was already hard.

J.R. reached for her belt, but Viv's hand caught him. "No," she whispered. "You shouldn't have to make all the moves. And lucky you, tonight you don't have to make any."

"I was only teasing." J.R. tried for her belt again and Viv backed up.

"Now, now, play nice." She pushed on his chest until he sat on the bed. "Just relax."

J.R. decided not to fight this sexy woman as she kicked off her sandals. Then she slowly pulled off her shirt and J.R. was ready to let her do anything she wanted. Her belt came next and rattled lightly to the floor. Seductively she unbuttoned and tugged down her jeans. Even better, J.R. noticed she had no underwear on and she was left in a flimsy lavender bra and her tattoo.

Reaching for her hip, J.R. let his hand skim up to her bra. The material felt like a T-shirt but softer. Viv quickly reached back and removed his hand while unhooking her bra herself. Tossing it on the bed, she dislodged the clip from her hair, setting it free.

"Are you trying to torture me?" He was ready to drag her down to the bed.

"Things had to go fast last night. Tonight is different. I think you're enjoying yourself." Viv rested a knee between his legs and his cock throbbed for attention. Slowly she leaned forward until her body fitted against his. Her mouth slowly nipped at his while her breasts pressed to his chest. The silky feel of her thigh against his cock was enough to make him come now but he fought for control. This woman triggered a lot in him. The sight of her breasts alone made him rock-hard.

Casually she moved them closer to the center of the bed. J.R. knew if he pulled her underneath him he'd ruin whatever plan was underway in her mind. What kind of gentleman would he be if he did that?

Her lips slipped from his mouth, down his throat and J.R. watched as her tongue and teeth worked both of his nipples before kissing a path south. Viv had a clear target in mind and J.R. was not about to change her direction.

Finally her soft pink lips were around the tip of his cock. As far as he was concerned, Viv could make every move from now on without any objection. Her tongue moved to the base and flicked quick strokes up to the head of his cock before her mouth engulfed as much as she could. Slowly she sucked and released, teasing him to the edge. Then she licked and sucked each ball into her mouth like it was candy.

J.R. groaned at the loss of contact. "Don't stop now, Viv."

"Don't get bossy or I'll tie your hands up with my belt." She dropped another kiss on the tip of his now completely hard shaft. The last bit of her lip gloss was now off her mouth and on him.

J.R. held on to his last strands of control at the image of her tying him up and then the reverse. Her at his mercy made him want it even more. Both were good but for now he preferred to be able to touch her. "I'll be good," he promised. "I just can't take much more."

"Me either." Viv's hand stroked him slowly and J.R. stifled a moan.

"But I've barely touched you," J.R. argued. He couldn't believe she was anywhere near ready for him but she was full of surprises.

Viv leaned over him. "You have no idea what you do to me," she whispered in his ear. Slowly she put a little protection on him then straddled his hips and rubbed her wet slit along his erection.

His mind went blank. How could she be this ready? J.R.'s hips rose to increase the pressure and Viv moaned. Her pussy tightened around him, telling J.R. she was more than ready.

"See what I mean?"

Kneeling up, she eased down and J.R. fought for control. As she began to ride him, he met her at every stroke. His mouth finally got access to her hard pink nipples, sucking and biting at them as she arched in encouragement. Holding her hips, he tried to swallow her firm breast. It was an impossible but pleasurable goal.

The noises coming from Viv's throat were no longer soft but deep and demanding. Clearly she had no objection to his actions now but he wasn't about to change positions. As she pushed down, she ground into him, adding friction and pushing them both closer.

J.R. braced Viv with one arm across her back while the other hand cupped the back of her head and kissed her hard. Her muffled climax triggered his and J.R. pulled her down with him, as her body turned to jelly in his hands.

"See, I can make the first move," Viv mumbled against his neck.

"You sure showed me." J.R. inhaled her scent as he toyed with her hair. Viv might've started it but the night was young. As she cuddled against him, J.R. knew they'd both be asleep before long. He kissed her forehead and looked into her satisfied blue eyes. Neither of them would forget this night.

Chapter Nine

Viv dozed in J.R.'s arms as they recovered. His warm hand ran up and down her back possessively. She felt more content than she ever had. J.R. rolled her gently and Viv looked up at him—the glint in his eye told her he was up to something.

"My turn." He kissed her.

"What?"

"You had your way. Now it's mine." He straddled her hips, his thumb sliding between her closed legs—teasing her pussy.

Viv moaned. "You can tell me. I'm not a prude. You know I'll do whatever you want." She pulled a pillow under her head and folded her arms above.

"Good." He licked his thumb and slid his half hard cock between her thighs, rubbing her pussy.

Viv started to open for him.

"No. Keep them closed." J.R. sank into the tight space.

Viv felt teasing friction that made her wetter. "You're not planning on missionary, are you?"

J.R. lifted an eyebrow and released her. "Roll over."

Her eyes widened as Viv's body kicked into high arousal. Slowly she turned over and rested on her stomach. J.R. could do anything he wanted—she wanted to see all of his desires and passions free. After he'd fucked her breasts, Viv knew he had variety in him. He was a great match for her in bed.

Fingers tangled in her hair and Viv knew he'd take his time. His hands roamed over her back and ass and legs. The warmth of his mouth teased her tattoo and then his sharp teeth nipped it.

She looked over her shoulder. "There's a tattoo place in the hotel if you want one."

"Thanks, I'll just enjoy yours." J.R. ran his fingers between her cheeks.

Viv tensed and grew wetter as his fingers dipped. The heat grew as he leaned on top of her.

"You want something different?"

Her body tingled with a rush of need. "I want you to do whatever you want. And I know you're creative."

J.R. kissed the back of her neck. "Get on your hands and knees," he ordered as he reached for a condom.

For an instant, Viv's body went weak with desire. She wanted it and eased back on her knees and then propped herself up on her hands. She was vulnerable and on display but it was J.R. She'd never trusted anyone more. The thought scared her but she focused on her desire. "Are you going to wait until I beg?"

His hands molded her breasts as he moved in behind her. The feel of his hard cock against her pussy made her push back but his hands braced her hips.

"When I'm good and ready."

Viv moaned. He could play his power trip all he wanted.

J.R.'s slowly eased his cock into her pussy. Her body tightened, pulling him in and wanting more.

"Please." She lifted her hips.

But J.R. didn't change his pace. When he finally filled her, Viv took a slow breath and rested her forehead on her arms. Without warning, J.R. pulled back and thrust into her.

Viv groaned and grabbed a pillow as he fucked her hard. With the same steady strokes, he let his desire set the pace and Viv relaxed, opening herself to his need.

The knowledge that his control was gone made Viv wetter and she pushed back, angling for him to hit the right spot.

His pace quickened and Viv tensed up to let him pound her G-spot—throwing her into a powerful orgasm. Viv shuddered, fucked back to meet him and screamed his name into the pillow as her pussy contracted, sending pleasure throughout her entire body.

She counted five more thrusts into her cream-soaked channel before J.R. shouted and exploded into her. Her body tightened around him and she groaned at the reflex to keep him inside her.

J.R.'s body sagged against her. "Better than missionary?" He wrapped an arm around her.

"Definitely." She kissed his arm. "But you didn't even try to fuck my ass. Don't be so uptight."

He eased them onto their sides and Viv relaxed her muscles as he spooned her. He quickly discarded the condom and pulled her more tightly to him.

"I've got to keep you wanting more. If I give you everything you'll be bored in no time."

"With you I always want more." Viv turned her shoulders enough to kiss him. The only thing she truly didn't like about doggie-style was that she couldn't kiss J.R. during. She was lost in the feeling of him.

When she woke, Viv looked over J.R.'s chest to the bedside clock. Midnight already. Viv stretched and did her best not to wake the perfect specimen of man underneath her. He was like a solid wall of muscle and Viv loved the feel, especially when he didn't know she was admiring him. Her head rested on his chest and the silence was soothing. The feel of his heartbeat against her ear was the only distraction and Viv was growing attached to the sensation.

A big part of her wished she could stay right here all night. But there was no way she could start her day at the office in the same clothes she'd worn tonight. Jeans and a snug T-shirt were not appropriate for her day job. On the plus side, she had a few hours before the hotel would be at its biggest lull. That was her best chance of leaving unnoticed. Until then there was nothing better to do than enjoy the feel of J.R.'s naked body. Her free hand molded over his chest and arms as she tried to memorize his body. Dawn's wedding would come too soon and J.R. would leave the hotel. Viv didn't let herself dwell on that thought. The time was going too fast.

"You can take a picture," he mumbled.

Viv put away the thoughts of him leaving and decided to enjoy whatever this was while it lasted. She smiled up at him and pinched the firm muscle on his rib cage. "I've considered it," she admitted. "But touching is so much better than just looking. I didn't mean to wake you."

"You like me unconscious for you to play with?" He pulled her close and kissed her.

Viv felt the jolt of his now-so-familiar kiss. How could she get enough? "Why not? You let me do whatever I want when you're asleep."

"I let you do whatever you want any time." J.R. twisted a piece of her corkscrew hair around his index finger and let it spring free.

"Smart man, but there are less interruptions when you're asleep." Viv watched him continue to play with her hair completely amused. "My hair is curly. Is that really so fascinating?"

"No, I was wondering something."

"Wondering what?"

"Do you get this blonde curly hair from your mother?" he asked matter-of-factly. "In the picture you have in your office her hair is all pulled back under some big hat."

Viv frowned. That was a weird question but J.R. had remembered the details of her mother's picture. It was sweet. "My mother is blonde too but her hair is board straight."

J.R. nodded. "Just curious. You must get the curls from your father."

Viv tried not to tense up. She knew J.R. hadn't meant anything by it. The topic of her father wasn't a comfortable one but he didn't need all the details. "I guess. I never knew him." Viv didn't like the direction of this conversation. It was an innocent question from J.R. but he had a habit of getting nosy.

Admitting that she didn't know anything about her own father only highlighted all of the fears and uncertainty she'd faced in childhood. She had no answer to give about her father. The truth was she had no idea what her father looked like. Much as she'd searched her house as a child for a clue as to her father's identity, no pictures or letters had ever turned up. She felt like she was holding back from J.R. but she wasn't. She didn't have anything to share.

J.R.'s hand moved up her neck to her cheek. "I'm sorry. I didn't mean to bring your father up. I just really get turned on by your hair."

"I know. I'm not used to talking about him. It's pure speculation for me. You know whom you look like. Probably have family pictures and everything." Viv let her fingers trace a pattern in his chest hair.

"Yes, I have family pictures. Everyone should. Didn't you ever ask your mother about him?" J.R. asked.

Viv stared at his chest instead of his face. "Naturally I asked, when I was little. It's not important."

"The hell it's not important. What did she say?" J.R. pulled her close.

Viv slipped out of his grasp and turned to face away from him. He turned on his side and Viv pressed his chest to her back. He gathered her close again. She wanted his warmth and strength to somehow transfer to her. Finally she took a deep breath. "It upset my mother. I could see the pain in her eyes. She wouldn't say a word for ten minutes. Then I would get a lecture about not being dependent on men or wrapping my hopes and happiness up in them."

"She never told you anything?" J.R. asked.

Viv shook her head. "After a while I realized that whatever my father had done to her was worse than never having seen me. I assume she felt it necessary to protect me from him. Eventually I had to accept it. I couldn't torture my mother every day over this."

"And no one else knew anything. Your grandmother? Your aunt?" He sounded amazed.

Viv had to admit that to anyone with a normal family hers would seem weird. "My grandma died when I was only six. Skin cancer. That's why I'm the pale one around here. When I was a little older I asked my aunt who he was but she got angry. She said I should never bring it up to my mother or her again. My guess is he landed in prison somewhere."

"I don't believe it." J.R. pushed her mass of hair out of the way and kissed her neck. "No one who is a part of you could be bad. You're too sweet."

"Sweet?" She sat up laughing and turned to face him. "You had too much champagne. No one has ever called me sweet in my life."

Smiling, J.R. tugged Viv to him for another kiss. "You are sweet and kind and caring. Deny it all you want but you are and I like it."

"I am not sweet." That went against everything she tried to be. "I'm a career-minded, independent and sexually adventurous woman."

"An independent woman who is too sweet to upset her mother by insisting on some very basic life information. You can't deny that. Viv, you have the right to know. There are medical records to be considered. Who knows what's on your father's side."

Viv reached for the blanket that had landed on the floor. "I am perfectly healthy. That's not a good enough reason."

"I could help you find him," J.R. offered. "I've got a friend who's a PI here in Vegas."

"No." That was too far. Letting him know she'd tried—sharing a little was one thing but she wasn't about to unearth those issues. Not again. "I appreciate the offer but that is out of the question. Any investigation would mean my mother having to answer questions that upset her. I won't do that to her. My mother and I are very close. If she couldn't tell me, she won't tell a stranger."

"Hasn't it ever occurred to you that she won't tell you because she's afraid you'll be angry with her? It's probably easier for her to just forget about it. Telling a stranger might be easier."

It made it easier for Viv to forget too. She wanted to know but not if it was something terrible. "So I should punish her now? Make her feel terrible even when she gave me a great life? How can I second-guess her when I have no info? What would have been better, give me up for adoption because she didn't have a husband? That way I could grow up normal, right? Have you seen the number of children in the foster care system? I had a great childhood any way you look at it."

"I'm didn't suggest you didn't. We were both lucky we didn't end up in the system. That doesn't mean you don't have a right to know his name. Is there any way to track him? Is Montrose his name?" J.R. wasn't letting this go.

Why was he so interested? What did it matter? Viv never had a man after her like this. Now he was after her family's dirty laundry.

"No, Montrose is my mother's name. She never married. My father's name isn't listed on my birth certificate either so don't bother looking there. I looked into all of this in college so there is no need to waste money on a private investigator. There are no records to look into. It's no use. My mom and my aunt covered him up very well." Viv was getting annoyed with J.R.'s insistence. If it were that easy she'd have found her father when she'd tried.

"You want to know." He had her there.

"Not enough to hurt the people who did love me and were there to take care of me." Viv reached for her clothes. Screw the time, she needed to go home. J.R. had gone too far and Viv didn't want to continue this conversation for two hours until the hotel was deserted.

"Are you sure he didn't die before you were born and your mother is just sparing you the pain?" Viv knew J.R. wasn't trying to hurt her but he wasn't helping either.

"That possibility crossed my mind. It'd be easier if he was dead and there were no doubts. But if he were dead and not a terrible person I have to believe my mother would've told me once I was old enough to understand death. My grandma died and I was at the funeral and I understood that she wasn't coming back. Any time after that would've been fine to tell me if my father was dead. She never did. As I got older there was this sense... It's stupid."

"What?" he pressed.

Viv was embarrassed that she'd admitted such things. "I don't think he's dead. I don't have any proof or way to check. Just a gut feeling. He's out there." Viv slipped into her jeans and T-shirt and then tried to rub the tension out of her neck.

J.R.'s hand rested on her shoulder and Viv didn't move. "I understand those instincts. The night of the car crash my uncle broke every traffic law on the books to get to me while my parents were in surgery. He sat with me while I got every stitch and they put the cast on my arm."

"He must be very good man." Viv wrapped her fingers around his.

"He tried to convince me my parents would make it and promised he'd look after me until they got out of the hospital. The doctor took him in another room where I couldn't hear to tell him my parents were dead but I knew. It was that same feeling."

"At least you understand. It's better not to dredge up the past. Just because your parents died, you didn't reject your aunt and uncle who did take care of you. I can't hurt my mother. My father wouldn't or couldn't be around but that's not her fault. I should go." Viv leaned down and kissed him softly.

This kiss was different and Viv knew he was under her skin. He'd also crossed that line of comfort. She wasn't about to admit her feelings but she had talked about her most private issues. For her that was more than any other man had gotten from her. "I have to go," she insisted. "It's getting late."

He held her arm. "I don't understand you, Viv. If I could have my parents back for a moment I'd do anything. You're willing to give up your father to avoid a fight with your mother and your aunt. They'd get over it. Don't you think they love you enough to understand?"

He didn't understand!

"My mother and my aunt are all I have. I won't hurt them for something that may make all of our lives worse. What if my father hurt my mother? Beat her? What if she was afraid for her life? What if he raped my mother? Is that what I am? How could I live with that? You have no idea the things that have gone through my head over the last thirty years. Good and bad. It's not worth it." She refused to let any tears start, no matter how much it hurt.

"How do you know it's not worth it?" he pushed. "You can't judge it unless you know."

"You know your parents were great people because you knew them. You have actual memories of them. I have no idea what I'd find in my family tree. Just because you lost your parents, don't try to fix mine into some picture-perfect family." Viv, now fully clothed, grabbed her purse and slammed the door to his suite behind her before he could respond.

Viv tried desperately not to look crazed as she headed for the elevators on J.R.'s floor. He'd had enough sense not to follow her into the hallway. She needed to go home, to remember what her life was supposed to be before J.R. Haddery waltzed in and swept her off her feet, into his bed, and out of her mind.

Turning the corner, she saw Mr. Lox in an elevator as the doors were closing. Viv stepped back before Lox looked in her direction. On the outside she kept an even smile and gave no reaction. On the inside, she cursed herself as a ripple of fear ran through her body. How could she take these insane risks with all that she'd worked for? If Lox had come down the hall just as she'd been exiting J.R.'s room, complete with dramatic door slam, she'd have been caught red-handed or at least blushing with guilt. It was midnight. There was no explanation for being here dressed like this. And no way to hide it.

Hours later Viv paced her condo, completely rattled at how close she'd come to being caught. This couldn't go on. Not for another minute. J.R. was great but he wanted too much, expected too much and could cost her far more than she was willing to risk.

She didn't want to give him up. He was the best lover she'd ever had but there was more to life than sex, right? There was her job and her family. J.R. might understand her better than most men but most men were idiots so what was so special about that? He wanted too much of her.

So why did she miss him already? Viv thought her condo would be a sanctuary for her to set her mind right but it hadn't worked. The wedding of her career would be a tacky affair with the choices Dawn made. Was Viv thinking of a tactful way of getting the bride to change her mind? No. Viv couldn't get her mind off J.R. no matter what she tried. What was wrong with her?

Why had she discussed her father? Viv had never told any man what she told J.R. tonight. While she felt exposed, J.R. had been that protective and reassuring man Viv thought only existed in movies. J.R. was wonderful but he wanted more than sex. Viv felt her self-control slipping. She had to stop this now.

Viv needed a shot of sense to overrule the emotional upheaval she felt. A few great days with a guy and she's sharing all her fears and secrets. She knew better than this. Her mother had taught her not to get all wrapped up in one guy. Taking a deep breath, Viv felt instantly better. The answer was right there and she'd completely ignored it. Mom would hear her out.

Dialing the phone, Viv crossed her fingers that her mother hadn't taken one of her sleeping pills. After one of those her mother could sleep through a Vegas floor show performed on her bed.

"Hello?" Mom answered, half asleep.

"Hi, Mom." Viv tried to sound only mildly frantic as she raked her fingers through her hair.

"What's wrong? It's two in the morning."

"I'm sorry about the hour." Viv paused to collect her thoughts.

"Honey, what's wrong?" Her mother sounded wide-awake now.

The fact that her mother put Viv's problem before sleep reaffirmed Viv's faith in herself and her plan. She could count on her family and her job. Men would always come and go. "It's just a man."

"What man? You don't worry about men."

"J.R.'s different," Viv admitted.

"J.R.? Who is he? Why is he different? You don't let men bother you." Mom sounded surprised.

Viv had no ready answer. He was entirely different from other men but she'd set it up like all of the others. "J.R.'s from Vegas. There's potential for more. I think he wants more." Viv knew it was an understatement but her mother's reaction could be dramatic.

"More what?" Mom asked.

"He hasn't said anything specifically." Viv tried not to let that worry her. She wanted it to be over. Right?

"What do you want?" Mom asked.

"You sound like a shrink," Viv laughed nervously. "It doesn't really matter what I want. He's affecting my job. That's the real problem. I can't focus."

"You have worked too hard to let anyone interfere with your career. It's just as important as his. You need to put your foot down and stop that." Mom was never shy with advice.

"It wasn't intentional on his part. I think I'm letting myself get too involved." Viv couldn't blame J.R. for what happened with Lox. He certainly hadn't helped but it was only indirectly his fault.

"You have to do what *you* think is right when it comes to men. But keep your head, don't let a man take over your life." That wasn't exactly the advice Viv expected. It was watered down and gentle for her mother but it was the middle of the night. Her mother would normally have advised her to dump him.

"You're right. I can't let this interfere." Viv took a deep breath and knew she had to tell J.R. they couldn't keep sleeping together. Hopefully that would end things naturally. "I'll deal with him first thing tomorrow."

"Good for you. If he's not some caveman he should understand that you have to take care of yourself and your career. Now get some sleep. You'll end up with dark circles in the morning."

"Thanks. Good night, Mom."

"Good night, honey."

Viv applied a thin layer of cream under her eyes. Giving up J.R. wouldn't be easy but whether she did it tomorrow, next week or next month it would still be hard.

She simply couldn't let J.R. ruin her chances at that promotion. Rumors could get around the hotel in minutes. Morgan was safe but if solid proof of a sexual relationship between her and a client got to Lox, Viv could kiss her promotion good-bye. He'd never promote her if she seduced the client on her first big assignment.

Finally Viv felt like she had a hold on what to do. Entering her bedroom, she shrugged off her clothing. She left the pile rumpled on her floor and slipped into a long cotton T-shirt with the hotel's logo across the chest. Viv crawled into bed and pulled the covers up over her head. Part of her wished she had one of her mother's sleeping pills because Viv knew she'd never get any rest tonight.

* * * * *

The next morning Viv entered her office with the dark circles her mother had predicted. Too bad she couldn't wear her sunglasses all day. A vase full of at least two dozen long-stem silver roses sat on her desk. There was no doubt in her mind who those were from. Viv opened the card and read it. "Viv, I don't give up that easy. J.R."

At least he knew better than to get sappy with her. She dropped the card on her desk, Viv flopped into her chair, relieved she had no appointments that morning.

"Mr. Haddery called twice already," Morgan called from her desk.

Viv was in no way shocked at that news. "I'm in a meeting." She busied herself with opening the blinds.

"Please." Morgan was now at Viv's office door. "He sent you those roses and you're in a meeting? Don't tell me the party is over already."

As Viv turned from opening her window shades to tell Morgan it was none of her business, Viv saw J.R. standing behind her assistant with a grin. He lounged against the doorframe as though he didn't have a care in the world "You can go, Morgan, thanks."

"Sorry," Morgan mouthed as she left and closed the door with J.R. inside the office.

"She's nosy." Viv shrugged.

"I knew the roses would get a reaction but I wasn't trying to impress Morgan," J.R. said.

"You think you're the first man to send either of us roses?" Viv glanced up at him confidently. All night she'd been a mess but faced with the man who'd nearly destroyed her career and gave her a pop quiz about her paternity, it was easier to be difficult. Flowers were a nice gesture but it'd take more than that to change her reality.

"I'm sure I'm not the first man to give you roses. You don't like them?"

"They're lovely." Roses were overdone in her opinion.

"What kind of flowers do you like?" he asked.

Viv shuffled papers on her desk. "That doesn't matter anymore."

"Don't do that. Don't shut me out because I asked about your father. I didn't judge you. An orphan judging a kid from a single-parent home? I'm jealous."

She could tell he was trying to lighten the mood and get her to smile. It wouldn't work. "This isn't about my father. Though you aren't the first man uncomfortable with that idea. You were very persistent last night. I'm a little worried you'll try to get a DNA sample and run it against every man in Nevada over forty-eight."

"Don't give me ideas."

Playtime was over. "Do you know who I almost ran into when I left your room?" Viv's hands braced on her desk.

"Siegfried and Roy?" he joked.

"Lox." Her voice dropped an octave.

"Oh." J.R. rocked back on his heels. "Did he see you?"

"Almost. In that state I'd have been caught for sure. I can't do this anymore."

"You're the one who wanted to leave so fast." J.R. reminded her.

"You're the one who wanted to send a PI to find my father. The party was over and it's really over now. This was for fun, not emotional torture."

"So that's it? We're done?" J.R. didn't sound convinced. "You're ending it because you almost got caught. I didn't make you leave. You can stay all night. Bring clothes. Whatever works."

"You knew I didn't want to talk about my father and you kept right on going. If you hadn't then I wouldn't have left when I did and I wouldn't have almost gotten caught. My father is not a topic I'm comfortable with."

"So we only deal with what's comfortable and easy?" He moved closer.

Viv stood her ground. "You knew I wasn't comfortable talking about it but you kept on talking. I've come to terms with my past and prefer to leave it there."

"So I know you that well already and you're just dumping me? Why can't you just have a fight like a normal person?" he demanded.

Viv had predicted that J.R. wouldn't make this easy. "I don't want to get that personal and I don't want to lose my job because of sex."

"You're going to finish out the wedding mad at me then?" He was getting closer again and Viv knew she had nowhere to escape.

"Your cousin is getting married. We don't have to be in the same room if we don't want to be. That'll make it easier." Viv knew seeing him every day would make it very hard to keep her hands to herself. If they avoided each other it wouldn't be as difficult.

"I don't know." J.R. shook his head. "Lox would notice that too."

Damn. He was right. They'd be even more conspicuous if they were suddenly never seen together.

"Fine, I can stay professional. But what happened last night can't happen again." Viv tugged at the hem of her suit jacket as if she were locking him out.

"Which part?" he teased.

"All of it," she snapped. "I won't take chances like that again. You're great in bed but no amount of fabulous sex is worth my career."

"Okay, you're right. We'll have to just be friends for a while." J.R. stuck his hands in his pockets but the disappointment in his face was clear.

"Friends?" Viv was uncertain of his definition. This was different from anything else she'd had with a man. Friends wasn't a normal concept.

"Sure. We both like Nevada and expensive food eaten in private while we're wearing jeans or nothing. I don't just like your body, Viv. I like you. If I have to settle for friends then I will, for now."

It was that *for now* that had her worried. Viv nodded slowly. To say she didn't enjoy his company would be a lie. Being with J.R. was comfortable and stimulating, mentally as well as physically. No man had ever clicked with her on that level. "You can never have too many friends. We're okay then?" Her question was careful and diplomatic.

"Perfect as ever." J.R. reached out and Viv tensed for a second, wondering if a kiss was in store. Instead he took her hand and shook it like he had that first day they met. Slowly J.R. released her hand and headed for the door. "See you later, Ms. Montrose."

That formal address from him made Viv panic for a second. "J.R.," she said to stop him. Pausing, Viv didn't know what to say as he turned to look at her. She had to say something. The rosebush on her desk gave her the answer. "I like lilies."

J.R. smiled as he let the door close behind him. Viv worried that he knew her too well. It was a good thing they'd backed off to friends. He was the one man who might be able to find a way around the carefully placed barriers to her heart. But as a friend he was harmless.

She hoped.

Chapter Ten

☙

J.R. knew he had seriously screwed up. He entered his suite directly from leaving Viv's office, without seeing a member of his family. There was damage control to be done. Friends. That was the best he could do on the spot. Lox almost catching her was out of his control but he understood Viv's reaction. He'd expected her to insist on more discretion, not a complete boycott of a physical relationship. J.R. knew Viv didn't want it to end any more than he did.

Why did he have to push her last night? He knew pushing her to talk about her father had been asking a lot. Too much, as he'd found out when she'd left in a panic last night. It had started as innocent curiosity, not an attempt to pry. She treated it like a resolved piece of her past. Clearly that topic was still raw emotion. J.R. had mistakenly thought they were ready to have those conversations. Viv might never be ready.

Last night she'd said men in her past had had issues with her nonexistent father. J.R. wanted to meet these men and personally toss them into a pit of angry scorpions. Because of them Viv didn't trust any man to accept her *as is*. Worse, they'd added to her pain. Now J.R. had to prove himself. How could he prove he didn't care what Viv's father or what her mother was?

The knock on the door pulled J.R. from his plan. "Who is it?" he snapped.

"Bruce," came the response from the other side of the door.

J.R. didn't move for a minute, deciding if he wanted to let Bruce in or not. Odds were if he didn't, the whole family would become aware of his hideout and knock down the door in concern. Opening the door, J.R. turned his back on Bruce and began pacing the suite.

"What's wrong?" Bruce looked around.

"You're not interrupting anything." J.R. knew Bruce was looking for Viv.

"I asked what's wrong," Bruce repeated. "You're acting weird."

"Don't ask."

"Too late. I already did. Come on."

"This isn't business-related." J.R. didn't need to discuss this. Bruce had already expressed surprise at J.R.'s choice of Viv. They didn't need to go into details about her family.

"Obviously this has to do with you and Viv." Bruce stretched out on the leather couch. "The doctor is in. What's the problem?"

"I don't need your advice on women."

"Want me to go get Dawn or Ginger?" Bruce offered.

"No."

"Want me to leave?"

"No," J.R. mumbled.

"Want me to keep asking stupid questions until you blow up?"

"No." J.R. knew he was going to confide in Bruce but he needed to work up to it. "Fine, Viv thinks I'm embarrassed by her family."

"As opposed to our family? I hope not. When did you meet them?"

"I haven't." J.R. paced.

"That makes it pretty hard to be embarrassed by them. What makes her think that?"

"Her mother was a showgirl." Maybe he was wrong. Maybe this was all to do with her father and she just hid it very well.

"Viv could be one too." Bruce winked.

"You want to leave the hard way?" J.R. pointed toward the window in a blatant threat.

"Sorry. I forgot you're crazy about her. Normally you're not this touchy about your girlfriends. I guess this is the first time I'm seen you in *love*."

"In what?" J.R. froze. Bruce was right. J.R. was trying to keep the relationship with Viv alive at all costs. If only it were that easy.

"Come on, why would she care what you thought of her family if this wasn't getting serious? Why would you care that she cares about what you think of her family? You're both sick over each other. Do yourself, Viv and me a favor, okay? Marry her. It'll put you both out of your misery," Bruce suggested.

"Marry her?" J.R. felt all of the blood rush out of his head and he sat down before he staggered. It wasn't the first time that thought had crossed his brain but it was the first time it had been verbalized. J.R. knew it felt right but convincing Viv wouldn't be possible now.

"Everything okay?" Bruce asked.

It wasn't Bruce's fault. He didn't understand recent events. No man had ever committed to Viv as family or anything else. That would be a massive step. "She demoted me. We're only friends. I don't think she'll be accepting any proposals right now. First I have to prove to her that I don't care that her mother was a showgirl, that her father was never around."

"Maybe her father was a gangster. I went on this tour yesterday and heard about the history of Vegas. It was practically put on the map by the Mob." Bruce's eyes glazed over at the excitement.

"She's too young to be the daughter of a gangster like you mean."

"She knows nothing at all about him?" Bruce asked.

"Not a thing. When I offered to try to help her find him she got all bent out of shape."

"Why? You're good at helping."

"I get the feeling she's afraid of what she'll find. A man who rejected her. A criminal. Who knows? The truth might upset her too much. I don't want her hurt."

"Why do *you* want to know so badly?"

"I don't know. She tried to find him herself before but had no luck. She deserves to know. I want to help her. Now she seems to think I care whether her father is dead or in prison. I couldn't care less."

"But she cares," Bruce pointed out.

J.R. stopped his pacing as Bruce's words clicked. Viv had put it behind her from what she thought but clearly it was an open wound. "You're right."

"If the truth bothers her so much then maybe it's better if she doesn't know."

"But what if he comes to find her?" J.R. posed the question that really had him scared. Viv had thrown out some terrifying scenarios last night. J.R. had played it off as impossible but he knew she could be right. This man could be anything and anywhere. The urge to protect Viv grew stronger the more thought he gave this.

"Wouldn't it be good if he showed up?"

"Not if he's some murderer."

"You're right. What if he was put in prison because he was a local mob boss and had people murdered? He could be dangerous. What if he gets out of prison and wants Viv to take her place in the underworld? It's better if Viv doesn't know him."

"It's probably not that dramatic but that's exactly why I have to find him," J.R. said.

"You lost me." Bruce sat up on the couch. "You're going to go looking for a guy because he might be dangerous to the woman you love. But she doesn't want you to and she demoted you to friend. Then what?"

"Protect her. If I know who and where he is then I can keep him away if he's trouble."

"He hasn't tried to find her or her mother in thirty years. Do you really think he'll try now?" Bruce asked.

"Now or later, it doesn't matter. If he's in prison there's no telling when he could get parole. Who knows if he's contacted Viv's mother or not. I'd sleep better if I knew where he was at all times." J.R. didn't care what he found so long as Viv wasn't hurt by it. J.R. couldn't let anything happen to the woman he loved.

"I don't think Viv will like this." Bruce cracked his knuckles.

"No, but I'm not about to tell her unless it's good news. I want to protect her, not hurt her more."

"So let me hire the private investigator and we'll find him," Bruce offered. "If Viv doesn't know it won't hurt her but you need to be prepared for what you find."

"I have a friend who does this stuff. How can he do anything without a shred of information? I know Viv's mother's name, and Viv's birth date, the fact that Viv's mother lived her whole life in Vegas until a few years ago and the fact that Viv was born here in Las Vegas. None of that is a definite lead to the father."

"Let the PI worry about that," Bruce insisted. "Look, you have to do something. Hire a PI. Buy a ring. Whatever. But you can't stay cooped up in here all day pacing. What good does it do? You're a man of action, J.R. I can't blame you. If it was my girl I'd do the same thing."

"You're right." J.R. ignored the ring remark. That was a step too far for his comfort. He had his mother's engagement ring in his safe at home and the idea of seeing it on Viv's finger made J.R. feel even more protective and possessive. "I don't want to handle this over the phone. No one around here needs to overhear anything. Viv knows everybody in this place. Plus the family could barge in here at any time."

"I'll go. Viv might change her mind about being friends and come find you."

J.R. wrote down the information he had on Viv and her mother and even what he knew about her aunt, just in case. Then he gave Bruce the name, directions to his buddy's PI office and keys to his Hummer.

"Yes! I love that tank." Bruce grabbed the keys with delight.

"I want it back in one piece." J.R. could just see Bruce mowing down a six-foot-tall cactus for fun.

"Okay, okay. I'll be safe." Bruce was off on the mission.

Bruce's joke about a ring replayed in J.R.'s head. If he showed Viv a ring she'd probably run the other way. The *friends* thing had been his idea. He had to play it up as much as he could so she believed it and relaxed around him. The idea of spending time with her with their clothes on and no expectations in that area wasn't the turn off she'd hoped for. J.R. needed her and it scared the hell out of him.

He had to take advantage of the *friends* situation. Spend as much time with her as possible. Bruce was right, J.R. was in love. All J.R. had to do now was get Viv to realize she felt the same way. No easy task but maybe finding her father would help. It might prove to her that he didn't care what he found. He wanted to put her mind at ease.

Of course if she found out and was mad, bad news or good news, it could ruin any chance he had for a future with her. He had to put her safety before a potential fight. Until the PI came back, J.R. would shower Viv with friendship and conversation. Make her forget her life before him.

* * * * *

With the girls by the pool and Bruce on the errand, J.R. spent the rest of the morning on business. His experience with

Viv, although brief, told him that she needed to cool off for her own good. But by the afternoon he was ready to shower her with friendship.

J.R. didn't find Viv at her office but Viv's assistant had pointed him in the direction of the spa. As he headed for that floor, J.R. wondered what she might be having done. Waxing?

As he entered the main area of the spa, he spotted Viv getting her nails worked on. The manicurist directed Viv's attention to him and J.R. smiled. The dozen or so other women staring at him held no interest.

"Is something wrong?" Viv blew on her nails.

"No. I knew the family was busy and thought you might have some free time. I didn't mean to interrupt." J.R. came closer.

"She's done." The manicurist chimed in.

"I have something I need to speak with you about, Viv."

"Okay." Viv grabbed her purse. Her tone remained professional and J.R. found that annoying.

"Thanks, Molly." Viv led the way to the elevators. "What do you need to talk about?"

"I figured with the family out and the plans in you'd have a little extra time." J.R. held the elevator door for her. Viv was off balance and her eyes looked him over and then looked away. The attraction would be hard to fight but he had self-control. The red nail polish taunted him.

"We talked about this. I'm not going to your suite." She pressed the button for the lobby as they entered the elevator.

"Of course not. I was hoping you'd help me pick out a tuxedo." J.R. gave her a few inches of space. They were alone and her perfume drove him crazy. Damn the security cameras he knew were everywhere.

"Are you getting married?" Viv asked. The look on her face was priceless, a mix of confusion and interest. The blush on her cheeks looked natural and he wondered what she was thinking about.

"No. I get invited to several charity and other formal functions. Renting one is fine for a wedding but I'd rather have one tailored and in my closet when I need it. You said you'd help me find the one that looked best on me."

"That's right, I did. I didn't think you were interested. You seem to prefer jeans." Viv's eyes ran down him and back up. "I think you look better in them too."

"I do prefer them but while I'm having to wear a tux anyway I might as well get it done." J.R. knew she couldn't resist the request.

"It's smart. If you attend enough functions it'll pay for itself in no time. I'm sure I know the answer but I have to ask. How much do you want to spend on this tux?" Viv sounded professional but her eyes kept surveying him as they exited the elevator.

"However much it takes to get the best. Let's go." J.R. followed as Viv expertly weaved a path through the lobby crowd, enjoying his turn to get a great view. He knew he shouldn't be but J.R. wanted to determine whether she had on a thong or no panties on at all beneath her sage skirt.

J.R. nodded to the doorman for a taxi.

"Don't you want a limo?" Viv asked.

"No. It's too much for the two of us around the city we live in. I'd drive us but Bruce borrowed my Hummer."

"Why am I not surprised?" Viv smiled.

"Surprised at what?" He slipped into the cab after her and sat very close to her. No limo, too much room for her to escape.

"A Hummer. You love nature but you drive around in something that could trample anything."

"It's not a tank, it's safe and good for the desert," J.R. insisted.

"I guess it is practical in some respects. I've never driven one myself."

"Sorry, you can't drive mine." J.R. glanced to see her sexy lips pout.

"Why not? I've been driving ATVs since I could reach the pedals because of Uncle Number Two." Viv crossed her legs, her calf grazing his knee. She was seconds away from being groped in the back of a taxi but J.R. restrained himself.

"I didn't dispute your driving abilities but I have a rule. I only let family drive my car. You're not family so I can't let that happen." J.R. wanted her to be family. Sitting next to Viv only made his need stronger.

"I guess I can't drive yours then. I'll take a test drive from the dealership one of these days."

They entered the upscale menswear shop and J.R. watched Viv in action. He could watch her endlessly and never get bored. She sorted through styles, checked vest designs, and reviewed tie patterns. Finally she seemed satisfied with her creation.

"See what you think." Viv handed him a tux. As his fingers brushed hers, J.R. noticed that she didn't move. Not even when he had a firm grip on the suit. A few seconds of direct contact seemed to be what she needed and finally she pulled her hand back.

J.R. changed as directed and stepped out to model Viv's choice. Her face lit up and he hoped it had more to do with him than with the tux design.

"How do I look?" He fished for a compliment.

"Perfect." Viv approached and ran her hands along the shoulder line and down to the small of his back.

Her touch was torture but better than no touch at all.

"Do you like it?" she asked.

Viv touched him more than necessary and J.R. had to fight the urge to grab her and kiss her. He didn't care that they were in a public place but Viv wouldn't react well.

"I'll take it." J.R. nodded. "Do you need to measure my inseam now?"

"That's not my area. At least not anymore. You were serious about the no-budget part, right?"

"How much is it?" J.R. looked for a tag but there wasn't one.

"Three thousand."

"Dollars? For a tux? My first car didn't cost that much."

"But I'll bet you didn't look this good in that car."

"Do you get a kickback for this sale?" J.R. teased.

"How rude. I'm getting the tailor. It's perfect for the man who has everything."

"Not everything." J.R. stared at her intently. He wanted her.

Viv paused but didn't turn back. Fighting with her was fun if they ever got the chance to make up. Being with her as friends was better than nothing.

Viv returned with the tailor who quickly assessed the necessary adjustments while Viv watched. J.R. handed over his credit card and changed back to his clothes.

It was over too quickly. The cab ride was painfully quiet but Viv was more relaxed than she'd been on the way there. J.R.'s arm stretched out behind her on the seat like a clumsy teenager's move but she didn't flinch. He tried to think of something else to keep her around but when they returned to the hotel, Viv spotted Dawn. He'd forgotten the food tasting was tonight. He could join in but he wouldn't have Viv all to himself.

He tagged along. Bruce was in on the food sampling. He gave J.R. the thumbs-up and slipped him his keys back.

"So what did you do today?" Bruce asked J.R. as Viv ran down the first menu.

"I spent it with Viv," J.R. replied.

"Good."

"I got her to pick me out a three-thousand-dollar tux."

Bruce stifled a laugh. "I know you've got money, J.R., but that's love."

J.R. nodded but didn't take his eyes off Viv.

* * * * *

After three days of friendly excuses to spend time with Viv, J.R. got the call from his PI buddy. Not wanting him at the hotel they agreed to meet at J.R.'s house. It was nice to be home again. J.R. hadn't realized how much his life had changed at the hotel.

His house was just as he left it, the cleaning service kept it spotless but it felt incredibly empty. He'd always enjoyed the solitude before. What he really wanted was Viv alone, here. No family interrupting. No work to take her away.

The doorbell rang and the door opened. J.R. was glad Drew knew him well enough to just come in. J.R. never locked the door when he was at home.

"How's business?" Drew joined J.R. in the kitchen.

"Good. You?" J.R. handed him a beer.

"Good. Bruce told me you're crazy about this woman and needed some information."

"Did you find her father?"

Drew shook his head as he sipped the bottle. "No luck. I've got every piece of information there is on Shelley and Vivian Montrose but no solid leads on who the father is."

"Nothing at all?" J.R. had been convinced some clue or bit of information would turn up.

Drew handed over a folder. "No. A lot of seniors in high school date college men. It's not like the UNLV campus is that far from Las Vegas High. There are too many possibilities."

"You're probably right." J.R. was disappointed.

"I tried to track down some of Shelley's friends or teachers from high school but most have moved away. Bad timing."

"What do you mean timing?" J.R. asked.

"You missed Shelley's thirtieth high school reunion by a week and a half. Las Vegas High had a pretty good turnout."

J.R. found the reunion announcement. "Did Shelley attend?"

"According to the records, she hasn't missed one yet." Drew nodded. "Never brings a date to them though. I followed every lead. If you have anything else I'll chase it down but I'm out of places to look."

J.R. drained his bottle of beer. "Nothing new. Viv doesn't know anything and won't ask her mother."

"Sorry I couldn't help," Drew said. "Viv must be amazing."

"She is." J.R. opened the folder Drew had handed him. The amount of information surprised him. A listing of her home, car, job, copy of her college transcripts, birth certificate, driver's license, medical history and notes on both her scar and tattoo done very professionally. A similar listing on Viv's mom went on longer but gave no indication as to the identity of Viv's father. Yearbook photos of both the women were included. Shelley was not alone in some of them. "Who's this with Viv's mom?"

Drew looked at his notes in the back. "I ran anyone I could. That's Lou Penton. Former high school boyfriend from the looks of things. I ran a check. He's now a university professor."

"Check him out some more."

"Sure. He went to college out East. I couldn't determine when they broke up."

"Can't hurt to check him out." J.R. saw something familiar in Lou.

"Serious about her?" Drew asked.

"I can't get her out of my head. Sound serious?"

"Terminal. Bruce said she's anti-marriage?"

"No father, no stepfather and serial uncles. She doesn't trust men. I'm not giving up. She's worth it." J.R. knew he had to prove to Viv that he wasn't going anywhere.

"She had it rough, no argument, but if she passes on a guy like you she's insane. If I had a nickel for every girl who was after you I wouldn't need to work — ever."

"They were only after the money." J.R. had experienced that out East and in Vegas.

"Viv doesn't care about the money?"

"No. I can tell when a woman is more interested in my money than in me. Viv is doing her job spending lavishly for the wedding, but she doesn't seem to care if I spend money on her or not. I never thought I'd meet anyone like her. We may not always agree but where it counts we understand each other."

"You're gone." Drew finished his beer.

"Pretty much." J.R. knew it was true.

"Then you'd better move her in here so we can meet her."

"I'm working on it."

"Good. Hate to drink and run but I've got to look into Lou. I can see it's eating at you. Good luck with her." Drew shook J.R.'s hand and showed himself out.

J.R. remained on the barstool. Move Viv in. The idea rolled around in his head. It was a step but not enough.

There was no way he could let the wedding day arrive and still be Viv's friend. J.R. headed for his home office and the wall safe. Unlocking it, he reached in and took out his mother's engagement ring. J.R. hadn't seen it since he'd moved in years ago. While it was worth very little monetarily, he hoped Viv would understand its value.

J.R. slipped the box in his pocket and closed up the safe. He had to get back to the hotel. There were only two days left until the wedding and he had a lot to do.

Chapter Eleven

Less than a week of J.R. as a friend and no sex had made Viv desperate. She wanted him all the more and had gone through more batteries than she was willing to admit with her nightly vibrator usage. It was good but not J.R. by any stretch of her very active imagination.

She thought that cutting off the sexual side of things would put distance between them but it had done the complete opposite. They were spending more time together and while she enjoyed it, not touching him was torture to her. She hoped he was suffering too.

Even as she sat in her office for yet another bridal meeting with Dawn and Ginger, Viv's mind was on J.R. It was a constant presence she'd learned to live with, wondering where and what he was doing for no real reason.

As Viv ran down the final wedding decisions, she reminded herself that it was her choice to stop sleeping with him. She couldn't blame anyone else. A comment by the bride brought Viv out of her fog. The wedding was tomorrow night and Viv was still letting herself be distracted by a man. "I'm sorry, what?" Viv asked.

"I think you were right." Dawn sighed at her oversized red bouquet.

"Right about what?" Viv prompted.

"I think I like the simple bouquet of roses for me and the tulips for Ginger. These are too loud." Dawn dropped the bouquet in the box and closed it.

"Dawn, your wedding is tomorrow. You can't change things now." Ginger rolled her eyes.

"It's my wedding and I don't like these flowers." Dawn folded her arms across her chest.

The calm was over and the panic had set in. Viv only wished the bride had taken her advice from the beginning. "If you're sure, I can place an emergency order today. We'll get the flowers in time," Viv assured them. Panic wouldn't help and those flowers weren't Viv's first choice.

"Really? That fast?" Dawn seemed surprised rather than delighted.

"Last-minute changes happen. We can accommodate them."

"Okay." The bride sat uneasily.

"Good, that's settled." Viv ran down her checklist. "We've finalized the food, the music, the flowers with that one change and you chose the location for the ceremony. The final dress fitting is all we have left."

The women proceeded to the bridal studio for the final fitting and Viv braced herself for the tears and the excitement that normally went along with the reality that the wedding day was here. The bride seeing herself in the dress normally triggered all sorts of waterworks. Ginger went quickly and happily through her fitting, saving the bride for last.

But the emotional overload didn't happen. The bride took a rather long time alone in the dressing room and refused all offers of help from Viv or the staff. Finally Dawn emerged with a frown.

"Is something wrong?" Viv asked.

"I look fat." The bride's jaw clenched.

"No, you don't." Ginger waved it off.

"That cut of gown is meant to billow," Viv explained as she had at the previous fitting.

"I look pregnant." Dawn whined.

"You loved it five days ago," Ginger pointed out.

"I look terrible. I need a different dress." Dawn stamped her foot.

Viv looked over at the owner of the bridal studio and sighed. What could she do? "Okay. Go change and we'll pick something else."

Inwardly Viv wanted to strangle the bride but had no choice other than to deal with it. This was her promotion on the line and if she let herself lose control now, Viv knew it would only make things worse. This had to go well.

"You'll never get the dress altered in time." Dawn put her hands on her hips.

This girl was more of a test than Viv had given her credit for. "Let me worry about that. Change and find the right dress."

Stepping behind the counter, Viv informed the owner she'd need emergency alterations on a different dress. Viv had seen cold feet before but rarely did it take the form of changing everything. In case Dawn changed her mind back, Viv would keep both sets of flowers and both gowns. As long as the bride was happy it would be a successful wedding.

Viv returned to the bride and selected the two dresses she felt would best flatter Dawn's frame. "I recommend these two."

Dawn looked less than enthusiastic but took them into the dressing room and modeled them both. "I want to try some others," Dawn declared and dove into the racks.

Three hours later Dawn was back to Viv's first pick. The seamstress did a detailed fitting and promised the dress would be delivered and a final fitting would take place at the hotel tomorrow morning.

Viv breathed a sigh of relief as they left. The bride didn't seem as happy as she should but there was little Viv could do for wedding jitters. Changing things didn't ease the traditional cold feet. Of course Viv's intuition still told her there was something more to it than normal nerves.

When they got back to the hotel, Dawn and Ginger ran off to enjoy their last day of vacation. Viv headed for her office to arrange a gift for the seamstress who would work her fingers to the bone today.

Viv didn't approve of Dawn's frivolous spending of J.R.'s money but it wasn't Viv's place to control the budget. J.R. had made it very clear that there was no limit to what he'd spend. She admired his generosity but there was repaying your family and then there was letting them run wild with what you've earned.

She attempted to focus on the wedding but she'd been so consumed with J.R. that it was impossible. Viv would have nightmares of Dawn changing everything again unless she found a way to have more pleasant dreams.

It was nearly noon and Viv had yet to see J.R. once. Maybe he'd lost interest. That wasn't the relief Viv had wanted it to be. The thought hurt and scared her. No man had ever done this to her. All the distance of friendship hadn't gotten him out of her system. She'd have to go another way. Unfortunately she wasn't sure what that way was.

"What's this I hear about changes?" J.R. was in her office doorway.

Viv nearly jumped out of her chair. She was happy to see him but he'd caught her daydreaming and Viv knew her cheeks were red. "Hello to you too, J.R."

"Sorry, where are my manners?" He entered her office and closed the door. "How are you?"

Viv felt her stress level drop the closer he got. "Fine. Yes, there were some changes. The bouquets, thankfully, and the dress. It'll be a lot of work but it'll get done in time. At least it's an evening wedding."

"I have complete confidence in you." J.R. appeared totally unconcerned that it would all be over tomorrow. He hadn't made any requests of her and once he moved out of the hotel… Viv didn't want to think about that.

"Is that what you came here to discuss?" Viv couldn't help but wonder if he didn't care that things would end.

"You're busy. I'll leave you alone." J.R. started to leave.

"No, don't go. I'm not the one who is sewing my brains out. Did you need something?" Viv didn't want him to leave. He'd mistaken her question for a dismissal when she wanted the opposite.

"I was thinking one friend could take another friend out to dinner." J.R. leaned against her desk. "Since the wedding is tomorrow and you'll be rid of me soon."

Viv felt a rush of warmth and dread. All she wanted was to be with him. This couldn't end. She didn't want it to end. Her mouth wouldn't say those words. "I'd like that. Dinner sounds great."

"I'll make reservations somewhere special. Don't worry, not here."

"No. I don't want to be in a crowded restaurant with all that noise. Why don't you come to my condo? We can order pizza or something. Very casual."

"You want me alone." J.R. leaned across her desk with a grin.

"If anyone can make me forget about the wedding tomorrow and the stress I'm feeling it's you." Viv surprised herself with that much honesty.

J.R. got off the desk and pulled Viv into a kiss. It felt like forever had passed since she'd had her hands and lips on him but he tasted as good as ever. Viv knew she wanted to keep seeing him. The more time they'd spent together, the more she wanted to be with him.

Why shouldn't they stay together? Viv couldn't think of one good reason why not. Before she could deepen the kiss J.R. pulled back. "I like pepperoni." He released her as quickly as he'd grabbed her.

Viv recovered and wrote down her address. "See you at seven o'clock."

"I'll let you work until then." J.R. slipped the paper in his pocket.

As she watched him leave, Viv wished it felt right. He went away when she asked and she still wanted him.

* * * * *

Later that night, Viv was alone in her condo and the anticipation was driving her crazy. The wedding plans were under control and there was nothing she could do until tomorrow on that front. This evening was all for her and J.R. It was almost seven as Viv carefully lit candles strategically placed around her condo. She hadn't been this nervous the first time she been with J.R. and now she was acting like a virgin. Truthfully, Viv hadn't been this nervous when she was a virgin.

Almost an hour before she'd begun trying on outfits. After exploring several options, Viv finally settled on a pair of jeans so well worn they were soft and a pale pink top with a hint of shimmer in the fabric. Viv opened a bottle of wine and checked her makeup for the fifth time. Finally the doorbell rang.

Counting to ten so she didn't look too nervous or overeager, Viv opened the door and smiled. Her attire was a good choice. He'd come in jeans and a T-shirt. Even after picking out his expensive custom tux, Viv preferred him this way. "Any trouble getting away?"

"No, the young ones are out dancing all night. No one will miss me."

"You didn't want to go?" Viv teased.

"A night alone with you or a loud nightclub? Like there's really a contest." J.R. leaned in to kiss her but paused.

Viv resisted the temptation to pull him the rest of the way. "Something wrong?"

"I just wondered if Lox was going to come around the corner."

Viv smacked his arm and pulled him into the kiss by the back of his neck.

Once his lips touched hers, Viv's playfulness and urgency slipped away. There was no immediate need for a deep and probing kiss, the contact was enough. She pressed her body against his and snaked her arms around his shoulders slowly. "I missed this," she whispered against his lips. The gleam in his eye told Viv he felt the same.

"Me too." He looked up from her and around the condo. "I like your place. Cozy."

"Is that a nice way of saying it's small?" Viv had driven by J.R.'s estate on a lark one evening. It was huge and to think he lived there alone with no neighbors for miles. She envied him but would also miss the convenience of being in the city.

"Small but comfortable." He roamed through the few rooms, tugging Viv along by the hand. Viv was glad she'd straightened up.

"I don't take up much room." Viv shrugged.

"I don't smell any pizza."

"I see. You came for the food?" Viv didn't believe it for a second.

"You promised me pizza. I'm starved." J.R. was being deliberately difficult. Good thing for him Viv liked it.

"It should be here any minute." Viv leaned up and pressed a few soft kisses to his throat. He tasted better than pizza. She had missed him so much it was ridiculous but Viv couldn't argue with her feelings.

J.R.'s fingers slipped to her waist. It felt wonderful to have his hands on her again. The wedding was just twenty-four hours away and then he wouldn't be a client anymore.

The doorbell rang and Viv snapped out of the gravitational pull of J.R. to get the pizza before J.R. could pay. He was weird about money but she could certainly spring for an extra-large. "Pepperoni as requested." Viv set the box on her butcher-block kitchen table and flipped up the lid. The scent of pizza filled the room.

J.R. leaned over to inspect it. "Four Brothers from Italy. Not New York pizza but not bad. You didn't have to get it all only pepperoni."

"Don't flatter yourself, we happen to like the same kind of pizza." Viv poured the wine and handed him a paper plate. "Dig in."

"Are you a sit down for dinner type or a plop on the couch and eat on your lap type?" he asked.

"Couch, definitely." She and her mom had spent many Friday nights eating pizza and talking or watching a TV movie. Of course after the pizza and movie came the beauty lessons. Viv had different after-dinner plans for J.R.

"Good. I hate fancy women." J.R. grabbed the plates and pizza and deposited them on the coffee table while Viv brought the bottle of wine and glasses.

They both grabbed a slice and ate and talked until the pizza was nearly gone. The conversation was light, Vegas in the summer, cars but nothing about their relationship. It was more comfortable than Viv had imagined possible. The unspoken gnawed at her.

Viv didn't want to spoil the evening with talk of the future and she suspected J.R. felt the same way. He seemed at ease in her little condo and helped clean up. Viv knew the mood would have to change. There were things to sort out but Viv didn't want the good part of the evening to end.

As she washed her hands, she contemplated asking him. How would he respond to the idea of continuing to see each other? Obviously they weren't bored with each other yet but why ruin the night by getting serious? Viv opened her mouth to say something but felt J.R.'s arm slip around her waist as he crowded her from behind and kissed her neck.

"I missed you too," he whispered.

"Good." Viv turned and smiled at him. Suddenly she got nervous. There were too many emotions racing around in her. "Ready for the wedding?" There were a million other things she wanted to say to him but didn't know how.

"Oh no. We're not talking about weddings or flowers or anything else like that. Not tonight." He pulled close and trapped her with his body.

His warm hands cupped her face and before Viv could blink he erased her nervousness with a kiss that sunk deep into her. It was the burning sensation of drinking vodka straight but coursing through every vein in her body.

When his lips finally released hers, Viv went up on her tiptoes to hug him. Her face buried against his neck as she held him tightly. J.R. followed her lead and captured her in an embrace that made her feel completely safe and content. Viv didn't want to lose this feeling.

"I want more," she whispered.

"You can have anything you want." J.R. relaxed his grip on her and kissed her forehead. That began a trail of kisses down to her mouth and Viv felt the shift instantly. How two kisses from the same man could be so different she didn't know or care. J.R. could be tender one minute and dazzle her with his passion the next. She loved it. She loved him.

The thought shocked her but didn't prevent her from responding to his kiss. Suddenly Viv felt like she was floating but J.R. had actually lifted her off her feet. "When did you turn into Tarzan?" She held on tightly.

"You've got a huge bed back there and that kitchen table will never fit both of us without breaking," J.R. quickened his pace.

"I like a man who plans ahead." A man had never in her life carried Viv. It was an odd sensation, a mixture of being spoiled and yet out of control. That summed up how J.R. made her feel and she liked it.

Finally he dropped her on the bed and stretched out next to her. "What do you weigh, ten pounds?" He ran a hand up her thigh and squeezed.

"Very funny." Viv pulled his shirt off in the process. "You don't have to flatter me. I think we're both dying for another night together."

"Not just any night." J.R.'s hand slid under her top and tugged it free from her body.

Viv worried he'd add that it was their last night. Luckily his mouth found her sensitive collarbone and proceeded to torture her. He was a mix of things tonight. The passion was there but the pace was less frantic than their other encounters.

Slowly their fingers worked off the rest of each other's clothes. Viv wanted to savor this night and it seemed J.R. was on the same path. Hands caressed rather than groped as their lingering kiss drew them in deeper. When Viv finally came up for air, she found they had made their way to the top of the bed.

J.R. half pinned her and Viv felt an odd surge of need. Her body arched but she didn't move to change positions. Instead she pulled him on top of her, handed him a condom from her nightstand stash and spread her legs.

"You sure?" He pressed his forehead to hers and stared into her eyes.

Looking into his green eyes, Viv was sure. She wrapped an arm around his neck and pulled him closer as he hurried to get the condom on.

J.R.'s mouth took hers as Viv curled her legs around his waist. The smell of his body, the taste of his mouth, and the feel of his hard cock pressing to her slit made Viv wetter. She didn't feel trapped by him but free and open.

As he eased into her, Viv pressed her breasts to the rough warmth of his hairy chest and let her tongue explore his mouth. Her hips relaxed and met every thrust as her body warmed toward climax. He pushed into her deeper with every stroke and Viv kissed his neck as she tightened her pussy around him. He filled her to the hilt, stretching her in the unusual position.

Viv dug her nails into his back, holding him to her as she came — her body convulsing as she bit his shoulder while the waves of pleasure hit her.

"You okay?" J.R. kissed her.

She nodded — not trusting her voice. He was still hard inside her. "More," she whispered.

J.R. eased back gently and Viv felt the loss. She relaxed her fingers on his back and enjoyed the feel of him under her hands as he filled her again. The contact sent a new wave of pleasure over her spent pussy.

The feeling of him tensing toward his orgasm fascinated her. Viv watched his face as he drove into her one last time and groaned. The look of ecstasy on his face thrilled her even before the rush of him coming inside her gave her a more physical reward.

"You okay?" His fingers brushed the curls away from her face and tipped her chin up so he could look her in the eye.

"It was perfect." She kissed him softly and let her fingers trace his jawbone.

"Your lips are all swollen." J.R. touched them and Viv kissed his fingertips.

"That's your fault. You're too good a kisser. You don't have to go back to the hotel, do you?" She needed him to stay.

"No, you're stuck with me all night. Unless you kick me out."

"No," she said quickly and blushed. "I don't want tonight to end."

"Good. Neither do I." J.R. removed the condom and rolled them until Viv was on top of him.

Viv let her hands roam his muscled chest, clinging as she arched into the kiss. Her tongue traced up his chin and around the edge of his lips until he groaned. Viv knew they were just getting started. Her brain turned off as she kissed him back. "I love you," she whispered.

Chapter Twelve

J.R. woke happier than he had in his life. Not only had their night together been as close to perfect as possible, but Viv had let slip those three little words that made him sure he was on the right track. Finally she'd admitted how she felt and for a stubborn woman like her that was the equivalent of shouting them over the Grand Canyon to echo.

How he'd fallen for such a stubborn woman he wasn't sure, but J.R. knew he couldn't let her go without her making some sort of commitment. If she got any distance at all she might give in to those ideas she was raised on and put her brick wall back up. That couldn't happen.

Glancing at her alarm clock, he realized it was almost time to wake her and give her quite a surprise. It was a big day in more ways than one. The wedding was tonight and hopefully the success would give Viv the promotion she'd worked so hard for. That was later. For now, she was all his and no one could interrupt them.

Viv sighed softly in her sleep and rolled over to his side of the bed. Her fingers laced through the hair on his chest and J.R. contemplated the best way to wake her. After days of no real physical contact last night both of them had given in and he felt restored. He decided against waking her with anything shocking. She was in for a surprise already.

Slowly he kissed her forehead as he pulled her body closer to his. He trailed kisses down her nose, over her cheeks, and down her throat to that familiar spot behind her ear that caught her attention every time. She made a soft sound and leaned closer as her fingers kneaded his flesh with those manicured nails.

"Good morning," he whispered.

"Definitely." Viv moved to a better angle and began kissing him with clear intentions. She stirred against him. Without hesitation her hand roamed his chest and lower to tease his cock.

J.R. tried to resist but his cock stood at attention for her.

She barely gave him enough time to get the condom on before she shifted on top of him, fully lining her slit up with his hard-on while teasing his chest with her hard nipples.

It was the best morning he'd ever had. J.R.'s hands went to her waist and pulled her up. Viv steadied his erection and pressed back until the tip was snug inside her. Soft moans of desire and contentment mixed as they kissed. Viv slowly inched back and took more of him.

J.R. felt her finally surround him and he lifted his hips for the extra pressure. The ideal morning with Viv, her draped on him like a sexy blanket was what he needed. She showed no inclination for a hard ride as she rotated her hips. He thrust up, creating more intense friction than he'd experienced. He looked into her blue eyes, sparkling with love and pleasure.

This was what he wanted—always. As the intensity built, he felt Viv squeeze harder. Her eyes were closed and her sounds became lower and more demanding. Her body jerked and her fingernails dug into his arms as her face pressed into his neck. He'd seen her come plenty of times and every time he wanted to see it again.

The tight spasms around his cock triggered his release and his fingers sank into her hair.

She was breathless. "We could conserve water and shower together."

"Insatiable. First I have a surprise." J.R. sat up and removed the condom. He then propped Viv up on pillows.

"What sort of surprise?" She played along.

"You'll see. I'll be right back." J.R. rolled toward the edge of her California king-size bed.

"Where are you going?" She wrapped an arm around his bare chest and reached lower to get his full attention. "I want you here."

"You'll like it. I'll be right back." J.R. dropped a slow, deep kiss on her and gently removed her arm before returning to business.

"What? Why are you so mysterious?" she pressed as he vacated the bed. Viv reached for his discarded T-shirt and pulled it on, it was well over one hundred degrees outside but Viv had her air-conditioning cranked for comfortable sleeping.

J.R. had every intention of warming her up again but first he had something else to do. "You'll see." J.R. found his jeans tossed over her television and fished the ring box out of the pocket. Keeping it out of sight, he slipped back into bed and wrapped an arm around her.

She snuggled closer and tried to peek. "What's the surprise?" Viv reached around him to try to grab it.

J.R. caught both of her hands and pinned her gently with his body. "Close your eyes."

"If this is some kinky thing you don't have to be secretive. I'm up for anything."

"I know but it's not sexual. Just close your eyes."

With a sigh, she finally closed her eyes and J.R. took a second to admire her. Even first thing in the morning, her hair a mess of curls, she was gorgeous. He had to ask her now or he'd regret it. He opened the box and put it square in her line of sight so she couldn't miss it. "Okay, open them," he prompted.

As her eyes opened they dilated as her eyebrows arched in confusion. "Marry me, Viv?" he asked.

"Is this a joke? Are you testing to see if I lied to you?"

"No, no joke and definitely not a test. I love you, Viv. Marry me?"

"What is it with Vegas? People get the marriage itch because it's everywhere and easy. J.R. Haddery, you've completely lost your mind." Viv dropped her face into her hands.

"No, it's not a joke and not the Vegas effect. I want you, a home, kids and everything that goes with it." He still hadn't gotten an answer. Viv clearly hadn't expected this. J.R. knew she'd be shocked.

"How can you do this?" Viv pushed him away. "How can you ask me that?"

"Because I love you. You have to know that by now. And you love me. You said it." J.R. was confident she'd calm down.

"I didn't know *you* were going to go over the deep end. You don't want this to end and you're overreacting. You agreed that this would *not* get serious, J.R. I never pretended. We never changed the deal."

"That's how you wanted things and at first I was happy with it. I never expected you'd be the one but you are. I know this is sudden but I'm not subtle. I won't give you up."

"So marriage is the answer? Is that your family's answer for everything?"

"What are you talking about?"

"Dawn is only twenty-one and she's getting married. I thought that was odd at first but you propose in under two weeks of knowing me just tells me your family is marriage-crazy. What's the rush?" Viv moved to corner of the bed up by her nightstand like the ring would bite her.

"Most people want to get married, Viv. You're the crazy one. You've had this idea in your head that Dawn doesn't want to get married because she's not your ideal client or acting the way you think she should act. You'll see today how wrong you are. I hope you haven't poisoned her against marriage with your strong opinions. She's young and you're opinionated."

"I want this wedding as much as you do, but I know a shaky bride who is avoiding me when I see one. I've predicted divorces down to the month in some couples. I know what I'm talking about. I could always tell you were the marrying kind but you knew I wasn't. I was honest and upfront from the very beginning. We've had a lot of fun. Why do you want to ruin it with marriage?"

"I've lost enough people in my life already, Viv. I'm not losing you too." He saw her eyes soften and knew she loved him. Why was she fighting herself?

"I'm not going anywhere. We can still see each other. Why do you need such a drastic commitment?" Her voice shook and J.R. knew there was a lot of fear in her. Carefully he slid in behind her and held her.

"Because I don't let what I want in life slip through my fingers. What do I have to do to prove that? I won't walk out of your life like your father did. I won't give you the opportunity to put distance between us. You tried that once before and it didn't change anything."

"You didn't let it. You spent more time with me than ever, only with our clothes on. I should have known then that you were too attached, too needy."

"And you enjoyed every minute of it. In or out of clothes you can't get enough of me. You'll just have to get used to that fact. I can live without sex, for a while, but not without you. Like it or not, you love me and you admitted it last night."

Her forehead rested on his shoulder. "I'm not denying it was good, great actually. Better than great but I never expected or intended for it to go this far. Usually I lose interest or the man realizes I'm serious about not being serious and he loses interest. Why do you have to be so stubborn?"

"I'm stubborn? You've never had a serious relationship in your entire life and you're thirty years old. It's one thing for a relationship not to work but you're afraid to even try. I won't hurt you but you've got to stop running."

"I'm not thirty yet," she argued.

"That's what you want to fight about?" He almost laughed. "So take a chance and start a new decade of your life as Mrs. Haddery."

"Oh, so now I have to change my name. What's next, be barefoot and pregnant until I'm forty? What about my job?" she shot back.

"Keep your name and I never asked you to quit your job. All I want is you. As for kids and houses, we can figure that out. I'm not asking you to move to New York or quit your job or marry me today. Just trust me and say yes. Over the past week I realized that the only way to prove to you marriage isn't hell on earth is to get you into one. It won't hurt, I promise."

"I never thought you'd hurt me. Don't you get it?" Viv got to her knees on the bed for distance, still wrapped in one of his shirts.

"No, explain it to me. If you're not afraid of getting hurt or ending up like your mother then what are you afraid of?" He matched her stance with a gentle hand on either side of her face so she couldn't hide.

"I don't fail, J.R. I've worked hard my whole life, at school, college and my job. Even if our marriage weren't a total failure do you really think I'd be good at it? What kind of wife would I be? What kind of mother? I'd screw it up for sure. I'd end up hurting you and I can't stand that thought."

He processed the new information. "No, you wouldn't."

"Yes, I would. I don't want to mess up your life or some innocent kid's life because I don't know what I'm doing. Do you think my mother or my aunt and her laundry list of ex-husbands are any kind of role models for family life?"

Viv was full of surprises. She didn't want to hurt *him*? "I think you'd make a great mother. Your mom obviously did a good job." J.R. couldn't think of anything better to say. She wasn't afraid of being hurt as much as hurting others. Clearly the fear was deep.

"Is that the grandmother you want for your kids? A Vegas showgirl who wore next to nothing at work and took me to school in full makeup, hair and high heels? You're normal. Stay normal and find someone normal to marry. I had a weird childhood with no father and that'll always be a part of me. At least I know it and accept it. I'm not right for you. I won't warp my children."

"You're not warped. Everyone's family is weird. You're not the only one in this room who had a different childhood. I could've let my parents' death keep me from caring about people. I did for a while but I got over it. You've got to let go of the fear and move on. I know it's harder with a father still out there and no answers but you can't let it paralyze you."

Viv held her ground. "What would I tell our kids? You just don't have a grandfather. How would that affect them? It's not like he's dead and that's just reality. I'll know it's a lie. I know how hard it was when my mother wouldn't answer those questions. I'm not about to lie to our children."

"Then you can't answer and don't. Do you love your mom any less because of those unanswered questions?"

"No, of course not," she admitted. "But there is this tiny part of me that resents her. Even if the kids don't resent me, wouldn't they resent their grandmother? I want this cycle of secrets to end. I turned out okay but I won't do it to anyone else. I'm sorry you don't understand."

J.R. knew he was about to jump off a cliff but he had to tell her the truth. "I couldn't care less about your mom being a showgirl or whatever your dad is. I want you. You might as well know I tried to find him. The PI couldn't find anything concrete about your father's identity. The information wasn't there without a solid lead from your family. But we can keep trying."

"You what?" Viv froze.

"Your mother and aunt weren't contacted at all. Which probably had something to do with the brick walls the private investigator kept hitting. I tried and we can again if you want." J.R. wasn't about to make this worse with a lie.

"I asked you not to do that," she reminded him through a clenched jaw.

"I thought it'd help. You need to have the truth. Viv, you deserve that much. I can at least visit my parents' grave but you have a mystery for a father. That's not fair."

"Life isn't fair. You had no right to do that. This is my family. My personal business. If I want to tell you about it, fine, but you have no right to go behind my back," Viv shouted.

"I have every right. I love you. I could see how not knowing tore you up inside. And all those scenarios of what kind of man he could be. I wanted to protect you from him if he turned out to be dangerous. Like it or not, I love you and you need to stop treating men like the enemy."

"Why? All you did was go behind my back and try to control my life and make decisions without me. I don't need to be protected. Is that the kind of marriage you want? I don't."

"No, I wanted to do it together but you were so against it that it would've gone nowhere."

"What does that tell you? *Don't do it!*" Viv flung a pillow at his head.

"You were against it because of your mother, not your own feelings. If she doesn't know then no harm done. I'm sorry I went too far. I did it because I love you. Stop avoiding and give me an answer." He held up his mother's engagement ring and saw Viv stiffen.

"Why today?" She broke eye contact and climbed off her bed. Viv traded J.R.'s shirt for her light purple robe. "The biggest wedding of my life with the bride from hell and you have to complicate things. I have a promotion riding on this and you pick today to make me an emotional wreck."

"I want to make you happy and Dawn's wedding isn't an excuse. You're running out of arguments." J.R. was out of patience. She could make him crazy and yet he wasn't ready to give up. Viv would have to give him a real answer if she wanted him to stop.

Viv padded out of the bedroom, pulling her hair back into a ponytail. She wouldn't get away—J.R. pulled on his jeans and shirt and followed her into the living room stopping short when she spun unexpectedly at him in mid-step, stabbing a finger right in his chest.

"This is *my* career riding on this wedding. I've already spent more time under or on top of you than with the bride but somehow I managed to pull together a fabulous wedding. I can't afford to be distracted today. Every detail has to be perfect." Viv took a deep breath, pressing her fingers to her temples. "When you're in the midst of a huge business deal do you make life-altering personal decisions?"

"This isn't a hard decision. We don't have to get married today. We don't even have to announce it yet if you think it'll interfere. But it shouldn't be hard to decide, Viv. Do you want to marry me or not?"

"What I want is for you to leave so I can get dressed and get to the office early. I have a lot of details to take care of. This isn't fair."

"Yes or no?" He stood over her, not letting her eyes avoid his. One way or another she was going to answer him, she owed him that much.

"For what it's worth, I wanted us to keep seeing each other. I do love you." Viv's voice was full of sincerity and affection.

Ten minutes ago those words might have been enough but now all he wanted was a one-word answer. "Yes or no?"

"No," Viv whispered.

"Have it your way." J.R. stalked back into the bedroom and grabbed his shoes and walked right past her out the door, letting it slam behind him. He had the horrible feeling that Viv would never want to see him again.

How could she do that? Every other signal was yes but her mouth said no. J.R. got in the elevator and shoved his feet into the well-worn gym shoes. The ring his mother had worn mocked him from its box.

Snapping the lid shut, he stuffed it in his pocket. Maybe it was too late. Viv might be incapable of change. An hour ago he'd been convinced Viv would take a chance if it were offered. He'd never felt like this.

Outside, J.R. got into his Hummer and threw it into gear. The pain was getting to him already as he flew along the highways of Vegas. Viv was running from him and herself because it was easier. She wasn't going to win.

His cell phone rang and J.R. looked to see if it was Viv calling. Damn, it was Bruce. J.R. didn't answer and glanced back at the road just in time to jerk the steering wheel and swerve out of the lane. He'd come within seconds of plowing into a stalled semi.

J.R. took his foot off the gas and got control. The accident that killed his parents flashed through his mind. There was no way he'd die in a car wreck. He'd bought the Hummer because it was a tank. His thoughts were wrapped up in Viv and his common sense was gone. If he wanted Viv back he'd have to do something but ending up in the hospital was a last resort.

As he entered the casino, J.R. spotted Bruce and avoided him.

Bruce was all smiles as he hustled to catch up with J.R.'s pace. "Out all night, J.R.? Don't think I need to ask where you've been."

"Leave me alone," J.R. snapped.

"What the hell happened?"

J.R. boarded the elevator and punched the button.

"Business?" Bruce asked.

J.R. shook his head.

"Viv," Bruce concluded. "Is she okay?"

"She's fine. Happy and single."

"I don't understand. What happened?"

J.R. paced the small area, feeling caged with enough pent-up rage to climb the walls. After doing everything he could to try to argue and convince Viv, he now understood why cavemen would carry off women over their shoulders. "She said no."

"No, she won't see you anymore?" Bruce filled in.

"No, she won't marry me. I proposed." J.R. felt like a fool. Marry a woman he'd known for two weeks? Anyone would call him crazy and he'd agree. "What was I thinking?"

Bruce put a hand on his shoulder. "You were thinking you wanted to marry her. I'm sorry, J.R."

"Am I a complete idiot?" J.R. needed someone to tell him the truth. His aunt would mother him, his uncle would tell him to suck it up and be a man. Bruce was his only hope for a reasonable answer.

"J.R., you've never been an idiot. You always do the right thing and take the right risk. I don't think this is any different. Go with your instincts—you'll do the right thing."

"Easy to take risks when you have nothing to lose," J.R. defended. His parents were killed, the expectations on him were about as low as a kid got. He'd inherited his father's ambition to make something of himself.

"I'd hate to see that record tarnished just because the woman you love said no. You can't fail."

"So forget about her?" J.R. knew that was not an option. He needed to get Viv back.

"Hell no, fight for her. Did you get the first business deal you made on the first offer?"

"This isn't a negotiation. She either wants to marry me or she doesn't. It's not that complicated." J.R. yanked the ring box out of his pocket and wished he had the strength to crush it in his palm.

"Maybe for her it is. What does your gut tell you?"

"She wants to marry me. She's too damn scared to admit it and take the risk. I can't play hardball or force her hand. Business tactics won't work here."

"I'm not so sure about that."

"This isn't a hostile takeover."

"No, but you can put the ball in her court, as they say. Force a review."

"I already did that and she refused."

"No, you offered her the ball." Bruce took the ring box from him and tossed it in the air. J.R. caught it. "If you give her the ball it might be harder for her to give it back."

"She won't take the ring. Viv looked at it like it was poison." J.R. stalked out of the elevator on his floor with Bruce behind him.

"Viv was in shock. Don't let her know she has it right away. Slip it in her purse or her pocket when she's not looking. She'll find it fast enough. It's not like she's got so many men proposing that she won't know who it belongs to. Viv'll take good care of it. What do you have to lose?"

J.R. thought it over as they entered his suite. "What made you think of that?"

"You're the one who always says talk is cheap, you need to pay attention to what people do to know the real deal. Viv can't leave you alone any more than you can leave her alone. So make her act on the ring rather than just *say* no." Bruce shrugged. "It's a dumb idea, right?"

"Actually I think you're on to something." J.R. kicked off his shoes and tore off the rumpled shirt.

"Really?" Bruce smiled.

"Maybe I came on too strong."

"You didn't give her any room."

"Viv is a planner, not a risk-taker. Wild or not, she has spent her life with enough surprises and problems. It's her whole job. Maybe that was too much uncertainty thrown at her. Saying no was easy. Giving the ring back might be harder."

"Maybe she needs to feel like she's in control too. You did kind of spring it on her."

"I know. I have to be ready." He put on a clean shirt.

"Ready for what?"

"For the wedding tonight and for Viv not to change her mind. I can't ruin the wedding by acting like this." J.R. rubbed his face with his palms, trying to get a clear head. "Viv said she wanted to keep seeing me even after the wedding." J.R. felt a glimmer of hope.

"That's great. Why didn't you settle for that? At least for now." Bruce got J.R. a bottle of water from the little fridge.

"I told her I had that PI look for her father. It all went to hell after that. She blew up."

"You told her that?" Bruce rolled his eyes. "You are crazy."

"The results were in, I couldn't lie to her. Then she'd have a real reason to say no. She deserves the truth."

"It didn't do any good. There was no news. Why screw yourself?"

"Because she wants to know who her dad is. It's a long story but she was more mad that I did it behind her back than that I actually did it."

"At least she knows you're honest." Bruce dropped onto the couch and massaged his forehead. "Anything else you did to help your case?"

"That was the last nail in my coffin. Think the ring will work?" J.R. sat down next to Bruce, both men with their heads resting on the back of the couch so they were staring at the ceiling.

"It can't hurt. You look too miserable to give up now. Want me to try a different private investigator?" Bruce offered.

"No. The truth won't change how she feels about me. I doubt they'd find him if Drew couldn't. The truth is she equates marriage with misery, hers or whomever she's with. I don't think she'll change."

"It's hard to deprogram that kind of stuff when it's been since childhood. Viv's a strong woman. If she wants to I'll bet she can change her mind. Maybe you just have to sweeten the deal."

"I'm not enough?" J.R. asked. "Then it's not right."

"I mean meet her halfway. Try compromise. You know something about not having family. Show her you understand."

"I tried, I told her I got over it and so can she. Didn't help."

"That was very sensitive of you and a lie."

"It's not a lie," J.R. scoffed.

"Then why do you always downplay how proud everyone is of you? How much you've done? You worked hard to prove you're worth something. You're still trying to make up for being the one who survived that car wreck."

"So what if I am?" J.R. folded his arms over his chest.

"So nothing. I'm not a shrink. It's your life and it works for you. But that's how I knew Viv was right for you." Bruce grinned.

"How did you know?"

"For the first time in your life you were selfish. You put your work on hold, juggled everything in your life all to be alone with her. That right there told me you wanted something for yourself finally. Maybe if she knew how hard this was for you she might feel differently."

"It wasn't hard." J.R. lied. He wanted Viv so much it felt easy but it wasn't his pattern of a relationship at all. "It started out as just fun."

"Right, but you changed the rules. You made the decision to change things. She might not be on your schedule. Relationships are compromise."

J.R. let the silence hang there as he pondered Bruce's words. It was true. For once J.R. had been selfish. He hadn't thought about anyone but himself. He didn't care what anyone else thought. He just wanted Viv. "If I can get her to talk to me maybe I'll tell her. It might be too late."

"But you're still going to try the ring thing, right?" Bruce asked.

"Yeah, the ring is a good step. Even if she returns it she'll have to talk to me." He couldn't give up yet.

Chapter Thirteen

Viv sat on the edge of her bed, shaking in anger. The tears that continued to roll down her face didn't help either. Why did he have to do that? She'd had it all planned. At the reception she'd wanted to ask him if they could keep seeing each other. Instead he jumps to the extreme. Marriage!

The word gave Viv a chill. If he wanted to call it fear, fine. She was afraid. As much as she loved J.R., she didn't want to hurt him.

She needed a voice of reason. Viv grabbed the phone and punched in her mother's number in Arizona. When the machine picked up Viv tossed her phone across the room. She needed a plan. Her life worked much better when there was a plan.

First she needed to shower. Get herself looking decent and get to the office. Once things were under control with the wedding she could call her mother again. Taking a deep breath, she found her phone and left a voicemail on her mom's cell. Viv hung up the phone and grabbed a towel from the linen closet. With any luck she could avoid seeing J.R. until the wedding itself and she would stay busy. Then her job would be over and her life could go on, hopefully promotion in hand. She couldn't think about J.R. right now. He'd been so angry Viv couldn't imagine he'd want to see her ever again.

An hour later Viv entered her office with the most fake smile she'd ever had at work. The wedding would be a distraction at least. She hoped it would be her day to shine. The bride's tacky choices had been replaced by better ones so that was one positive.

"Good morning." Morgan was too chipper. "The limo is set to pick up the bride's parents. I took the couple to get their marriage license today so that's all taken care of."

"Wonderful. Thanks. Good morning." Viv tried to sound upbeat but knew Morgan would see through it.

"What's wrong?" Morgan followed Viv into her office.

"Nothing." Viv sat at her desk so tense she knew she wouldn't last the day without telling someone. Morgan could be trusted not to gossip. "Everything."

"That makes no sense. Is the wedding off?"

"No."

"Did J.R. dump you?"

"I wish." Viv instantly regretted her words. That wasn't true. She didn't want it to be over. But being dumped would be easier than being proposed to.

"No, you don't wish. What did he do? Did he cheat on you?" Morgan asked in a whisper.

"No, of course not." Viv was suddenly offended at all of these things Morgan was accusing him of. "I thought you liked him?"

"I did but he obviously did something terrible to you." Morgan was a loyal friend.

"Not exactly," Viv hedged. "He did something but you wouldn't consider it bad."

"What do you consider it?"

"I don't know." Viv didn't want to be difficult but she knew she wasn't making sense.

"What was it?" Morgan pressed.

"He proposed." Viv felt a weight lift off her as she verbalized it.

"Proposed?" Morgan looked skeptical. "Proposed like you're in the middle of sex and he blurted out 'Let's get married' or proposed like he got down on his knees and had a ring?"

"He had a ring and then we had this huge fight." Viv leaned back in her chair to stare at the ceiling.

"You said no?" Morgan sat with a shocked expression and stared at Viv.

"I said no. What did you think I'd say?" Viv fought back tears. "I've only known the man two weeks and he wants me to make a commitment for the rest of my life. That's insane. J.R. is insane!"

"First of all marriage *in theory* is a lifetime commitment. You do realize the divorce rate is something like fifty percent so you're technically not stuck with him forever if he turns into a jerk. Second, you can be engaged for as long as you want if you need to get to know him better. It's not out of the question. It doesn't mean you don't love each other. And third, what in the world made you say no? I've never seen you as happy as you've been these past two weeks."

"I don't want to end up like my aunt. Serial marriages. I can't do that. It's just not me." Divorce didn't appeal to Viv but she'd never seriously considered marriage either.

"So the truth finally comes out." Morgan grinned.

"What truth? What are you smiling for? I'm miserable over here and you're smiling."

"You're a romantic."

"Ridiculous." Viv rolled her eyes to keep from crying.

"You are. No serial marriages for you. You'd only do it once."

"I never said I'd do it at all."

"But it all makes sense now. Your mom never got her knight on a white horse and you won't settle for anything less. All these years you've just talked a good game so we'd think you didn't really want what we all want. There are no sure things, Viv."

"Everyone has fantasies but no one gets them in real life." Viv would admit she'd love to have it all on but that was unrealistic.

"J.R. is gorgeous, rich, smart, sexy, he loves you and he wants marriage and a family. Plus you said he's the best sex you've ever had. Which part of that isn't your fantasy?"

"It was an ugly fight but let's just say that nothing is perfect."

"Welcome to reality. That's not the point. You're not perfect either. You love him and you're acting like he told you he already was married or had a bunch of kids or something. You can't expect him to be perfect but you must love him or you wouldn't be so upset."

"He did something behind my back." Viv couldn't overlook that. If he hadn't hired a PI to investigate her father she would have suggested they keep seeing each other. They might have made some compromise but he'd crossed the line. She couldn't let that go no matter how well intentioned.

Her mother's mistakes were not J.R.'s to pick through and judge. People had always judged her mother. Not so much Vegas natives but the tourists and outsiders her mother routinely got involved with for brief relationships. Viv wasn't going to let J.R. do that to her or her family. Even if that wasn't his intent, if the truth was as bad as Viv feared he'd have to make a negative opinion about her father. That was human nature. "I don't think I can get past what he did," Viv mumbled.

"Was it something mean?" Morgan asked.

"He didn't mean it to be mean but it hurt. That just proves we don't know each other well enough yet. I can't marry someone who doesn't understand me."

"As you pointed out you've only known each other two weeks. Maybe you need to spend more time together, not less. The more you know about each other the fewer big mistakes he'll make. He's a man. He'll always make some mistakes. If I dumped my man every time he made a mistake I'd have a revolving door and he'd be gone by now. You're not perfect either."

"I heard you the first time." Viv knew she could be stubborn about change but it worked for her. At least it had until now. It didn't feel like it worked anymore. "I don't know if I can be flexible enough to deal with this."

"You got the bride from hell to make choices and do everything she needed to do. You've handled a lot worse than a guy you're in love with."

"This bride will be gone tomorrow. Short bursts of the ridiculous are one thing but the rest of my life. Morgan, it's just too much." Viv rubbed the back of her neck, trying to relieve the tension.

"Then maybe you did the right thing by turning him down. Does it feel like the right thing?"

"I don't know. I can't think about it right now." Viv had to change gears or she'd throw something else. "Is everything ready for the wedding?"

"Ready as can be. I've got the bridal party set up in the spa midday and all of the final fittings were done this morning. The decorations are going up as we speak and the kitchen has the schedule. The dresses are in the rooms with the bridal party. Tuxes are ready and in the right rooms. Smooth sailing so far."

"Good." Viv exhaled slowly. "I need to make a phone call. Do you mind?"

"Of course not. Calling J.R.?" Morgan got up to leave.

"No. I have to deal with the wedding. If he tries to call or come in find some excuse please. When I'm ready I'll find him."

"You're the boss."

"I hate when you say that. That means you think I'm wrong." Viv reached for the phone as Morgan reached the office door.

"Bosses can be wrong." Morgan closed the door behind her.

As she dialed her mother's phone number, Viv hoped she wouldn't get voicemail again. She did.

A knock on her office door made Viv look up. "Can I help you?"

A short fifty-something man with curly gray hair stood in her doorway. "Are you Shelley Montrose's daughter?"

Panic gripped her. "Yes. Did something happen to her?"

"No, no." He patted the air. "I'm sorry. I didn't mean to frighten you. She's fine."

"Yes, she is." Shelley came up behind him. "What are *you* doing here?"

"Mom, what are you doing here?"

"You sounded so upset this morning when I got your message that I flew up. Why are you here?" Shelley stared at the man like he was a ghost.

"Who is he?" Viv stood up to get attention from the two of them. Never in her life had Viv seen her mother so stunned. She looked confused and on the verge of tears.

Viv's mom sighed and closed the door to the office with a shaky hand. "He's your father."

Viv sat down, dazed. "What?"

"What are you doing here, Lou?" Shelley turned to him.

"Some PI called and asked about us in high school and said something about a kid and you. He said he'd arrange a meeting but I couldn't wait. I came back to Vegas but didn't find you. I did find a listing for Montrose and went by the address given. Luckily, a neighbor was able to point me in this direction."

"So you just show up and barge in on her? Don't even talk to me?" Shelley turned to Viv. "And you hired a PI?"

"No." Viv cut in. "I didn't. The man I was seeing did. This is really my father?"

Shelley nodded and looked at him. "I'm sorry, Lou. You never came back and the next thing I heard you were married."

"I was. I've been divorced for ten years. Never had kids. I wish you'd told me." Lou stepped closer to Shelley.

Viv saw sparks between her parents.

"Really, divorced?" Shelley leaned in.

Viv walked over to her father. "Lou, is it?"

"Lou Penton." He held out a hand.

Viv couldn't bring herself to shake it yet. "Can I have a minute alone with my mother? The admin at the desk can show you where there's coffee and tea."

"Sure. I understand." He left.

"Just hear me out." Mom sat in a guest chair.

"What the hell is going on?"

"Please don't be mad. I never meant for this to happen."

"Tell me the truth."

"I was sixteen when I met Lou. He was so cute and had a great motorcycle. We had so much fun and loved being together. I was really in love, Viv. I know you don't know what that's like." Shelley stared at her long fingernails.

That sentence made Viv's jaw clench. She did know and it hurt. The pain of J.R. was still raw. "Go on."

"I convinced you single was better because I wanted to protect you. But true love is something that can't be denied. Once you find it you'll know it."

Her mind went to J.R. and back to her father. The shock would have to wear off in its own time. "He had a motorcycle and you were two crazy-in-love teenagers," she prompted.

"Right. We dated our junior and senior year in high school. He got this great scholarship to a Big Ten school back East and he was so excited. Then right around graduation I found out I was pregnant with you."

"So Lou really is my father. There's no question?" Viv wanted to be sure before she let that idea sink in and got attached to it.

"Oh honey, no, he was my first and until you were about three—my only. I know it's hard to believe that with the life I led after him but it wasn't the life I wanted."

"Go on." Viv leaned back in her chair. Seeing her mom in pain made Viv hurt but she had to know it all.

"I didn't want him to give up his scholarship so I didn't tell him. By the time I started to show he was off to school. Your aunt wanted to call and tell him not to come back ever. I was sure we'd be married once he was done with college. He said he'd come back. Then your aunt ran into someone he had gone to college with and found out he got married. I gave up at that point."

"He never knew about me?" Viv had never thought of that as a possibility. Her scenarios were always a father who walked out on her mother or landed in prison. This had never occurred to her.

"No. I thought it was best not to put any pressure on him. Single mothers didn't get the child support back then that they do today. I could support you. I didn't want to leave my job or for him to leave his wife. It wasn't his fault. When you asked I didn't tell you because I didn't want to get your hopes up. I was so heartbroken over losing Lou I couldn't ask you to go through that too."

"So you always loved him?" Viv was confused.

She nodded. "I wanted to be a showgirl. I loved my life here. Vegas was all I knew. I didn't want to give it or you up. Then your grandma got that cancer and we had our hands full. I don't regret a thing. I hope you can forgive me."

"He seems normal." Viv couldn't believe it. Numbness set in and Viv wished she'd eaten breakfast or at least had some coffee. It was more than her system could handle.

"He was a good man. Still cute."

"You really loved him?"

"Yes, seeing him again is odd. He never went to any of the reunions."

"But you always did. You wanted to see him again." All of this secrecy and her father wasn't some random one-night stand or a criminal in prison. None of her fears were true. Viv's hand slapped her desk with frustration. "How could you do this?"

"Lou was a good man," Mom assured her.

"Exactly!" Viv snapped. "There was nothing wrong with him. I thought you were protecting me from someone bad. I thought he'd hurt you or raped you or murdered somebody. Why couldn't you tell me the truth? If not when I was little how about when I went to college? Do you have any idea what a relief it would've been to know my father was a normal man?"

"I honestly thought it'd only hurt you. You turned out so great I didn't want to mess that up. I didn't realize it still was bothering you so much. Please don't hate Lou."

"How can I hate him? He didn't do anything." Viv twisted the cord on her phone and tried to take it all in. Her mother had loved her father. J.R. was right, she'd wanted a father and now she had one.

"Do you hate me, Viv?"

Taking a deep breath, Viv ran the whole thing over in her mind. "I can't hate you. I'm stunned but relieved."

"I know I taught you to be independent and I still believe in that. There were too many girls in my graduating class who got married and never earned a dime. They're stuck. I see them at every reunion and they're not happy. I wanted you to have all the options in the world. Look how far you've come."

"But you always loved my—Lou?" It hadn't sunk in yet. Calling him father wasn't feeling natural just yet. She hated that her mother had endured all of those years of heartache. Her mother as a romantic was a new vision for Viv.

"Why do you think I could never marry anyone else? We don't settle. That's why I'm so proud you haven't settled for anyone less than the right one. When it's the right man, you'll know."

Viv wanted to ask how she'd know but her mind was too cluttered.

Viv's philosophy of life was now gone. Her code, her map, her mantra—it was all a lie. "Why don't you and Lou catch up? Go to the Windsor Room and put lunch on my name. I have a wedding tonight. I have to get some things done."

"Wait. This isn't what you called me about this morning, is it?"

"No. I actually called you about something else."

"What's wrong?"

"I don't want to talk about it. I doubt you'll be on my side now." Viv didn't know what to think but telling her mom about J.R. right now might not help.

"I'm your mother. I'll always be on your side. You couldn't do anything I wouldn't support. What's the problem?" Mom wanted to help.

Viv sincerely doubted it. "You remember how I told you I was seeing a man?"

"Yes. Did something go wrong? If he broke your heart I'll have Lou talk to him."

"No, Mom, J.R. and I had a fight. A big one."

"Fights happen but they blow over. I'm sure you'll work this out." Mom patted Viv's hand.

"Thanks. You and Lou go have lunch." Viv couldn't go over it again. Not now.

"You're sure you don't want to talk any more?" Mom looked concerned.

"Not right now. We'll talk later, okay?"

"Okay, honey." Mom left.

Viv needed to be alone as the world caved in on her. Viv was now a woman with two fairly normal parents who had loved each other. At least they had in high school. True love did exist.

Chapter Fourteen

J.R. wanted to talk to Viv but she clearly didn't want to talk to him. Every attempt to call her had gone unanswered.

As he stood in the hallway near her office, J.R. could see her mother in there. The woman from Viv's picture had aged well but the apparently serious conversation between them brought out her age lines.

Looking around for Viv's assistant, J.R. noticed a man about fifty waiting near the offices as well. It was the man from Viv's yearbook. "Are you a client of Viv's?"

"This is personal," J.R. replied. "You're Lou Penton?"

"How did you know?" The man stared.

"I'm the one who hired the PI to find you. Why didn't you contact me first?" He kept the edge out of his voice as he approached the man.

"I have a daughter." The man looked into Viv's office again. "I wasn't going to wait to meet her."

"Does Viv know?" he asked.

"She does now. You're the boyfriend?" The man looked J.R. over carefully.

"More or less. You picked a bad day."

"Would there be a good day?"

"Good point." J.R. could barely believe his ears.

"I dropped everything and flew here. Didn't know Shelley would be here."

"You really didn't know?" J.R. had been ready to hate the man.

"No idea. Never had any kids until now. Never forgot Shelley though." Lou looked toward the office again anxiously. "About you and my daughter."

"Bit early to pull the protective bit."

"You hired the PI for her. Must be serious."

"I'm trying." J.R. decided he could use an ally in Viv's family. Lou had experience with Viv's mom.

"Why haven't you succeeded?"

"She's stubborn."

"Like her mother." Lou nodded. "How long have you been seeing her?"

"Two weeks." J.R. shifted his weight to the other foot.

"You're sure about her?"

"Yes." He tried to see Viv again but her blinds were half closed.

"I have a few more questions."

There was no point. "Viv said no when I proposed."

"You're going accept that?"

"No."

"Ever been married?" Lou asked.

"No."

"Do you have any money?" Lou stepped closer.

"Quite a lot," J.R. admitted.

"Live in Nevada?"

"For over ten years." J.R. nodded.

"Why did she refuse to marry you?"

J.R. paused. He had no right to assume what he thought was the truth. "You'll have to ask her that."

"You must have a theory or you wouldn't be here trying to talk to her."

"I moved too fast. Viv wasn't ready for that level of commitment."

"What's wrong with you?" Lou looked puzzled.

"What do you mean?"

"If she doesn't want to marry you there must be something wrong with you." Lou shrugged.

"You'll have to ask her." J.R. saw that Lou had a blind spot for Viv before he even knew her.

"Does she love you?" Lou asked.

"Yeah."

"Then fight for her."

"I deserved her reaction." J.R. leaned against the wall, feeling defeated.

"Why?" Lou came a few steps closer to J.R.

"I hired the private investigator to try to find you. Viv didn't appreciate my meddling."

"She didn't want to find me?" Lou asked.

"She did. Viv didn't know what she'd find. It wasn't my best move."

"Why did you do it?"

"I figured if you were a dangerous person I could protect her."

"From me?" Lou chuckled.

"How did I know you weren't serving twenty to life for chopping up a hitchhiker?"

"Fair enough."

"I should have asked her first. Talked her into it." J.R. knew he had probably ruined any chance with Viv.

"If she loves you, she'll get over it."

"Maybe you're right." J.R. had a lot to think about.

"When did you propose?" Lou asked.

"This morning."

"Big day." Lou looked back at the office door, content to wait.

"I'll see her later," J.R. said.

Lou waved as J.R. headed for the elevators.

This was not the time. The plan still seemed good but things were getting more complicated.

J.R. dialed Drew's phone.

"Drew," he answered.

"What happened?"

"J.R., I've been trying to get a hold of you since last night. I left five messages on your cell. I found him. Lou is the father. Swears he was her only boyfriend junior and senior year. Viv was born a few months after graduation."

"I know. He's here."

"What? I told him we'd arrange the meeting. I'm sorry, J.R., I didn't get the impression he'd hop a plane."

"Well, he did." J.R. kept back all of the nasty things he wanted to say.

"Christ, it's not like there's even DNA to back it up. Her mom could've cheated on him and we screwed it all up."

"I don't think so. Her mom showed up and apparently confirmed it. This isn't what I needed today."

"Sorry, man. I swear Lou gave no indication he'd try to contact Viv. I never even gave him Viv's name. I asked only about Shelley."

"It's not our fault. Viv comes by her impulsive and stubborn traits naturally. Both sides." J.R. hung up his cell.

He needed to find Viv. Talk to her soon.

* * * * *

Half an hour later, J.R. entered the Grand Ballroom and saw Viv with her back to him. She studied the head table but he knew her mind was elsewhere. The news of her parents wasn't what either of them expected to deal with today but life with Viv would never be boring.

Quietly he walked up behind her. Rejected or not, he couldn't stand to see her in pain. She should be happy but he knew Viv's reactions were rarely average when it came to men in her life. Until she threw a screaming fit to get rid of him he wasn't giving up.

"You okay?" he asked softly.

Looking over her shoulder, Viv shrugged a shoulder. "You know?"

"I got to talk to your dad briefly. You and your mom were having a private conversation when I came to find you. Gave me the third degree for wanting to marry his daughter. He seems like a good guy. The PI left a message but I didn't pick it up until this morning. I'm sorry I didn't get to warn you." His hand squeezed her shoulder supportively. J.R. could feel the tension knotting her up.

"I don't know what to think right now. It's not what I expected. Nothing about today has been normal." Viv turned to him as she wiped her eyes.

"Rough day." He brushed a curl back from her forehead and stepped closer. "At least you know he didn't walk out on your mother. He wants to know you. I told him if he hurts you he'd answer to me."

"You have no right to act all macho like that over me," she began.

J.R. put a finger on her lips. "I'm kidding." He could see the flash of anger disappear fast.

"I can't believe it. He didn't do anything to my mother or me. She is so happy, J.R." Viv leaned forward, her head resting on his chest. "I can't believe this day is really happening. I go thirty years without any men in my life who love me and in one day I have a man who wants to marry me and another one who is my father. I'm afraid to actually believe it."

"Believe it, Viv. He is your father. You can't change that even if you wanted to. The worst thing you could do is cut him out of your life." J.R. pulled her in and held her. The tension seemed to drain from them. "I envy him. You won't be able to tell him no."

"Why do you say that?" Viv lifted her head.

"You may not be comfortable with men loving you but you want a father. You can't lie to me. You've wanted a dad all along."

"I guess it's human nature," she admitted. "But I'm not a little girl. The fantasy is gone. It's not the same but it's real."

"You deserve to know him. Maybe it'll be a good influence on you. Drew said your father is divorced and lives in Arizona. Looked cozy with your mom in the restaurant. Things are looking up." J.R. felt her tense in his arms.

"Don't propose again. I don't think I could take that right now." Her eyes showed a vulnerable side he'd only seen in brief flashes.

"One is my limit, Viv." He slipped the ring into her pocket, careful that she didn't notice. "When you're ready, you'll let me know."

"You're awfully confident." Viv's voice caught in her throat.

"I may have bad timing but I'm right." He kissed her forehead. "Things will look different after the wedding is over and you can focus on your life again."

Viv looked at her watch. "Dawn's wedding. There is too much going on today. I need to go make sure the women are manicured and pedicured. Will you make sure the groom has everything he needs to get ready?"

"Sure." He leaned down and kissed her mouth gently. "I get all of your dances tonight."

"You don't give up, do you?" Viv looked him in the eye. "I can't believe you're speaking to me after this morning."

"When I make up my mind I can be very pushy. You're an impulsive woman but not when it comes to marriage." J.R. laced his fingers with hers. "We both had it pretty rough as kids. I'm not about to lose you if I can help it. And you're fun to fight with."

"My father showing up doesn't change things. It doesn't undo my life as I've made it. You went behind my back and I don't know how to deal with that."

"When I saw that picture of your mother you seemed a little on edge and then all the talk of your father. It sounded like you were worried I'd judge you over your family. I thought if I found your dad you might realize I wouldn't love you any less if he were an ax murderer. I love you and the family that comes with you." He shook her shoulders gently.

J.R. braced for impact as Viv crossed her arms. "I'm not ashamed of my mother. Although most men have reacted badly when they found out."

"I'm not one of those men." They were actually having a real conversation again. J.R. started to feel level.

"I know but I can't have someone else running my life. That's not me. You took that control away from me, that choice of if I wanted to know or not. I can't live like that. I'm not even that good at sharing. Only-child syndrome, I guess. Call it what you want but letting someone else take over isn't something I can deal with."

"I've seen you share, Viv." J.R. wasn't going to let her off that easily.

"That's not my point. I know if I make a conscious effort to work with someone I can do it. But this went far beyond that. I appreciate the apology but, J.R., you're the one who fixes everything. It's your nature and I can't ask you to change."

"What are you talking about?" he asked.

"Dawn wants to get married in a fancy and expensive place and you take care of it. Even when she has another wedding in the works. Dawn falls in a nightclub and they get you even when you can't do anything. They just assume you'll always take care of it. I don't have a dad so you hire a PI to find him."

"I help the people I love. That's a bad thing?" J.R. defended.

"It's not a completely bad thing but I won't let you do that with me. Do you think it helps Dawn to learn to fix her own problems?" Viv threw her hands up. "You can't fix everything and I won't let you fix me."

"My family did a lot for me and they didn't have to. I'd like to return the favor if I can. Maybe I need to learn to share too."

"Maybe."

"Just think about what I said. Believe it or not, there is *nothing* about you I want to change. You love me. It might take a little time but you'll trust me." J.R. couldn't say anything else so he headed for the door.

"J.R.," she said.

Turning, he saw a confused smile on her face.

"I do trust you." Viv bit her lip and turned back to the wedding decorations.

He wanted to hold her, make the confusion and the pain go away. Unfortunately she had more on her mind than him. He had to practice letting people handle their problems on their own. Viv was overwhelmed and right now he needed to let her sort out her family, her life and her answer.

The ring rested in her suit pocket and eventually she'd find it and either chew him out or change her mind. He hoped she'd understand the meaning.

Fortunately the ring wasn't that big so when it came flying at his head it wouldn't do too much damage.

Chapter Fifteen

Viv walked into her office and the silence made the reality of her day more vivid. All she wanted was to go home and start the whole day over. J.R. had proposed and she'd turned him down. Yet somehow he wasn't mad at her anymore. Any other man would have stayed as angry as he had been when he stormed out of her condo that morning. But J.R. was not any other man.

J.R. seemed to defy all of what Viv expected out of men. So did her father. Even worse, Viv had let J.R. into her heart. It was too late to undo it now.

Her life suddenly made no sense at all and Viv had to reevaluate. What if J.R. was the right man? She couldn't deal with that now. The tears welled up and confusion raged. Her only solace was that the wedding wasn't in ruins. The bride had picked a final dress and everything else was proceeding as planned. It had been torture to get here but the work was done so they just had to get through it.

Reviewing the agenda, Viv had to make sure all of the women were ready. The wedding wasn't until seven but Viv needed to focus on it or she'd have to deal with J.R. or her parents or both. She wasn't ready for any of that yet.

Viv exited her office and noticed Morgan was on a rather serious phone call. Viv paused by Morgan's desk as she hung up the phone, looking very concerned. "They need you up at the Haddery suites immediately."

"What's wrong?" Viv asked.

"One of the rooms had a small fire. The sprinklers contained it but you need to get up there."

"A fire? Is everyone okay?" Viv asked.

"Yes, they said the room was empty."

"Which room was it?" Viv had a bad feeling about this.

"The bride's suite." Morgan confirmed her worst suspicions.

"Damn." Viv couldn't believe this. "Call Security and have them bring up the surveillance tape for that hallway to the room. I want to see it myself."

Morgan's expression registered confusion but she didn't argue. "Okay."

Viv headed for the elevators and wondered how everything in her life had gone wrong in one day. She reached the room in record time. The door had been propped open to help clear the smoke and she immediately spotted the bride crying on her mother's shoulder. "What happened?" Viv asked Ginger, who looked the least traumatized. Looking in the room, housekeeping was airing it out with fans and scrubbing the ash away.

"Someone must have broken into the suite and smoked one of my cigarettes. We found one smoldering on the floor by the window. Probably some kid." Ginger pointed toward the scorched curtains.

Viv gave Ginger a suspicious glare. "Someone broke in?" Viv didn't believe that.

Ginger held up a finger. "I never leave my cigs even a little smoking and I wouldn't leave it on the floor. Our dresses were hanging on the curtain rod."

No, not the dresses. "We'll have to find out who did this later. What caught fire? The curtains? The bedding? Don't tell me the dresses."

"My dress!" the bride sobbed.

"It didn't even burn really, it just sort of melted into these pellets and gave off this terrible odor." Ginger sniffed and rubbed her nose.

"Here is what is left." The maid showed Viv the half melted gown. "The sprinklers turned on so the fire didn't spread but the gowns are ruined and the curtains."

"Thanks, Maria. Poly blends do this." Viv could see it was a lost cause. The wedding couldn't be ruined because of this mishap. "I'll call the bridal studio and get another dress. It won't be tailored of course but it'll work. I can find a seamstress to do a quick take-in. Unless you'd rather push it back a day or two."

"No!" Dawn stomped her foot.

"That was the only dress like it in her size," Ginger reminded Viv.

"What happened?" J.R. arrived with Mr. Lox at the perfect time. Viv wanted to jump out the window if only they opened.

"There was a little incident with a cigarette." Viv didn't need them here now. "We can overnight another dress. I'll find one."

"The dress? Who was smoking in the room?" J.R. turned to Ginger.

"We were all getting our nails done. Someone must've broken in," Ginger snapped back.

"This is the security I paid for?" J.R. turned to Viv and Mr. Lox.

"No one without a pass card to that room or an employee could get in. The locks are electronic and the door was clearly not broken down," Viv said.

"Are you saying an employee did this?" J.R. pressed.

"Whoever did this I assure you we will look into prosecuting them for arson, trespassing and whatever else we can," Lox said angrily.

"Prosecuted?" Dawn sniffed.

"No, no staff member would do this. Who would want to destroy a wedding dress?" Viv defended as she studied

Dawn's nervous face. "Don't worry, I had Morgan call Security to bring up the videotape from the hallway."

"What tape?" the bride asked.

Viv pointed to the camera concealed in the ceiling fixtures. "With as many people and as much money as changes hands in the casino we have cameras everywhere. Not in the private rooms but in the hallways, elevators and all public areas. They capture everything."

"Mr. Haddery you have my assurance that we will deal with the vandal very harshly," Mr. Lox said.

"No, we don't need to do that. I don't want to get anyone in trouble." Dawn fidgeted with her hands.

Viv and J.R. both turned to stare at her in disbelief. "We most certainly will to find out who is responsible and see that they are fired," J.R. said.

"The hotel needs to know what happened so we can prevent this in the future." Viv knew J.R. had every right to be angry. He had a lot invested emotionally in making his family happy today. There was little Viv could do to change that now.

The bride's desire not to view the tape clicked with Viv and she suddenly knew exactly who set the dress on fire. Dawn had expressed no desire to have another dress brought in. Now Viv was very glad J.R. and Mr. Lox were here to witness this. All they needed was the tape and they'd be home free.

The fear in Dawn's eyes was enough for Viv but the proof would be what saved her neck with J.R. and Lox. Lox could give her that promotion or not based on this but J.R.'s lesson was harsh. She wanted to comfort him.

"Ms. Montrose, you wanted this." A security guard made his way through the crowd and handed Viv the tape.

"Thank you." Viv entered the suite despite the stench of melted polyester blend. "Here we go." She popped in the tape and they all crowded around except for Dawn who hung back.

Viv fast-forwarded the tape to the time when the bridesmaids and bride left the room.

"There we go to our spa appointments," Ginger said defensively.

Viv let the tape play and it revealed the bride returning fifteen minutes later.

"You said you were going to the bathroom," Ginger snapped at the bride now caught in a lie. "I thought you were gone so long because of nerves. You don't smoke."

The tape played on, showing the bride leaving as the smoke detector registered and sprinklers went off. "Well, I don't think it's a staff problem." Viv ejected the tape. "Why, Dawn?"

Dawn's tears now looked real and Viv couldn't help but feel sorry for her. The girl clearly didn't want to get married.

"Why would you burn your own dress?" J.R. demanded.

The sniffling bride couldn't meet his eyes. "I'm sorry, J.R."

"Sorry. You ruined your own wedding on purpose. Why?"

"I don't want to get married," she admitted.

"What?" J.R. moved closer to her.

Viv should've been enjoying this. She'd known all along something didn't feel right about Dawn's wedding. "Why didn't you say something if you'd changed your mind? Brides do it all the time." Viv tried to defuse the situation delicately.

Dawn glanced uneasily at her parents. "Bruce and I were dating when I finished college. Dad liked Bruce and wanted to know my plans. I didn't want to work in the family business. I wanted to enjoy life. Mom was a wife and mother with no day job so it sounded good."

"So when it didn't sound good anymore why not break the engagement then?" Viv asked.

"I didn't know what else to go. My parents have planned everything in my life. I couldn't disappoint them. I didn't know what to do."

"So you wasted his money instead?" Bruce asked.

"Shut up, you're as relieved about this as I am," Dawn spat back.

"Forget the money," J.R. cut in. "You deliberately ruined this wedding. The ankle? The missed meetings? Changing everything at the last minute? I told Viv that you were just nervous but she was right all along."

"How could you do this to J.R. and Bruce?" Dawn's mother demanded.

Suddenly the hallway was a sea of shouts and finger-pointing. Most of it was in Dawn's direction but clearly the family had issues to work out.

"Excuse me," Viv shouted to be heard and put her hand on J.R.'s arm. She pulled it back quickly. The feel of him only reminded her that she wasn't sure what was between them. First she had to handle this chaos. "I'll cancel everything and return what we can. I'm just glad no one got married who didn't want to. We'll move the girls to another suite and you can finish up your vacation with your family. Obviously you have a lot to discuss so Mr. Lox and I will leave you alone. I do suggest that you might want to move this conversation into a private room."

"I'm sorry I kept screwing things up," Dawn said to Viv. "You did a really great job. It was hard to find ways to cause trouble."

"You were definitely a challenge." Viv patted Dawn's arm.

"Come on, Dawn. We need to talk." Her mother wrapped an arm around the girl's shoulders. "Breaking the news to your grandmother should be punishment enough."

"Ms. Montrose, may I speak to you in private?" Mr. Lox asked as the family slowly dispersed.

She nodded but wanted to stay with J.R. He had wanted this so badly that Viv couldn't help but feel for him. The verdict of her promotion was important but was no longer what mattered most.

* * * * *

Viv stood in Mr. Lox's executive office and wondered what her fate would be. She hadn't actually screwed up the wedding but it was not her finest project.

"Not an ideal affair," Mr. Lox began as he sat behind his desk.

"No, unfortunately not. I did try to speak to the bride about it and alerted Mr. Haddery to my concerns but there wasn't enough evidence to get at the real problem. I'll get everything canceled and smoothed over."

"I'm sure you'll handle it." Mr. Lox seemed unconcerned. "Please sit down, Viv. We need to discuss the future."

She sat and wished he'd just get to the point.

"You handled the blowup and fire this afternoon very well. The situation was completely out of your control and yet you had enough presence to manage the crisis. I'm amazed you managed to get a wedding planned at all with full bridal sabotage."

"Thank you." Viv still wasn't sure what to think.

"You're perfect for this job. Congratulations."

"Thank you," Viv managed as the relief washed over her. Things might be looking up. If only J.R. hadn't been so disappointed about the wedding.

"I know you need to get back to the cleanup so we can discuss your new salary and the other perks later. I'm sure not all of our high-profile weddings are as eventful."

"Thankfully, no." Viv left the executive office and headed down to her office to find Morgan.

"J.R. is looking for you," Morgan warned.

Viv could top that news. "The Haddery wedding is off."

"Oh no. What did Mr. Lox say about that? What about your promotion?"

"That's the weirdest part. Dawn was sabotaging her wedding. Lox was so impressed that I made it that far with such a difficult wedding party I got the promotion." Viv smiled deeply for the first time that day.

"That's great." Morgan hugged her. "You deserve it. That bride was rough."

The promotion was good but Viv couldn't stop worrying about J.R. "Did J.R. look mad?"

"No, he wanted to talk to you. He looked concerned. What happened with you two now?"

"Don't ask."

"I just did. You don't want to talk about this?" Morgan confirmed.

"I don't know what happened."

"If you want to avoid J.R. you'd better go now. I just saw him go into your office again."

"Thanks, I'm going to hide out in the bar for a bit. If there is another emergency you can find me but other than that you don't know where I am. I need a quiet couple of minutes to myself."

"Have a drink while you're at it. After a wedding dress goes up in flames you deserve it."

"That's not going to clear my head." Viv headed for the elevator with a bad headache. That drink did sound good. At least the pressure of the wedding and the promotion were no longer issues.

* * * * *

The bar was a nice place to people watch and be anonymous. Viv's mind was so busy she barely noticed other people in the room. She needed to think things through. But what had all of her thinking gotten her? That's how she ended up turning down J.R. and look how happy that had made her.

"Here you go, Viv." The bartender placed a shot of vodka in front of her. Viv was both confused and grateful. She hadn't ordered anything.

"Thanks but I'm still on the clock." Viv knew she needed that drink. A wedding dress up in flames. A proposal! Her mother was still hanging on her father. Her father a nice and normal man. Well, those last two weren't bad so much as not normal for her just yet. If she ever needed a drink, today was the day.

"Call it a celebration for your promotion. Morgan called down to tell me to make sure you got a drink. If I ever get married you're the only one who'll do the wedding. I want it classy."

"Thanks." Viv smiled as the bartender turned to deal with a customer. Out of the corner of her eye Viv saw her parents heading for her. She downed the shot and cleared her throat.

"Congratulations on the promotion, honey," her mother gushed and hugged Viv hard. "We ran into Morgan while we were looking for you."

"Thanks, Mom." Viv knew it was good news but with everything else going on it wasn't her first thought. J.R. wasn't happy and it bothered her that his grand plan to repay his family hadn't turned out the way he wanted.

Her mom smoothed Viv's jacket after the hug wrinkled it. "What is in that pocket?" Shelley patted Viv down like a cop to find the violation of good fashion. She could spot a speck of lint from across the room. "It's ruining the line of your suit."

"I don't know. I only carry my employee access badge with me." Viv dug in her pocket. Feeling the ring, she slowly pulled at it and felt a spark of longing. He wasn't done with her. "J.R. must have slipped it in when I wasn't looking."

"He proposed?" her mother asked.

"Yeah." Viv stared at it seriously. "He doesn't listen very well."

"What are you waiting for?" Viv's father asked.

Viv looked at her mother and shook her head. Her father wouldn't understand and Viv didn't have it in her to dredge up the truth right now. "I don't know if I can."

"You don't love him?" Mom sounded totally unconvinced.

"It's not that." Viv wasn't sure what was stopping her except her own stubbornness.

"It's my fault," her mom said.

"No," Viv insisted. "This is my problem."

"You're my daughter and I taught you this. All of your life I let you think men weren't worth your time. I taught you that love and marriage made you weak because I was too hurt and ashamed to tell you the truth." Mom wrapped her arm around Lou's arm. "I didn't want you to get hurt the way I had. It obviously backfired. You're even more hurt and miserable now. You have everything right in the palm of your hand to be happy but are too afraid to take it."

"I've only known him two weeks." Viv knew it was insane to be in love so fast. To know deep down this was what she wanted and needed forever. So why was that the message her heart kept giving her?

"That long? I knew after only a week with your father. We Montrose women know what we want. I was eighteen and scared. You don't have that excuse. Don't let him go if you want him. I went thirty years without the one I wanted." Mom poked a fake red fingernail in Viv's shoulder to add emphasis.

Viv wondered how her day had gone so out of control and it was only four o'clock in the afternoon. This was what heartbreak felt like.

Viv suddenly felt very sorry for her mother. Thirty years without the man she loved. There was no way she could have endured it as gracefully as her mother.

That possibility made her feel sick to her stomach. Not having J.R. He pushed so hard to be in her life she never thought she might not be able to have him. Touch him. The idea of losing him was unbearable. He was the one. She didn't want to wait thirty years like her mother. Viv wasn't going to let that happen to her. She had to find J.R. and hope he hadn't changed his mind.

"You okay?" her mom asked after the silence had gone on too long.

"Absolutely." She wanted J.R. "Are you guys ready for a wedding?"

"Whose wedding?" Lou asked.

"Mine!" Viv got off her barstool. First she had to make sure her groom was on board.

"Are you sure?" Her mother smiled.

"Definitely." Suddenly Viv felt the emotion she saw in all brides and never quite understood. It wasn't just a day. It was her day. "Why don't you call Auntie and see if she can make it?"

"I'll call her right now." Viv's mom pulled out her cell phone and dialed.

"I have some things to do." Viv had to let J.R. in on the change of plans.

She headed for the nearest security phone. First she made sure he hadn't checked out and then told them not to let him leave if he tried. Working at the Royale had its advantages and there was no reason to let her hard work go to waste. Dawn's canceled wedding was going to get a quick revamp and become her own.

Chapter Sixteen

J.R. stormed through the wedding consultant offices for the third time looking for Viv and finally he found her talking to Morgan. He half expected her to go the other way as he approached but she headed into her office as though she'd been expecting him.

"I've been all over this place looking for you," he informed her.

"Me too." She folded her arms behind her back and smiled at him.

"I'm sorry I doubted you about Dawn. It wasn't your imagination." He had to get that out first. J.R. had been so set on the wedding he'd been blind. He hadn't given Viv's professional observations enough credit.

"I'm glad you realize that. I didn't poison Dawn against marriage. And I'm sorry that your present to your family didn't go as planned. I know how much it meant to you." Viv took a step closer.

She wasn't herself but it had been a very weird day. J.R. knew she had the stubbornness to walk away from them if that was what she wanted. He couldn't let her go without all the facts. If he had to compromise to keep her he would. "Look, I know this thing with your parents is still settling in but I have to say this before too much time passes. I understand if you think I moved too fast or put too much pressure on you but I'm not giving up."

"Really?" Viv began but J.R. cut her off.

"If you're not ready to get engaged we can keep seeing each other but you're not going to get rid of me. It's not like I'm going back to New York. I live here and I'm making you my top priority." He closed the distance between them and towered over her but she didn't move except to tilt her head up to look at him.

"No."

"No what?" Had she just ended things with one word?

"No, we can't keep seeing each other."

"You found the ring? I'd like it back." That chip of a diamond wasn't worth the cost of his suit but it was his mother's.

Viv held up her left hand. "No. It's mine now. I was afraid because I do trust you and love you. It scared me. I'm not about to settle for dating you when you proposed. At least you'll get to try out your new tuxedo. We better hurry up, we only have two and half hours before the wedding." She stood on her tiptoes and kissed him before J.R. could respond.

Wedding? Married? She had his mother's ring on. This was beyond teasing. Viv was serious. Her true meaning finally dawned on him and he pulled her to him and smothered her with a hard kiss. "Does this mean you really changed your mind and actually want to?"

"Yes, I'll marry you." Viv kissed his roughly shaved chin. "And I don't need to think about it. I want to do it tonight."

"Tonight? What about your aunt? You'll need a dress." J.R. didn't want her to rush into something and have a disappointed bride on his hands.

"You're trying to fix things again," she warned. "My aunt can be here in no time and don't worry about the dress. Morgan's called to have one delivered. If there is anyone you'd like to invite you'd better call them now. We need to get the license in person."

"You said you would never get married and yet you know what dress you want? You phony." He squeezed her tighter.

"Not a phony. I just know which dress style will look best on me. I've seen most everything out there. That's all I'm going to say about it because it's supposed to be a surprise."

"That won't be the first surprise we've had today," J.R. replied.

"If my impulsive nature is a shock to you then you should've thought harder before you proposed because now you're stuck with me." She ran her hand up his arm.

"There are worse things to be stuck with." J.R. took her left hand in his and ran a thumb over her ring. It meant a lot to him that she was wearing the ring but he wanted to give her the world. "I'll get you a ring that really sparkles."

"No, you won't," she said. "I'm the bride! This is my day and I'll have things my way, including the rings. This is a family heirloom and I won't have it changed. Now how expensive you go on the wedding bands is up to you. That is traditionally the groom's expense."

"This morning you swore you'd never get married. Now you're drunk with bridal power." If she wanted to keep that ring it was fine with him. He had the rest of his life to spoil her.

"I like power." Viv winked. "You can take back the proposal if you want but I'm pretty sure there's a mob of your family and mine that would kill you."

"They know?"

"Of course."

"You're really that sure?" He looked into her eyes for any sign of doubt.

"All my life I tried not to make the same mistakes as other people. In the process I almost made a huge mistake of my own. There's no reason for us to wait."

"You're right." J.R. pulled her close.

"I just hope Dawn doesn't think we're stepping on her toes." Viv looked concerned.

"I'll talk to her. My guess is she'll be glad to have the attention off her for a while. I think she learned a hard lesson."

"Dawn just wasn't ready. I've seen it before. Though she's more creative than any of the others. I've had brides run off, lock themselves in the bathroom and leave *Dear John* letters. She's the first to methodically sabotage her own wedding. Good thing for you that I'm not prone to that sort of behavior. I'm very clear about what I want."

"Good because if you get cold feet, I'll drag you up that aisle."

"You have nothing to worry about there. Once I decide something I'm committed."

"Glad to hear it." He subtly glanced at his watch and leaned over to kiss her neck. "We have some time. What are you doing between now and the wedding?"

"Tempting as a last round of premarital sex is, I don't think we have time for that. We have to go announce things, invite people and get dressed in time. I also need my nail polish changed and my hair done. There's too much to do." She grabbed his hand and pulled him out toward the door.

"Wait. First I want you to admit it."

"I said I'd marry you." Viv tugged at him again. There was concern in her face that he might change his mind.

"No, you have to say you love me." He wasn't a sap but it was his wedding day.

Relief washed over her face. "I thought men didn't like the mushy stuff. I guess you are unique. If that's all you want I'll say it until you're sick of it."

"Try me," he challenged, pulling her close.

"I love you and I trust you." Viv's arms encircled his neck firmly and she kissed him. "I love you so much, J.R."

"No, not sick of it yet."

"Good because I'll never get tired of saying it. Now I have to decide if I'm going to change my name or not." Viv headed for the door as two deliverymen with baskets full of lilies knocked on the door. Viv opened it and looked at J.R. "What did you do?"

"You like lilies." He kissed her.

He grabbed one of the baskets and pulled Viv into the elevator. Selecting the floor for his suite, he waited several floors before hitting the stop button. The alarm sounded as he tugged Viv's jacket off.

"What are you doing?" Viv didn't fight as he kissed her neck.

"I know the wedding stuff is important but it's our wedding. We can push it back half an hour." His hands pulled her near so she was against him.

"Here? Security will come and the cameras," Viv protested. "J.R. I'm management now."

"So you'll come to my suite?" He kissed her mouth slowly as the alarm rang.

"If it means that much to you." She hit the resume button and the alarm stopped. "You're so stubborn."

"That's good compromise. See, we can do it." He held the elevator door as she exited. They entered his suite and J.R. set the flowers on the table and dropped his jacket on the floor.

Viv dropped her jacket and stepped out of her skirt. The blouse went next and she was in nothing but her underwear but instead of the bed, she went for the couch.

J.R. stepped out of the rest of his clothes, his erection straining for her already. He sat next to her. "Bored with the bed?"

"No." Viv straddled his lap and kissed him. Her slit teased his cock. "I just remembered that we never got to finish what was interrupted by Dawn's little fall."

J.R. groaned. "You're right." He pulled her up so he could suck her beautiful breasts. "I'll never let you go."

"Me either." Viv shivered in his arms. "Now we don't have stop ever."

He pulled her down slightly and Viv rode his cock while his hands steadied her. As she tightened and bounced, J.R. ran a thumb over her clit. Rotating clockwise and then counterclockwise until she screamed into his shoulder. Her tight spasms pushed him to orgasm. He exploded into her, holding her hips tight to him.

"The couch was a good choice," Viv muttered.

"Very good. You do like it on top." He held on to her, knowing she was his forever.

"Thank you for the lilies." She kissed him softly.

"Your office will always have fresh lilies. Now all you have to do is decide if you want to go to Hawaii or Alaska for the honeymoon." He stroked her hair.

Viv pressed her forehead to his. "I can't believe this is real."

"It's real. And so is the wedding. What do you think about joining me in the shower?"

Viv's eyes sparkled. "I think you're insatiable."

"A perfect match."

Also by Cheryl Dragon

൩

9 1/2 Years
An Extreme Haunting
Black on Blonde
Opal: Curse of the Mexican Opal
Outsmarting the Moon

Also see Cheryl's books at The Lotus Circle (www.thelotuscircle.com):

I'm Okay, You're Dead
I'm Okay, You're a Fake

About the Author

୨୦

A lover of unusual things, Cheryl Dragon enjoys writing unique stories of sinfully hot erotic romance, pure erotica or paranormals with a psychic twist. Never at a loss for ideas, there are plenty of stories yet to be written. Her two favorite settings are Las Vegas and New Orleans--where anything can happen.

Cheryl lives in the Chicagoland area with her deaf albino cat. By day she analyzes numbers as an Assistant Controller for a division of a large international company, which leaves her creative side free for writing.

Cheryl welcomes comments from readers. You can find her website and email address on her author bio page at www.ellorascave.com.

Tell Us What You Think

We appreciate hearing reader opinions about our books. You can email us at Comments@EllorasCave.com.

Why an electronic book?

We live in the Information Age—an exciting time in the history of human civilization, in which technology rules supreme and continues to progress in leaps and bounds every minute of every day. For a multitude of reasons, more and more avid literary fans are opting to purchase e-books instead of paper books. The question from those not yet initiated into the world of electronic reading is simply: *Why?*

1. *Price.* An electronic title at Ellora's Cave Publishing and Cerridwen Press runs anywhere from 40% to 75% less than the cover price of the exact same title in paperback format. Why? Basic mathematics and cost. It is less expensive to publish an e-book (no paper and printing, no warehousing and shipping) than it is to publish a paperback, so the savings are passed along to the consumer.
2. *Space.* Running out of room in your house for your books? That is one worry you will never have with electronic books. For a low one-time cost, you can purchase a handheld device specifically designed for e-reading. Many e-readers have large, convenient screens for viewing. Better yet, hundreds of titles can be stored within your new library—on a single microchip. There are a variety of e-readers from different manufacturers. You can also read e-books on your PC or laptop computer. (Please note that Ellora's Cave does not endorse any specific brands.

You can check our websites at www.ellorascave.com or www.cerridwenpress.com for information we make available to new consumers.)
3. ***Mobility.*** Because your new e-library consists of only a microchip within a small, easily transportable e-reader, your entire cache of books can be taken with you wherever you go.
4. ***Personal Viewing Preferences.*** Are the words you are currently reading too small? Too large? Too… ANNOYING? Paperback books cannot be modified according to personal preferences, but e-books can.
5. ***Instant Gratification.*** Is it the middle of the night and all the bookstores near you are closed? Are you tired of waiting days, sometimes weeks, for bookstores to ship the novels you bought? Ellora's Cave Publishing sells instantaneous downloads twenty-four hours a day, seven days a week, every day of the year. Our webstore is never closed. Our e-book delivery system is 100% automated, meaning your order is filled as soon as you pay for it.

Those are a few of the top reasons why electronic books are replacing paperbacks for many avid readers.

As always, Ellora's Cave and Cerridwen Press welcome your questions and comments. We invite you to email us at Comments@ellorascave.com or write to us directly at Ellora's Cave Publishing Inc., 1056 Home Avenue, Akron, OH 44310-3502.

Cerridwen, the Celtic Goddess of wisdom, was the muse who brought inspiration to storytellers and those in the creative arts. Cerridwen Press encompasses the best and most innovative stories in all genres of today's fiction. Visit our site and discover the newest titles by talented authors who still get inspired - much like the ancient storytellers did, once upon a time.

Discover for yourself why readers can't get enough of the multiple award-winning publisher

Ellora's Cave.

Whether you prefer e-books or paperbacks, be sure to visit EC on the web at www.ellorascave.com

for an erotic reading experience that will leave you breathless.